MANTEIA

Jon East

*For Linda, encouragement and wisdom
are your legacy.*

"Time is the wisest of all counsellors."

PERICLES

Foreword

Mythology is the one thing in life that we can take for granted with impunity. It is the sole gift from powers long-unseen, but not forgotten, which we can freely craft and manipulate. That is its purpose: the more we tell and re-tell the stories of old, the more we interpret the truth of them, the happier those same ancient authorities will be. Doing this duty strengthens their case for immortality, and reminds us that we are but mortal.

Advisory Note

This novel contains explicit content of a sexual and violent nature, which some readers may find offensive.

Chapter One

I n life, I was acolyte to Athena. In death, I am *manteia*: oracle for all, gatekeeper of myth, guardian of the gods' timelessness.

I speak of love and fear, of hubris and legacy, and of Medusa. I am her fate and she is my own. They on Mount Olympus decree that I never forget it.

The rhythm up there alternates between chaos and peace, just as it does down here. The pattern allows mortal life to eventually, and entirely, claim the earth. The sliver-space between the extremes of chaos and peace - a deep and narrow valley of shadow - is where Mother Death rests. Just as a mother is necessary to produce a child, Mother Death is necessary to give meaning to life: death is legacy, and legacy is mother to all. We are only truly born when we die.

Medusa was the offspring of a man and a woman, themselves entirely mortal. No siblings were known: no other children shared her mother, but mystery surrounded the father. While Medusa was born with no divine blood flowing through her veins, at the end she was a gorgon: a monstrous apparition; an example of malice and magic, of pride and jealousy, of dark wonder that only the Olympians could design.

After she took up residence on the Isle of the Dead, half the rumours that had dogged her in life became truth: the fearful half. With Medusa exiled, Mother Death began to court me. As I kept to my room beneath the temple of Athena, Mother Death crept in the shadows. If I took the air among the temple's gardens of olive trees and strawflower, Mother Death lingered in the shade. If I hobbled to the altar, alone before the great statue of Athena, Mother Death knelt beside me. I would lower my wizened back in long-held piety, and my prayers craving exoneration would slip amidst those of habitual devotion. I wanted Medusa to forgive me, not the god.

We first met in the village of Tanis, when we were twelve years of age. We left that place together, sat aboard the market-train of the trader Menethus, baking under the sun of the relentless hot season that Greece endures each year. The cart we shared was not a mobile dungeon: Menethus took good care of his stock, and I had been in his charge for many years since he had acquired me in Libya.

The worn wheels and tired axels shook and juddered, quickly carrying us and others in the long train across the dry Argolian land towards the city of Mycenae. Whether it was because she had suddenly left her old life behind in Tanis, or because she was mindful of Baktria, her recently deceased mother, Medusa felt compelled to recall to me an early memory from her childhood: that of first witnessing her own reflection in a *musalu* - the old name for the common mirror. I was startled by her education; and by the way she could recount such a trivial event with clarity and emotional depth. Her mother had schooling beyond the academic and, before her untimely death, had devoutly passed on what she could to her daughter.

I already knew the history of the mirror (how so I shall return to describe), but I listened attentively as Medusa explained its origins. Even as a child her voice had a sensual husk: a vocal remnant of her Libyan heritage that had been tempered by an upbringing mostly surrounded by Greeks. It added a confidence to her tone. The sound of my own voice was unattractively coarse: I too had Libyan parents and good education but, unlike Medusa, my mother gave birth to me in Libya. I had been surrounded by harsher accents and warring temperaments since the cradle. Listeners would be drawn to Medusa's voice, to better hear its soft and assured quality. Some could consider it haughty or mighty: in fact it was that schooling of her mother's, rather than thoughts above her position in life, that gave her good vocabulary and a careful stance: a subtle awareness that she was an exception rather than a rule.

She candidly told the story of the mirror. At

the same time as we were pulled from our respective wombs, a man of science from the city of Byblos, beyond the sea that separates Greece from the eastern regions of the world, had perfected the polishing of thin metal sheets. He layered them with veneers of glass that were thinner still, creating what he called a *musalu*. Whatever was put in front of a *musalu* was reflected with great clarity. One's own beauty and imperfection could be perceived for oneself.

The man of science became a man of commerce and began to sell his invention: initially as something for the rich, for wealthy merchants and their wives and concubines; or for men successful in war. As the production of the *musalu* increased with demand, their value declined and soon it was affordable for all. The man became one of the wealthiest people in the mortal world, since his *musalu* was sold in all inhabited corners of it. But his genius as an inventor was now twofold: he was not only the man who designed the mirror, but also the man who created vanity.

Medusa's mother owned one. No sooner had Medusa seen her own reflection in the mirror, she could fathom her profound looks. She could understand the stares of admiration and the more complex coldness of envy, either of which she had noticed in the faces of people when they looked at her. Even as a child, she told me, she knew that boys and men mostly observed her with a curious, latent yearning: a polite wonder. Girls and women were not much different: some peered at her shyly, wondering if she was supernatural, descended from Olympus. Some studied her from afar, trying to understand how it could be that a little girl could look so unusually perfect. Some looked at her jealously, wondering why they had not been blessed with the same symmetry of face, or the same light green eyes housed amidst eyelids the colour and shape of unripe almonds. Thanks to the mirror, Medusa knew herself to be beautiful.

She interpreted her remarkable allure as a task that she had been called upon to undertake; a burden that she should carry. Already at that young age she wanted to share the weight of expectation surrounding her appearance. Already she sought a form of protection from the exposure her natural beauty would grant her; the unconditional and remorseless attention she seemed to know would continue and intensify as she grew into womanhood. It was apposite that she should look to me for shielding: a girl with the sort of face and body that were easy to ignore. I was the physical antithesis to her. While we became a unit, a bonded entity in friendship and sisterhood for much of our time together, my presence ultimately served to accentuate her stunning aura. I gave her the protection her instinct seemed to demand, and yet in doing so I enhanced her and strengthened the attention she received.

As we rolled across those dusty lands, I asked her if anything else made her special. I did not care whether she said anything, but I wanted to detract from the troublesome aspect of her looks.

After a thoughtful silence she said: "My mother taught me to listen very carefully."

"You have the hearing of a bat," I replied, repeating something I had heard earlier when we had been in Tanis.

She laughed and said: "Yes. My mother taught me to listen for approaching horses."

"The god Poseidon governs horses, along with the seas and the winds," I said pointedly, feeling the need to instruct her.

I may not have looked like her, but few children knew Olympian doctrine better than me. She acknowledged my sudden teaching with a slow blink and a thankful nod. She already had the sensibilities of composure and grace, but I feared she knew little of the powers that had brought us together; the powers that fated us.

She continued. "If you put your ear to the ground and listen carefully, you can hear the distant sound of hooves. Like a heartbeat through the earth. Boom, boom. Boom, boom. My mother taught me the rhythms to listen for, to tell what type of man was coming to the village.

And therefore prepare."

"What types of men?"

"Steady rhythms were soldiers coming to take their pleasures. That meant the chance of trouble was slim. They would be determined, but disciplined. My mother always relaxed and became happier with those prospects."

"And the other type?"

"Scrambled and rushed, the sound of excited workers. This meant trouble. These men had no masters while away from their labours. My mother used to worry before those nights began."

My value as Menethus' property was maintained by keeping me shielded from the harshness and hedonism of the world; to present me clean and virgin in body, mind and spirit to the buyers at our destination, the city of Mycenae. Listening to Medusa then, I was reminded of my inherent fear of what lay beyond my carefully managed lifestyle. And yet this unrest had bred fascination: I was captivated as to what life was outside of the sanctity of Menethus' care, and that of religion. Until I met Medusa, this intrigue had been confined to my imagination.

I looked at her keenly. "Would both types of men ever come to your village at the same time? Maybe the soldiers would protect your mother and the other women from the workers..."

Medusa's eyes pierced mine. She searched me for naivety, which I hid well. I broke her intense, kind stare by looking shyly at the floor of the carriage. Any longer I would have been locked in position, stone-frozen.

"My mother told me the two groups had an agreement. One would not come if the other had already set out from Mycenae."

"Men can make such agreements in a civil way?"

She shrugged slightly, believing she spoke the truth but was ignorant of the details behind it.

"I only ever knew one group or the other to spend the night in Tanis."

"If both types of men were there, I doubt the soldiers would protect the women," I said, answering my own question and labouring the point. "They would be off-duty."

I spoke without malice, but I felt uncomfortable believing I could have offended her. To compliment her exotic accent, Medusa had the gift of talking plainly without repent and with sincerity. I longed for that skill but my deep-held piety prevented it, providing me with a condition of guilt that either restrained my tongue when I needed it free, or polluted it when I had the chance to speak openly.

She suddenly took one of my hands and stared at me with those sharp, unmatched green irises. "Never be sorry for speaking truth," she said.

I looked at her mournfully. She looked at me brightly, trying to cheer me.

"I'll tell you some magic. Whore's magic.

Whores know how to conjure silence. How to move quietly. How to leave a bedroom the morning after the night before, before the customer wakes and wants without paying. How to hold their tongues if a man is too drunk to control himself. How to run away without being heard. How to arrive by a man's side without him knowing. Being a friend and mistress to silence is the whore's trick for avoiding violence and death, for survival. My mother taught me this from when I could barely walk. Better her customers not know I was there at all, she told me. Children could be a ransom, or a hindrance to business, or a target for unkind appetites."

"You can move without being heard?" I said, in awe of her again.

"I can run and dance on my toes," she said, smiling at me wide-eyed, sharing her witchery. "People think me a breeze. The shadows of corners befriend me naturally. I know every part of my body that makes a sound, and I control each one perfectly. My mother told me it is my life-long gift."

Her gifts served her well. Not only her soft-footing, but that of attracting men to her presence. Even when exiled on the Isle of the Dead, the men still came. Not to try to fuck her, but for glory and for power: to prove their courage and to test their resolve against the sheer, whispered dread she had become. Beauty and terror are close cousins.

She crept around the Isle's temple ruins in ways that caught countless near-heroes unawares. She could hear them coming even as they set a single foot on the shores of rocky sand, grey-white like the colour of corpses. Their first steps from the ferryman's boat would be taken so carefully: an effort to begin a habit of sure-footed quiet that could guarantee victory. The more skilful would get deep into the broken temple, where she slithered and hissed. Most perished.

Olympian love and hate for us are fleeting and capricious. Unless you are a rarity, whose mother or father inhabits Mount Olympus: such demigods are either adored or loathed unconditionally and permanently; an Olympian child is either a successful conquest or a damned embarrassment.

Like a bodily deformity, Olympian desire to end us all is always present. But only Zeus, the father-god, can truly finish what he started. Only he can form the ultimate alliance with Mother Death and obliterate us all. He never will. Pride and foresight stay his hand.

His family's tolerance of mortals is more fickle than his own. Zeus obeys the need for chaos and peace, and often requires the forbearance of his relatives. They all have the power to punish, which for them is as much an entertainment as it is a chance to discipline. Penance is more feared than death by the mortals, and more preferred by the Olympians. Mother Death, though sometimes necessary, is a solution too simple and crude. To the Olympians, having a mortal live a nightmare trumps leaving life altogether. Our suffering, like our piety, forms their existence.

They all concoct mischief, devise schemes, hatch plots, make plans, curry favours, harbour inclinations. Those things satisfy their urge for chaos or peace when one extreme has embedded itself for too long. Those things make way for disorder among the deities. Those things make way for mayhem among the mortals.

Zeus supports the schemes, quashes the plots, rearranges the plans, doubts the favours and announces the inclinations of his wife, his brothers, his sisters and his children. The father-god permits their quarrels be reflected as earthly deeds: these the vitality that sustains our belief in them. Love, fear, beauty and pain are the conduits. We mortals are compelled to embrace those mediums, willingly or not - just as the gods are compelled to give us reasons to believe in them, willingly or not. They are our fuel, and we theirs.

Olympian power depends on mortal reverence; mortal power depends on Olympian love and scorn. The longer we exist and breed, the less we pray and pay tribute and live as we believe they want us to. That is how the gods will eventually fade; Mother Death will one day have her way with them. What follows will be chaos and peace. Zeus knows this, his venerable pride and eminent foresight acting as both his ally and his enemy.

Zeus and his family are not isolated to mortal earth. Other realms he had once spawned can host them if they choose: *galaxies* are what learned men and women call these planes of existence. Poseidon, Aphrodite and Athena take the greatest interest in earth and have remained the longest: governors for what the father-god proclaimed to be his greatest creation.

If a god summons a mortal to commune on Olympus, warning is given though it is short-lived. We the summoned arrive in their halls and chambers amid darkness and light: a near-instantaneous period of chaos followed by peace. Mortal speech is impossible up there; we the summoned endured sealed lips and frozen tongues. We pray and we sacrifice and we invoke while on earth: that is enough speech.

I had been servant to Athena since the womb. Those very first communions with the god, those foetal visits to the vast Olympian halls, were the most comforting moments of my life.

My embryonic mind was awed and settled as she cooed and caressed me, and spoke of things in words I did not yet know. As I grew from baby to child, from child to young girl, from young girl to woman, the divine meetings were not so innocent. Their aftermath affected me like obsessive memories of vivid dreams: uncertain in their truth, but with the power to generate substantial feelings of joy and dread, of contentment and longing.

Chapter Two

Before Medusa and I were first introduced, I experienced the most profound communion from a summons by Athena. While Menethus' market-train was under attack by thieves, an event that I shall return to describe, I felt the familiar, potent sensations of the summons prior to communion: the unusual, bitter taste in the mouth; the sudden exhaustion; and the clouding of vision. The preparation for Olympian meetings was a sickness in itself. But I should endure any discomfort to see the glory of Olympus; my earthly piety should be strengthened by being a witness to its glory.

Zeus had just returned from another of his *galaxíes*, ending a long absence from earth. Poseidon, Aphrodite and Athena could have been forgiven into thinking he had lost interest in the mortal cause. His arrival back to Olympus implied a pivotal moment was nearing: one the three had overlooked, or not suspected.

Zeus sat back on his throne, gladly resting into it and recalling its familiarity, as if his incredible, cosmic journey had been tiring. The seat was carved from the single white bone, a thorax or backbone, of some long-dead giant beast. The father-god's blueish, mortal-form eyes danced with anticipation; he knew his return would spark debate among his family. He had missed their arguments. He even enjoyed a feud, but despaired at long-held animosity.

On Mount Olympus they were flesh and blood, by Zeus' decree; a reflection of the organisms they inspired. In his mortal form the father-god took the body of an older man: white-haired and bearded with wisdom and authority. The physique he had chosen, however, was muscular and lean. His skin was as dark and supple as a walnut tree. He had the stature of a man whose bodily prime had come at the same time as the sageness that reaches most long after. No robe covered his frame; no clothing covered any of them: they wandered Olympus' great halls, and schemed in their private chambers, unashamedly naked.

Zeus spoke in careful query to Poseidon, Aphrodite and Athena, his voice rich and steady: a mature statesman not quite gone to seed.

"I have not been here since we established the Black Lands, as they were called then. How do the mortals there fare?"

"The lands thrive," Poseidon said warmly. The sea-god stood at over six and a half feet, and had the physique that could feasibly be perceived to hold the weight of the oceans he controlled. His form was more handsome than Zeus: his face more youthful, sleek with high cheekbones and beardless; and his arms and legs rippled with tanned muscle, covering bones that were harder than the rocks his waves on earth eroded. Yet his dominating body overshadowed a shrewd and secretive demeanour: his mortal form was impossible to miss, but his actions were difficult to anticipate. And while Zeus' voice was sure with age and experience, Poseidon's own was youthful and no less confident: disarmingly friendly and optimistic.

The sea-god continued. "The mortals have done well. They no longer call their home Black Lands. Now they call those lands *Kemet.*"

"*Kemet,*" Zeus repeated distastefully, as if the name brought him some unkind memory. "A harsh-sounding name."

"They thrive under harsh weather. A broad and powerful river runs through their vast territory. It cuts from north to south, splitting it lengthways for two thousand leagues. They have as much sand as fertile soil. That soil is dark and rich. Still black lands, just not in name. They entomb their dead kings and queens in enormous, triangular mausoleums."

Zeus stared into the space ahead of him reflectively. "They have evolved a great deal. I have truly been away for too long," he said, his voice pierced with regret. "Which of you do they worship? Such a resourceful, earnest people must ally their hopes and fears to you, Athena."

16

"Not me," Athena said flatly. The despondency in her voice did not reflect a lack of spirit or thought to the matter, though the god seldom gave way to excitement or zeal. Beneath her tall, athletic frame whirred a mind that was in constant calculation. Her face was well-proportioned and her eyes were intensely brown: they asked more questions than her tongue. But her beauty was an acquired taste: strikingly attractive to some, not feminine enough to most.

Zeus seemed deflated by her answer. "Then such a copulating people must be obsessed with you, my fierce and beautiful Aphrodite," he said.

"Certainly not," Aphrodite said tartly, as was her way. She was sensually curvaceous, porcelain-skinned and chestnut-haired. Unlike Athena's squarish jaw, Aphrodite's own face was delicate and slight. Wide, blue eyes granted her wear innocence like she owned it. Her breasts were generously endowed, as if recently lactated, and she moved in a way to exploit the bounty of her beauty. The form she took personified her idea of mortal perfection in a woman; the god probably lusted after herself.

"I have seen them," she said, continuing. Seldom could Aphrodite not elaborate her opinion. "Mud-dwellers, snake-worshippers. Not my kind of mortal. If only their forefathers could see what has become of them."

Zeus let out a joyous laugh and clapped his hands. "You are so impressive, dear daughter.

I've missed your sweet venom. Just as I have Poseidon's pragmatism. And Athena's calculated restraint. Where would the mortals be without you three?"

Poseidon offered Zeus a slight, aloof smile, perhaps expecting a greater compliment.

"Thank you, brother. The Kemet people worship the sun. Like the hill-dwellers over the seas in the west. And like those savages, the Kemet rip the hearts from virgins atop their stone monuments honouring dead royalty. They believe it guarantees the harvest."

Athena interjected. "They're wrong," she said with a note of accusation.

Poseidon turned to her politely, forcing patience like a tired parent of a too-curious child.

"Indeed they are. Consistency of temperature, strength of wind and spread of rainfall determine the harvest," he said.

"Things that *you* can control. Yet you continue to let the Kemet kill each other, honouring sham beliefs," Athena replied.

Aphrodite, sensing conflict and none more sweet than one between Athena and Poseidon, positioned herself to take the same view as her father.

Athena capitalised on Poseidon's delayed reply. "Those same sacrificial virgins could fill our temples in Mycenae, in Argus, in Pylos, in Thebes. Not much use a temple without acolytes."

Poseidon shrugged, as if he was powerless to affect change. His enormous shoulders lifted his pectoral muscles, which were like oversized haunches of cooked meat.

"The Kemet people must find their own way," Poseidon said conclusively. "You cannot be one to sympathise with cruelty, Athena. Why not ease the suffering of your own acolytes? I hear the new girls are whipped in front of naked men, to associate the male mortal form with pain and distrust, and quash any feeling of temptation."

Aphrodite smirked as she watched Athena. She took issue with the mortal form her half-sister had taken, which did not rival her own in looks and perfection of female physique. She had done it to spite her, Aphrodite thought; Athena had no need for beauty, content to rely on her ancestry. They shared the same father in Zeus, but different mothers: the source of an underlying hostility between them that was fuelled by envy; envy denied by Aphrodite and provoked sparingly, but effectively, by Athena. While Aphrodite had inherited her sea-nymph mother's bitterness, the sprite having been one of Zeus' seductions at a point in the distant past, Athena had the purity of unadulterated lineage: her mother was Hera, Zeus' absent wife. Athena was legitimate Olympian royalty, and it annoyed Aphrodite that Athena did not use her entitlement more openly. Aphrodite hated subtleties.

"Initiation is merely part of the price that allegiance to my temple costs," Athena said modestly. "I offer my acolytes and priestesses great things - among them no false hope."

Poseidon sighed dramatically. "One thing worse than a short life is one lead in denial of pleasure."

Zeus rose from his throne and spread his hands out for calm.

"Peace, peace," he said warmly.

Athena, who had been poised to continue sparring with the sea-god, said nothing. Poseidon was also silent, pleased at having had the last word.

Zeus continued. "I want to confirm something I was told while in my long absence from this mortal world. A powerful notion. A way of organising their existence has been fashioned. By identifying the start and finish of weather systems, a cycle of four seasons has been established. They have agreed that the sun rises and sets ninety-one times in each. Those adept have created circular tools to measure the phenomenon. The shadow of the sun carves up the day, and the light of the moon portions the night."

Zeus looked at them all, amazed and hoping they would share in his wonder. Their faces were straight, betraying no embarrassment for the father-god, until Poseidon broke and laughed.

"You have been away a long *time*, brother," he said. "Your understanding of this is very delayed. Perhaps your grip is loosening."

The sea-god's smile was on the edge of condescension. Zeus peered at him with scrutiny.

"Perhaps, in another reality, you may know what it is to spawn a universe," Zeus said. "But not in this plane of existence. This realm is mine. Our creators awarded *me* chaos and peace to own and nurture. There is no grip to speak of. There is only Zeus."

The father-god's face shifted to a look of challenge, inviting Poseidon to make more of his comments. A battle between them would have been chaos itself but with only one winner, and Poseidon knew it would not be him.

"I only mean to say," the sea-god said smoothly, "the phenomenon you speak of is custom throughout the mortal world. The mortals rise and fall by the hour of the day. They have quantified their existence. They all live and die by *time*."

Zeus massaged his beard and walked slowly in thought, crossing the seemingly endless atrium of sheer white rock, once hewn and hollowed into the heart of the mountain with an unfathomable power. The eyes of Poseidon, Athena and Aphrodite followed him.

"How long have I been away from here?" Zeus said gravely. "Speak how the mortals would calculate it."

"Nearly two thousand years," Poseidon said obligingly. "Four seasons is a single year. A lifetime for most men is seventy years. If they live

21

well and don't become victim to war."

"Women tend to live longer," said Athena. "If they live well and don't become victim to men."

"We three," Poseidon said and then paused, ignoring Athena's comment and gesturing to himself and to Aphrodite and Athena. He sought to remind Zeus of their importance. "We three took up permanent residence soon after you left. The city of Troy had just been established, you may recall. We three have invested ourselves in the mortal cause more than any. The others have been here only on scant occasion."

Athena spoke up, more gently than Poseidon and seeking to educate her father.

"Troy was a small settlement when you left. Now it thrives, and has sprawled closer to the western coast of those unnamed lands east across the sea from here. They have established trade, pioneered education, amassed an army, expanded populations further eastward. Their dynasty of kings has blood from these mortal forms you insist we assume."

"The Trojans are certainly pious," Aphrodite said. "I have visited a few of the men before, to test them."

"I'm sure they worshipped you on bended knee," Athena said snidely.

A flicker of doubt crossed Aphrodite's face, as if suddenly revisited by an old and unwanted memory.

"Two knees, if you must know," she said

curtly. "Trojan men can look enticing, but are usually a disappointment. Few have shown me the apex of mortal pleasure. Most disintegrated when they entered me. Therefore I have learned that cities are reflected by their populations. Troy is beautiful and powerful, but impressionable and tactless. Troy will one day suffer its share of trouble."

"I applaud you," Zeus said, no mockery in his voice. "Their survival has been built on us remaining a power they rightly believe exists and affects them, but whose wonder is kept mysterious by being seldom seen, seldom felt."

"We could walk among them as equals," Athena said, as if answering a profound question never asked. "Take these forms permanently. Renounce our immortality."

Bewildered, Poseidon and Aphrodite looked at her with narrowing eyes. Zeus suppressed a small smile; only Athena could have uncovered something the father-god believed was private only to him.

Aphrodite spoke first: "A foolish idea."

"I agree," said Poseidon, staring at Athena witheringly. "For all the wisdom bestowed upon you, you sometimes scrape the barrel of stupidity."

"I only suggested it as a relevant hypothesis," Athena said assertively. "We will eventually lose the mortals, be separated from them permanently. It is inevitable. So if not what I suggest, what is the alternative? We must discover how to survive, or assume mortality and live and die as they do."

"*Survive*?" Poseidon said with sharp disbelief. Whether he considered what Athena said to be true was unclear. "Not a good bedfellow for immortality."

"Athena, ever-wise and with sharpness afforded by her mother, is right," Zeus said. "We are bound to the mortals, as we are to any of my creations. But the longer we are invested in any cause, the more our power diminishes. This venture will only be successful if we are disciplined enough to embrace inevitability and detach ourselves from them. We must continue to leave them be more often than we intervene."

The father-god paused and looked upon their faces: Athena solemn, Aphrodite suddenly fearful and Poseidon attempting to be reflective, in fact calculating, as Zeus' words hit their brains.

"The chaos of our origins has gradually made way for mortal order," Zeus continued. "This *time* you speak of is their greatest invention. We can only know it through observation. We have no concept for it but theirs. Divine interactions must become rarer and rarer. We will influence, but only at key moments. And then, when the *time* is right, our activities will cease altogether. We will detach ourselves fully from the mortals. In doing so we will guarantee our timelessness."

"We should abandon them immediately,"

Aphrodite said, panicked and seeming not to grasp the issue. "We should seize our timelessness now!"

"There is no such urgency," Zeus said smoothly. Aphrodite calmed.

"Soon?" Poseidon said, an edge of worry in his voice. He was unaffected by Aphrodite's alarm but, beneath that serene and aloof exterior, his concern was for the stability of his own schemes.

"As long as I say it takes."

"There is still much we would do here," Athena said.

"The mortals *are* a work-in-progress," echoed Aphrodite. "As Poseidon says, we three have invested more than any in them. Hera has not come since you were last here."

Zeus smiled ruefully and bowed his head slightly, guiltily.

"She will come when she is ready, though she does not like it it here," he said. "And I will not stand her temper, so I do not encourage her. She seems to like this arrangement."

"Demeter handed me control of the harvest," Poseidon said, sensing the opportunity to swell his importance. "She has visited once. She prefers your other *galaxies*."

"And Ares," Athena said, unifying the veritable trio of reason. "He is the same, chasing war in other corners of your universe. He has visited twice, briefly each time, scouting for inspiration by witnessing the long-held tribal war among the Kemet, which has been fought since they rose from the soil."

"It is Apollo who surprises me the most," Aphrodite said. "For all the lauding of his protection over the mortals - consider his distribution of medicine and truth - his visits have been fleeting and not recent."

"Apollo knows I can be trusted to preserve and uphold his skills," Athena said with mild reproof. "Consider Artemis - she did not appoint any of us when she left."

Zeus smiled coyly. "She did not appoint any of you because she is still here."

Poseidon frowned unhappily. Aphrodite let her mouth drop open. Athena pressed her lips together tightly in annoyance. Before any could speak, Zeus continued firmly.

"I permitted Artemis to assume the form of a wolf and roam the earth at will. Before I left earth, the huntress superior and guardian of the moon suggested to me that at least one of us should be among the mortals. She volunteered and I agreed. One of my more sensitive moments - she chose her approach wisely. In fact I chose two others to do the same - Hermes and Dionysus have also been disguised among the mortals. Hermes has been nurturing languages, and performing the occasional favour for me in my absence. Dionysus has been teaching them entertainments of the mind and of the flesh. The mortals call these things *art*."

"We know their art," Poseidon said dismissively, but he could not hide his surprise that Zeus, despite his absence, had made such secret, long-held arrangements. "It precedes their languages. When you deem it necessary for us to leave the mortals be once and for all, will they all come? Demeter, Apollo, Hera..."

"All but Hades. He will stay in his beloved underworld," Zeus said, not without apathy. "But he is different. He and Mother Death are closest allies. He feeds partly from her power, which supersedes my own. But she cannot use hers on a whim, as I can. Her power *is* her weakness. No, Hades will not leave the mortals. They must experience the afterlife, for the good or ill they affected while flesh."

Zeus paused and looked at them proudly. A smile grew on his lips.

"I do owe a debt of gratitude to you three - my brother and daughters. So have no fear, our work with the mortals is far from complete. Many more civilisations will be built, many more grand wars will be fought, many more lands will be conquered and split, many more kings and queens, heroes and tyrants will rise and fall. All before we are no more. The mortals still need to learn certain things fluently."

"Such as?" Athena said.

Zeus looked at her keenly. "Love and fear, chief among others. We shall ensure they are

taught, and therefore learn them better ourselves."

Conversation among the Olympians shifted between subjects that were extraordinary and
mundane. They enjoyed revelling in profound
matters, just as they did in trivial things. Discussion regarding mortal inventions excited them
most. During that long and intense communion
they debated the merits of the *musalu*: from
their conversation I learned its history.

They treated the mirror with a mixture of
disgust and wonder. Athena would not have it
in her temples, considering them a distraction
from her teachings of wisdom, skill and justice to her acolytes and priestesses. Aphrodite,
professed mother of beauty, had banned the device long before it was prominent. She wanted
to stop her acolytes and priestesses convincing
themselves they could be more lovely than she.

"I think it is a wondrous thing," Poseidon
said, in contrast. "What better way for the mortals to understand themselves, by first knowing
how others see them? Better a mortal knows for
themselves if they are intolerably ugly or ravish-
ingly beautiful."

Poseidon said this knowing it would provoke,
which he tried frequently to do if only for his
own entertainment. In Athena he saw a com-

petitor; in Aphrodite a target to antagonise. His dominating posture and rash manner were too much for Aphrodite to resist, however, and satisfying her needs with mortal men had its limitations. This was no secret and Poseidon knew and played on it, nurturing his ego by sparring with Aphrodite, spurning her to spur her on. Occasionally Poseidon accepted Aphrodite's advances; rarely did he make them on her himself. Familial relations on Olympus are not the same as mortal blood-bonds, there could be no pollution.

Aphrodite took his bait and her voice rose. "Users of it should be blinded and every *musalu* cracked beyond repair. And the maker of them ought to be exiled somewhere, humbled and surrounded by a mountain of mirrors so he can see nothing but his own miserable reflection. The island of Paxos is small, out of the way. People would eventually forget about him and his invention."

Zeus smiled indulgently as he listened. He gave his family a long tether from the rock of his judgement, only drawing it taut when it served his purpose.

The father-god addressed Aphrodite good-humouredly: "Then we would have scores of mortals scrabbling around, if you had your way. Falling over each other. This *musalu* - an ugly name - is so popular, the blind would have to lead the blind. Love and fear would not be taught in the way I wish. The mortal world must learn to be wholly responsible for itself. And we must learn to intervene less."

Zeus permitted nothing be done to stop the existence of the common mirror. This did not sit well with Aphrodite, and it took her a great effort to keep her lips sealed. Athena did not challenge Zeus and made no show of any consternation, though I knew she too was aggrieved. Both goddesses, usually distant from each other's beliefs, were aligned in the fear that their temples would be overrun with secret mirrors; allied by the threat of being undermined by a mortal invention.

The father-god turned his full attention to Aphrodite, his brows of white hair frowning in scrutiny as he revisited one of her earlier statements.

"You said that Troy will suffer its share of trouble. Can such a mighty city ever fall?"

Aphrodite considered her answer, compelled to do so since it was her father's query.

"I predict those strong, high walls will be shattered by beauty and jealousy. A great war will rage over the love of a woman, which the mortal power-brokers - Greeks and Trojans opposing each other - will interpret as lust and treachery. Love will be revealed for the poison it is. Hence I sparingly advocate its use."

"Love a poison? That's your nymph mother talking," Zeus said. "And when will this great problem befall mighty Troy?"

One of his thumbs supported his chin, the digit consumed by beard and supporting his weighty stare. Aphrodite narrowed her eyes in concentration. They seemed to blacken as her lids thinned, their brown hue forming darker pools as she summoned the response to a question she did not expect to answer.

"In mortal terms, as soon as ten years or as far as a thousand."

"I would be most grateful, dear daughter, if it could be at the latter end of your scale."

"I will not necessarily be responsible for Troy's fate."

"I say you will be."

"War doesn't interest me. It might never happen if it is left to me."

"You said beauty and jealousy will bring Troy to its knees. Whether that is through lust, or even poisonous love, both are your expertise. You must be responsible for it. Look upon it as a test. I will take no refusal."

Beleaguered, Aphrodite withheld a sigh. "As you wish. In no more than a thousand years and no less than half that, as the mortals count time, Troy will fall."

Athena had been keenly observing this exchange. "Why the interest in Troy's demise?"

Zeus filled his ample lungs, as if soothing a

latent excitement that threatened to overspill into the Olympian hall.

"I want to establish a new city. One to rival and, eventually, supersede Troy."

Poseidon spoke, protesting mildly. "Mycenae, in the Argolis region, is already a major city. Seen by all as the centre-point of Greece, and by some as that of all the civilised world."

Zeus leaned forward, reinforcing his announcement. "And it will continue to be, until my new city overtakes it. Mycenae's problem is that it is too far inland. It is missing access by the sea, and for that reason can never be much more than what it currently is. Piraeus is a port and gateway to what will be the capital of all Greece and the centrepiece of all the world, civilised and not. I envision Piraeus being the mouth to feed a place where every skill bestowed by us upon the mortals can meet and harmonise. Where love and fear can flourish."

Zeus allowed a moment for his words to be challenged, but his brother and brood waited for more.

"I have commanded that a citadel be constructed atop a hill but two leagues from the port. This *Acropolis* will be a beacon to guide and compel people there. The population at its foot will swell and exceed that of Mycenae, and become a counter-weight to glorious Troy. This city will be the new nucleus of civilisation. It will birth Republics. Its essence will be replicated the throughout the world. This city will shape the future of all mankind."

Zeus sat back, satisfied. Aphrodite raised a single eyebrow, curved and dark as a raven's wing in flight; she seemed impressed. Athena stared into the space in front of her, her brain whirring to calculate the possibilities. Poseidon straightened his muscular back and stretched, heaving his shoulders up proudly, as if presenting himself for duty, and was the first to speak.

"Will any of us be this new city's champion?"

Zeus peered at the sea-god thoughtfully. Athena was now paying strict attention. Aphrodite gently felt the contours of her graceful jaw, her fingers stroking the delicate skin in thought.

"There will be temples for all of us like any other city. However," Zeus paused and raised a finger so his next words were marked well, "to show my gratitude to you three, for showing such particular loyalty to the mortal cause, one of you shall be its figurehead. You shall have the new city named after you. When the Acropolis is complete and the city is as busy and expanded as I would like, a contest will be held within its walls. It shall be a moment when you may display a small measure of your power for all to witness. Whichever of you appeals to the people the most will win the naming rights. The winner will be immortalised in the forums, in the homes and in the minds of the people. I foresee this city standing long after we have departed.

This prize is a bequest."

Aphrodite narrowed her eyes with scrutiny. "Why not destroy Troy now, and give this new city a capital advantage?"

Poseidon, locked in thought, said absently: "Cities need competition to grow and prosper."

"Is Mycenae not enough competition?"

"Domestically perhaps. But as people flock from the expanisve east to Troy, people will flock from the east, west, north and south to this new city."

"It seems Poseidon can be relied on to take part. Daughters?" Zeus said.

Poseidon did not contradict Zeus. Athena opened her mouth to speak, but Aphrodite blurted first.

"I'm not interested," she said.

Poseidon and Athena both looked at her with careful surprise. Zeus frowned, but let her explain herself.

"I am satisfied to represent what I consider to be the pinnacles of mortality - beauty, lust, even love when I must, and all the things that connect those beacons. They are older and more powerful than any city. If it is love and fear you want, there will be enough for me to be occupied with. I do not need any further confirmation of my power."

Zeus could not hide his disappointment from his face or voice.

"Very well. Since you are also going to arrange

34

Troy's destruction - eventually - I can accept your decision."

"I do not decline," Athena said steadfastly. "I can think of no better chance for wisdom, skill and justice to be exemplified. No three attributes will spawn more love or fear, or teach the greatest lessons in them. A great bequest to us, a greater gift to the mortals."

Aphrodite turned to Athena. "Wisdom, skill and justice are entirely dependent on beauty, lust and love. Our father wants love and fear to be well-learned among the mortals, as immortalised within their essence as the winning god will be in the city's name. I *am* love, and despite my reticence towards it whoever wins the city will ultimately have to answer to me."

Irked, Athena faced her. "You hinder progress. Mortal history is plagued with the adverse results of your whims. Our father is asking for something more than what you perceive as love. Fear is poison, love is the antidote - and you are terrified by it. You cannot be trusted to spearhead this new city, so I applaud your decision to withdraw from the game to rule it."

Aphrodite, slender and delicate, squared her body in challenge to more robust Athena, who stood a head taller than she.

"And what of war, which you cannot be trusted with? Don't forget war, which is in your charge while Ares does as he pleases. The prayers for victory in battle and skill with weapons you often honour, rarely scrutinising them, with little regard for the mortal consequences. That has caused just as many *adverse results* as love, if not more."

"War is beneath wisdom, skill and justice," Athena said. "I lament it being the solution to the tangles of other disciplines. So often your obsession with beauty and lust - and your too-cautious use of love - pollutes my powers. I am often left with no choice but to let the battle rage freely."

Aphrodite gave Athena a pitiful smile. "You treat war in the same way you claim I treat love - with fear. Too afraid to take responsibility when your own disciplines backfire. You wield war as an errant weapon, as a hot knife to be quickly rid from your hand. I say that you, Athena, cannot be trusted. This new city would be ill-equipped to handle *your* whims."

Poseidon stepped between them eminently, playing peacemaker.

"Then all is fair between you," he said.

Athena and Aphrodite backed away from each other, the tension defused but lingering in the Olympian air.

"Let me be clear," Zeus continued. "Whoever wins the city will *be* the city. Its champion - whether you Poseidon, or you Athena - shall use their powers to embody love and fear, purposes so vital to the mortal cause. Either your wisdom, skill with healing and sense of justice, dear

Athena; or your power over the seas, winds and horses, Poseidon, shall dominate. You, my proud and ravishing Aphrodite, will not have the control. You are love itself, I grant you that, but the burden of that, along with beauty and desire no less, must now be shared. All of you will know its difficulties, which Aphrodite has carried alone since creation."

"Fear we know well enough," said Poseidon. "We are experts at instilling it."

Zeus looked at his brother solemnly. "Do not be too quick to celebrate your dread achievements. A host of new challenges awaits. Whoever wins this contest, you must all go deeper in your search for new terrors, and new passions. This city will truly mark mortal and Olympian progress."

"I have changed my mind," Aphrodite said suddenly. "I have profited from the lesson Athena sought to give me." The god adopted her best and most sincere voice. "I revoke my declining of your invitation to take part in the contest."

"Not granted," Zeus replied without hesitation. Aphrodite's mouth dropped open slightly. "This is not a contest for those prone to indecision."

"But..."

Zeus raised a hand to silence her. "You had the opportunity to partake and you shunned it. Besides, a contest is so much more exciting with just two vying for victory."

The father-god paused for any further retaliation or comment. None came.

"Good, this is settled. And just as I was becoming comfortable on my long-awaited return, I fear I must leave again. Another one of my *galaxies* beckons. But I will not be away for long, and then I shall stay here on earth, here on Olympus. Then I shall confirm our immortality."

The mouths of Poseidon, Aphrodite and Athena all opened at once, but Zeus gave no chance for questions. In the blink of an eye he had vanished, leaving his remarkable throne empty.

"I already miss his arrogance," Poseidon said airily, idly wandering towards Zeus' vacated seat. "Without him here, I am unleashed. *We* must forge our own paths. Zeus is too used to ruling with impunity, and we too used to obeying."

The sea-god reached the enormous white-bone structure and eased himself down upon it. He was not immediately comfortable, the throne having been carved specifically for Zeus. He sat back and patted a knee, indicating that Aphrodite should sit on it.

Slow and coy she wilfully approached, putting one slender, naked leg of pale flesh in front of the other. Her ample hips and bottom shifted sensually, and a small smile was caught upon her lips. Poseidon watched her hungrily and he spread himself upon the throne, allowing his enormous phallus, mid-swell, to fall between his legs. Athena thinned her lips in prudish disapproval but said nothing.

Aphrodite circled the throne and caressed its curved backrest. She tempted Poseidon by not yet doing his bidding.

"He will know you said that," Aphrodite said. "Zeus knows his weaknesses, but does not like admitting them."

"He will hear nothing of what we say while he is absent," Poseidon said, craning his neck to follow Aphrodite. Both cared not for how they were perceived by Athena, herself standing spare. "I know his mind. The *galaxías* he is bound for now is so apart from this one. He will be back here soon enough."

"We are all responsible in his absence," Athena said. "But you would prefer my father do what Demeter did with the mortal harvest, and what Apollo did with art. You would have him entrust his kingship to one of us. You would nominate yourself, of course."

She had a mockery in her tone: normally an unwise strategy with the sea-god. But she could sense a coming argument and sought to bait him early; Poseidon was most vulnerable when agitated. Aphrodite finished her circuit of the throne to stand beside him. She draped an arm causally atop the seat's crest. They both studied Athena, the two of them united in preparation for the debate.

"Naturally," Poseidon said. "Wouldn't you? Ah no, of course not - not prudent, honourable Athena. Even if Zeus' authority were offered to you on a dish, if you alone were told to own the supremacy my brother covets, you would say: '*I refuse. I am humility itself. I know my place among the clever crones, the fumbling medics and the haughty judges.*'"

Athena laughed lightly. "You underestimate my ambition. And you overstate your own."

"Knowing *how far* to reach is the ultimate weakness," Poseidon replied. "To convince an opponent that they have limits is far more destructive than any hard weapon."

Aphrodite spoke. "Beauty and love have no limits. They are borderless. Timeless. Zeus may have denied me claim to his new city, but even he is at the mercy of what I stand for. He knows it."

"Well said," Poseidon said, and Aphrodite elegantly twisted her naked body to finally rest on his lap. Now she used Poseidon as her throne, settling into the crevice afforded by his pelvis.

"If that is so," Athena said carefully, "then he is also at the mercy of wisdom. And healing. And justice. Even war, dare I say. The mortals crave those things. There is beauty and love in them. Subtle, yes, but not unseen or unfelt."

Poseidon laughed. "Absurd! You have outdone yourself with that statement. And you expect to be the figurehead of the most glorious city this mortal earth has ever witnessed? I shall pray for its inhabitants if you beat me to it."

"As shall I," said Aphrodite.

"Wisdom, healing, justice...these are mortal toys," the sea-god continued. "Inventions to remind them that they only exist by our grace."

"Our inventions or theirs, Poseidon?" Athena asked.

"Ours of course," the sea-god said.

"I disagree. The mortals' are greater creators than us. Ultimately, after all is said and done, that is what Zeus wants - for the mortals to invent their self-sufficiency, to guarantee their own survival. We cannot do it for them."

"The mortals own nothing themselves," Poseidon said, aggrieved. "They may believe they do, but everything they have created is because of us." He shifted an arm from around Aphrodite's waist and loosely pointed a finger at Athena. "We allow them to believe what they create is their own."

Aphrodite wriggled slightly and pressed herself against Poseidon's lap. The god gently shifted the lower half of his body and a flash of pleasure passed across his face. Aphrodite gave him a brief, knowing glance over her shoulder and bit her lower lip. Athena looked on, aware these tactics were partly intended to discomfort her.

Aphrodite turned her attention back to Athena. "Wrongdoers and innocent victims *pray* that justice is either ignored or executed," she said. "Those who heal ensure the *altars* are well-stocked before they give their dose." The god closed her eyes and gasped without inhibition as Poseidon carefully eased his hardened phallus into her. She adjusted her hips to accommodate him, but kept her slender, inviting legs near-closed. She regained composure, able to withstand the stimulation. "And the wise are ever-sure to *thank* our power for their every new enlightenment."

Athena said nothing, but not from muteness or shock. To the contrary: she knew the way to deal with Aphrodite and Poseidon was to let their moment pass; let them have their fun and be aware for the moment of climax. She knew that a period of weakness immediately followed.

Now Poseidon and Aphrodite were fucking, gently and rhythmically. Poseidon kept his eyes on Athena, even as Aphrodite leant back against him, wanting the god to kiss her. She widened her legs slightly. Poseidon compensated for his disinterest in Aphrodite's face and neck by gently stroking one of her perfect breasts, alternately caressing beneath the heft and areola.

"Aphrodite speaks a great deal of truth," he said. "Beauty and love are the heralds of order.

They may prop up your own schemes, in a tenuous way, but they are all that really matter. Without them there is no mortal survival. There will come a time when the mortals will understand this. Beauty and lust, perhaps love, will be the sole religion."

Aphrodite's face reddened and she let out a sudden yelp of pleasure. Her body quivered and she grasped Poseidon's neck, digging her fingernails into his muscular nape. Her writhing upon his lap slowed to a stop and she caught breath, at the mercy of mortal-form limitations. Poseidon had maintained his stare upon Athena all the while, but his face showed the release of an enormous tension. Aphrodite appeared damp with orgasm: her face vaguely slick with sweat and her inner thighs, now spread wider, moist with residue.

"Finished?" Athena said flatly.

Aphrodite took the comment seriously and nodded briskly, smiling and easing herself off of Poseidon's lap. Poseidon's phallus, itself coated with semen and fluid, flopped lazily atop one bare thigh. She turned towards Athena and took a step forward.

"Are you embarrassed by how *obsessed* Poseidon and I are with each other?" Aphrodite said, catching breath.

"No," Athena said. "I completely understand. While we assume these flesh shells we must obey the urges."

"What we have is not an *urge*. What we have is..."

"Love?" Athena said. "Poisonous, unreliable love?"

"Something like it," Aphrodite said too quickly, and looked to Poseidon for support.

The sea-god smiled at her in a way that she would believe to be sincere, but to others would be a look of tolerance. She returned her spent, post-coital stare to Athena.

"Despite Poseidon's kind words, what really trumps beauty is water and the power to control it. That which gives life to the mortals, and what takes it away. The very essence of balance. The seas, the droughts. Tides that nourish and drown, rains that permit vines to grow and which cause floods. Droughts that give healthy thirst, and which make throats parch. When essential water causes death, therein lies more beauty and love - the beauty of being alive, the love for survival."

"We crave what they crave, while we take their form," Athena said evenly. "All of our gifts bestowed to them are equally valuable. One's dominance would only suppress another."

Poseidon raised his voice and startled Aphrodite, his frustration echoing around the Olympian atrium. "Then *what* supersedes all? There must be something that dominates, something that *wins*. It is the natural order. All cannot be equal."

"Time," Athena said with authority. "The definitive mortal invention. Their identification and measurement of it is the first weakening of their bond with us. It makes us their secret enemies. You said there will come a time when beauty, lust, perhaps love, will be the sole religion. *That* is a limit. *That* is the ultimate threat. Beauty and love are not timeless. Neither is wisdom, nor justice, nor the skill to heal. Neither is water nor war. Time itself can only be timeless. Whoever wins Zeus' city will make a friend of time."

I was suddenly enshrouded in darkness again, and believed my return to the mortal world to be imminent. Athena, however, had further use of me: the blinding shadow across my eyes was my transportation to another part of the mountain.

The space I arrived in hosted tall ionic columns, vast in number and precisely set apart. They were made of a hard, black material that mortals may know in a fragment of the future. The darkness they cast was not of the sinister kind, but one of comfort. They were hewn and carved to smooth perfection, shined to spark a reflection from a distant source of light yet to be fully revealed.

They formed a dense forest in this daunting and sublime atrium. No randomness of their positioning was evident; they stood regimented, like a phalanx of soldiers awaiting orders before invasion. While their heights seemed immeasurable, their arrangement eventually ended: a semi-circular pool was exposed by their clearing. It was as wide as the atrium where this spectacle of simple architecture was housed; the pool a perfect half-moon with the curve steering closest to those approaching it. Its straight edge was bezelled by a power that reached as infinitely tall as the columns. This essence, this sorcery, slowly swayed and undulated, its stillness betrayed by occasional waves of fluctuation.

This remarkable arena was where the gods bathed, with a view of the universe. On the other side of the hypnotic, glassless window were stars and occasional spectrums of colour; bright patterns and shapes spawned from the chaos that they tamed, and then disordered again.

Poseidon and Aphrodite did not notice Athena and I lurking behind a column nearest the pool. Excellent concealment was granted; friendly gloom that had perhaps been created on purpose, as a secret tool with which to spy on others during personal and reflective moments. When plain truth could be most comfortable, and most disagreeable.

Athena had been waiting patiently for them to conclude their marathon lovemaking, which had begun in the throne room. She wanted to listen to them when they thought themselves alone; she wanted to evaluate the true extent of their alliance, whether it went beyond mortal satisfaction. The silvery waters (though no water on earth took the form of the pool's liquid) did not slosh and splash as Aphrodite clutched Poseidon between her thighs. The substance flowed about them like a second skin.

She latched onto him like a leech, her bucking enthusiasm for him barely controlled by Poseidon's muscles. If he had wanted he could have hurled her, screeching in failed climax, across the wide pool, a comet against the starry backdrop. Instead he channelled his energy to compliment hers, spurring her pelvic grinding and urging her growing shouts of pleasure. He eventually drove her to an explosive orgasm: her command of the mortal-form body was briefly lost and a shimmer of the goddess' true form was exposed. It sprang from the flesh like steam from volcanic lava suddenly cooled, before quickly returning inward, re-absorbed into her and condensing on the skin.

They detached from one another, her breaths quivering more than his. After a time she lay in the pool on her back, letting the liquid support her naked frame and buoy her. Poseidon lay on his belly, leaning against the straight edge of the pool and staring out at the shining space-scape. Aphrodite could not keep away and soon joined him. She kissed his broad back lightly, trying to coax post-coital affection, but Poseidon had become distracted by his thoughts. Their bodies glistened in the starlight and fluid, like twin suns radiating in a substantial blackness. Aphrodite pecked slow kisses upon his back.

Poseidon continued staring at the universe, and asked: "Have you ever loved any of your mortal lovers?"

The question was not ill-timed, but purposeful. Aphrodite stopped.

"Once," she answered truthfully. She sat up in the water; the sloshing of the liquid echoed around the atrium. "But it is nothing to me now. All of my visits to mortal men have only been to satisfy my curiosity. I will not admit to Athena that I have allowed pure love to birth between you and I. Only in loving you do I truly know what a terrible mistress love is. Permitting it more credence would weaken me against Athena."

"You have always been afraid of powerlessness," Poseidon said provocatively.

"I do fear you falling out of love with me."

"And you fear Athena knowing you have found love with me. Nobody has known fear until they have known love. You have found love with me, and you have found fear. You will discover it is a fair exchange."

A brief silence hung in the air. They both focussed on the space-scape, though Aphrodite sat awkward with unease. A streak of thin golden light shot across the blackness between the stars, a meteor's tail. It quickly fizzed out of existence.

Aphrodite attempted a lightness of tone, but her question was weighted with uncertainty.

"I could never replicate what we have with a mortal. The trust that goes beyond our intimacy. Could you?"

"There has never been a mortal woman to rival you for beauty," Poseidon said absently. "And I doubt there will be."

"That is a guarded answer," Aphrodite said. "I must be more to you than beauty."

Poseidon shifted his position in the pool, facing her as if to begin a test. He changed the subject of their talk, speaking what was truly on his mind.

"How should I compel the people of Zeus' new city to select me, and not Athena? *'Whichever of you appeals to the people the most will win the naming rights'* Zeus said. Should I host games, and establish a nation of athletes? Should I equip the city with the finest ships and start a naval war they cannot lose, for glory and plunder? Should I make a new breed of horse exclusive to the city, a symbol of magnificence and power that nobody could challenge?"

He looked at Aphrodite expectantly.

"I think...," she said cautiously, but aware of opportunity. "...Why not offer something beyond your usual expertise. Something new. Something that the mortals can congratulate themselves for eventually fathoming."

Doubt and impatience crept into Poseidon's voice.

"Such as?"

"Our love."

Poseidon either believed her answer to be one of genius and was speechless, or his silence was his great effort to control his disdain. Eventually he spoke, quietly.

"How would I appeal to the people with *our love*?" He could not hide his contempt for the idea.

Aphrodite persisted. "Conjure a flower that does not die. Or an orchard that bears fruit through all four earthly seasons."

"Peaceful offerings that show no real strength," Poseidon said tightly. He then looked at her accusingly. "You would use the opportunity I have for a true legacy on mortal earth to appease your own concerns and shortcomings, your own fears. You could have agreed to Zeus' proposition, but you didn't. This city will not be won on platitudes and unity among us. Zeus wants a contest, a war between Athena and myself. My weapon will not be our love - as you call it."

He returned to his view of the shining universe. Aphrodite lingered, dejected but brave; she seemed unwilling to further argue her case and yet desperate to fill the void in talk. She shifted her position to lie casually alongside Poseidon, as if his words had no effect.

"I have received a series of prayers from a mortal," Aphrodite said. "A reputable woman in one of the villages of debauchery outside Mycenae. Such powerful prayers, and for something so unusual."

"What did she want?"

"This woman has taken guardianship over a girl named Medusa. The girl's mother died from a sickness that swept their village of Tanis. The woman wants a particular trader and his train to stop there."

"Show me these mortals," Poseidon said. He would not normally care for such a plight, but he wanted to encourage Aphrodite's deviation from her unpalatable mood.

Aphrodite raised a hand, commanding the undulating window. A woman appeared, barebreasted and in supplicant pose. She was joined by a clothed child of age similar to my own, who I rightly assumed to be Medusa. Their features were distorted by the quivering, transparent mass: like shades of ancestors, ghosts to be brought into being for a time and then released back into the oblivion from whence they came.

"The child attracts much attention for her

looks," Aphrodite said. "But many do when in the comfort of youth."

Poseidon was silent, focussed on them. Aphrodite smiled to herself, aware she had regained his interest. She continued speaking.

"She may have men forever begging to insert their unworthy cocks into her, spraying their watery seed up her and producing less striking bastards. I may keep her as a virgin, for her sake. And for the amusement of continually watching mortal men suffer by her unobtainable beauty."

"Too much intervention," Poseidon said distractedly. "Why does her guardian want the trader to stop in Tanis?"

"She wants to offload Medusa, for the child's own good. The trader is a rarity among his type - fair in business and in temperament, though to look at the man you might think differently. He would be able to sell Medusa to a good family. More than the woman could offer since the disease has decimated their livelihood. He currently spurs his train on to Mycenae, with no intention of stopping at Tanis. Unless I honour the woman's request - made more piously than others I have granted in the past."

The image of Medusa slowly vanished. Poseidon was released from his staring at them, as if freed from a spell.

"To alter the trader's course would be acceptable intervention. But directly altering the course of the child's life, to keep her womanhood intact, would set an unfavourable precedent."

Aphrodite sighed. "You're right, of course. How should it be done, to affect the trader?"

"I have an idea, and for what to present to the people of the new city," Poseidon said. "I regret my earlier words to you. Some were harsh. I blame that post-coital weakness that affects the mortal form - that vulnerability and introspection. Your suggestion of subtlety is wise."

This pleased Aphrodite. "You have no apology to make. There is always a price to pay for pleasure. How will you compel the people? How will you beat Athena?"

"When the time comes, I shall summon a surge of sea water from the ground, which will reach into the sky. Simple and subtle, as you suggest, but a display of my strength and suitability to claim the city. The people will know it is I, and all that I entail, who seeks their favour. They will be a nation of seafarers with me as their figurehead - conquerors of distant lands and the forgers of empires with me as their champion."

"I can think of no better idea," Aphrodite said encouragingly. "Athena will struggle to match it."

"Allow *me* to intercept your trader. Permit me to steer him to Tanis. Consider it a gift."

"How will it be done?"

"I shall not compel the trader directly. I shall be more thoughtful - you have taught me well, and I obey Zeus' command for scant intervention. A clever arrangement."

Poseidon waved a hand at the throbbing transparence. The image became that of a group of men on horseback, riding hard, roughshod and armed, kicking up dust from the landscape. Their aggressive shouts were calls to arms, eager to attack in a throaty and garbled language. Their noise echoed around the atrium, breaking the peace.

"Thieves," Poseidon said. "I have altered *their* course. They have seen the trader's train and will attack it. There will be bloodshed, but your trader will survive. He will stop at Tanis to recover his senses. Your pious whore may get her wish after all. Salvation may reach the child Medusa."

The image of the thieves dissipated as the window quivered its last, revealing the starscape once more.

Athena retreated, slipping away without a breath of sound. I followed her. The innumerate columns gradually became darkness itself as I was released from the communion.

Chapter Three

Having been forced to stop on the fringes of Tanis, Menethus saw that I was finally awake. He got me to my feet, rousing me in a rough manner: he had much experience of the moments after I was released from the communion, and usually dealt me a gentler hand. But he was bloody and wary from the ambush by thieves that had diverted us, arranged by Poseidon. In my entranced state I had been fully aware of what was to befall Menethus, and yet oblivious to the fight as it took place on the ground around me.

Tanis served Mycenae as an outpost of vice. Its function was as a pleasure-village for the jobbing men and garrisoned soldiers, money burning a hole in their cotton pockets, eager to drink and gamble and laugh and fuck and hope. They would stay for a full night before sloping back to the city, their pockets and testicles lighter. Such satellites (for Tanis was not the only such place) served another useful purpose: in keeping Mycenae largely free from downmarket activities and as a bastion of regulation and honour that the city's authorities decreed. Pleasure-villages such as Tanis were left to govern themselves in terms of business, and serious trouble was mostly allayed by the threat of strict Mycenaean law that could be imposed.

Tanis' distance from Mycenae was farthest. A good rider could spend the same time reaching Tanis as it took a setting sun's full surrender to night. Plenty undertook the journey: the promises of the most exotic women, of rich games of chance, and of stories and sustenance of high repute were too tempting to resist.

Far beyond Mycenae, to the north-east, is the port of Piraeus. Long before Zeus marked it out as the mouth to feed his new city, workers and merchants had continually flocked to what was fast becoming a critical shipping gateway. Its outskirts had gradually burgeoned through trade and ripened with expansion. Zeus' command for a citadel to be built overlooking this vast and flourishing settlement was well-timed.

From Mycenae a fast rider could reach Piraeus within a single rising of the moon. A family with beasts and a cart could expect twice that time. A market-train, such as that owned by Menethus, would be more, eating into a small portion of the season if the weather was persistently poor.

Menethus' face wore injuries and urgency: he needed me, his dependable and pious property. He did not ask me to tend his wounds, and I did not offer. A puff-cloud of fine ash swirled and floated above the timbered dwellings. It was like snow that I had once seen when we crossed the Parnassus mountains. Unlike those frozen droplets, the ash came from searing origins. I knew what had caused it, the reason as clear in my mind as a recent memory: disease had swept through Tanis, as Aphrodite had proclaimed. The dead, I quickly concluded, had been burned on a communal pyre and their embers were now drifting over us. Menethus looked around, his eyes narrowed with trepidation and recognition.

"I know this place," he said. "I have been here before. It looks different, smaller, but I have been here before." He sniffed the air. "There is either disease or battle here. I see no evidence of a fight."

The dwellings of Tanis were indeed neatly arranged, and there was no sign of bloodshed or struggle. I summoned my voice, which croaked with tiredness.

"It is a disease. The ash we see is its last victims. It has moved on."

"Towards Mycenae?"

"No. It came from that direction. It touched Mycenae, but they were careful and it did not spread. Now it makes for the coast, out to sea. We may have met the plague in the wind had we not been attacked."

Menethus looked at me, searching my face for error. He was descended from barbarian stock, from the swamp-lands in the extreme north, far from Greece. His legs and arms were as thick as tree trunks, though his skin was pale and coarse with dark hair. He towered over most people like a temple column, not least myself who barely reached his waist. His manners were less gruff than his peers who shared his trade, and he seldom barked his words. Menethus had learned the value of an even temper, and it had served him well enough to become his habit, unchanged by his rough experiences and business.

Satisfied with my deduction, his great bearded head nodded once and we trudged onward into the heart of the village, from where the smoke and ash of incinerated corpses plumed. My child legs had to be quick to keep up with his stride. The market-train and all its cargo - human, animal and object - remained in the care of his drivers: trusted workers who had served him for generations. Menethus' greatest asset was the loyalty of his troop, and his ability to retain it.

We found the pyre with ease. No inhabitants walked among or challenged us. The huts stood as if in silent memorial for the charred. Their animal-hide coverings quivered slightly in the breeze.

"We may see no people, but I smell them," Menethus said in a low voice. "The odour of living bodies. I know no scent better. They huddle in these dwellings, mourning fearfully."

A cockerel lay at the foot of the pyre. Its body was half-decapitated and blood had spilled and spattered over the stones. The great red stain showed evidence of having boiled in the heat of the fire, its crimson edges brown as mud. The bird's white feathers had mostly been scorched away, revealing skin that was cooked crisp.

Menethus pointed a large, meaty finger at the pyre. "Why those?"

He referred to flowers: seven scarlet geraniums tied together, wilting and smelling bittersweet, draped over the slaughtered cockerel.

"Offerings to Athena. The cockerel's blood for the flames to be strong. Earnest heat to scorch away the flesh and the illness. Geraniums - one of the god's favourite plants. Seven - one for each recently brought dead to the pyre."

In the embers I counted hundreds of bones intermingled, and among them seven skulls in various states of disintegration.

"Athena seems happy," said Menethus conclusively.

I paused before replying, staring into the pyre and not allowing my thoughts to answer. Rather, I wanted the god to respond to me, as my own mother had first taught me. The number of the dead came to me like a memory.

"Thirty-two have perished from the disease."

"That is a waste of bodies," Menethus said, as if he had lost trade through the deaths. "Could the god not have intervened sooner? Banished the

59

sickness altogether, or healed the unwell?"

I swallowed down nausea, glad for it because I knew what followed: I felt the remnant oasis of discreet knowledge, seeped through in after-effect from the transcendence of the communion.

"This final burning was white-hot," I said. "That was the extent of the god's aid."

We became aware of a presence behind us, the soft crunch of leather sandals against the dry ground. Two sets of feet: an adult's and a child's. They stopped a respectful distance away from Menethus and I.

We turned to face them, Menethus half-prepared for a fight. I recognised them from communion. On closer, clearer inspection I could see that the woman was of no more than thirty years. Her face was pretty and with a look so determined it inspired desire to assist without even knowing why. A desirably feminine body was hidden beneath her conservative robe of white cotton. She draped an arm around the shoulders of Medusa, her loose embrace a symbol of guardianship, rather than motherhood, over the child.

Menethus was not a man who was easily swayed, but at that moment he stared at Medusa, instantly entranced. I wilted slightly as I beheld her for the first time in the flesh, and shyly moved closer to Menethus. He said nothing, transfixed by the alluring child. Vulnerability had been exposed in both of us by her arrival: a helplessness that, for our own reasons, Menethus and I had long-suppressed.

A gust of wind gently blew. Corpse-ash floated onto the woman and the child. The woman, lightly and without fuss, rid herself of it. Medusa did nothing to brush it off, instead allowing it to naturally coat her. It settled on her perfectly, its darkness tattooing her golden-tanned skin with black marks that seemed to carve out the symmetrical angles of her face.

To look at us must have been alarming for them. Menethus had not cleaned himself following the attack: one of his eyes was bruised blue-black, and a gash to his head, though clotted and no longer freely oozing blood, extended down to the top of his cheek and threatened to split with any sudden pressure such as a smile. I had not bathed in days: my pale-coloured robe was filthy; and my face was likely bone-white and under-nourished as I recovered from the potent communion.

The woman spoke, her voice strongly accented with the Libyan tongue. "Thirty-two have died. It's a fever-sickness. You will not find much hospitality here."

"I have it on good authority that the disease has passed," Menethus said. "And we need to stay for a brief time. I own a market-train. It was attacked by thieves."

The woman stared hard at Menethus, as if recognising him and trying to recall his identity.

"You can use the real term for your market-train," she said. "There are no strangers here to the slave's life, or masters."

"Very well," Menethus said, bowing his head slightly in rare defeat. This woman was savvy, but not unkind. "I meant no dishonour, only care. I am Menethus, and my business is the trafficking of humans, animals and objects. I am proud to be a fair man. My reputation is known."

The woman's natural approach was caution. From what I had witnessed in the Olympian bathing atrium, she knew Menethus - but she did not say or show it then.

"Whose authority says the disease has passed?" She said.

Menethus gestured to me. "Miranda. Twelve years old and a gifted agent of Athena from birth."

"Why is she not in temple?"

A pertinent question to ask, and one that Menethus had answered before.

"I acquired her in Libya. She has no family but my own offerings. Miranda will be sold to the temple of Athena in the settlement beyond Piraeus. She will be an acolyte, one day a priestess. She will have a pious life, and a good one."

The woman relaxed, her face mellowing to

one of wonder and hope.

Menethus continued. "There will be a new city there one day. Bigger than Mycenae, from what I hear from my messengers. Commerce, education, religion...it will be a place like no other. Even Troy will eventually bow down to its supremacy."

The woman nodded slowly in agreement. She studied me with increased interest.

"Were you born in Libya?" She said to me.

"The town of Gonia," I said softly, tearing my own stare away from Medusa, who had continued to look at me. Her expression had maintained a tenderness, but her slowly blinking stare was unrelenting.

The woman brightened. "I know it," she said. "On the coast. A modest journey east from Tobru, where I'm from. And Medusa's mother." She gestured to the child, introducing her. "Most of the women here are from Cyrenaica. Escaping between truces in the war."

Menethus interjected. "Libya holds difficult memories for Miranda. I found her decrepit and starving, kept out of sight of the marauding Haruj. The High Priestess in charge of the small temple thrust her into my arms, told me she would fetch a good price in Greece. Moments later the High Priestess was killed."

I could recall the hideous death of my old High Priestess, asphyxiated by the swollen belly of a venomous reptile. The invading Haruj had made no effort to attack Menethus; they knew he was not there for war. With him, I was immediately safe.

"She was pinned down and force-fed a pregnant krait," I said. "The Haruj believe the snake cleanses the heathen spirit. They see our gods as charlatans. They don't yet realise their gods are the same as ours. Heathen fools."

Suddenly Medusa spoke in her quiet, crisp voice. "You could entreat Athena to take revenge. My mother told me the god does not advocate it, but can be forceful if convinced."

She was correct. I had once appealed to Athena for the swift and gruesome deaths of those Haruj who slew my former High Priestess. She had been honourable, as loyal a servant to the Olympian cause as any, and a woman who willingly shared her vast knowledge. But it is a mistake to think that mortal prayers can be disguised as orders. I did not witness her murderers' deaths, and received no assent from the god as to whether they took place at all.

"The god is not mine to expect things from," I replied, neutrally.

Medusa broke her stare away from me, looked up at her guardian and they shared a look of understanding.

"You must be hungry and thirsty," the woman said to us, now friendly. "My name is Ashiya. Come with us."

Menethus answered: "I would be grateful. Let

us share more of our stories, so that trust might be earned. My workers and stock would benefit from your generosity, and I would pay for it. I do not believe in free trade."

◆ ◆ ◆

The abode we approached stood unclustered, set apart from the others, indicating it held some importance in the village.

Inside the dwelling was a large single room, the thick wooden borders of the structure rounded at its edges. Drapes of coloured fabric hung from ceiling to floor, segregating smaller, private areas. The fabrics were coloured in emerald green, brownish copper and dusky rose: shades that honoured Aphrodite in what was a dominion of sex.

An open fireplace occupied the centre. What sprung from it was remarkable: a fixture of iron, shaped into a rough tube, reached upward from the hearth and extended through the concave roof, neatly expelling most of the smoke created by the fire. I had seen similar fittings before, but none as adorned as this. The metal had been decorated with swirling patterns and symbols of a language that was foreign to me. Near its apex, before it spread into a triangle shape and was connected to the wooden roof, a series of faces circulated the fitting. Their expressions grinned and gaped with what I perceived as a demonic horror; some had small horns fashioned above their metallic brows.

We sat on sumptuous cushions that ringed the perimeter of the floor, our tired legs and backs finally supported by something other than our weary bones. Ashiya served us a rich, sweetly-spiced bread and an infusion of leaves. I distrusted the steaming bowl of brown, clear liquid, having never smelled anything like its bitterness before. Menethus slurped his noisily and greedily, drenching his beard. He whipped me a look as if to say *'drink or you'll parch, insult our hosts and embarrass me.'*

Ashiya caught the warning and smiled at me. "A herb grown in the far east," she said. "Lots of people drink it as an infusion. It won't harm you."

I peered at the liquid doubtfully but obeyed and, beyond the sting on my tongue from the heat, the drink did not taste as sharp as its odour. With the bread it was comforting.

We finished our meal. Medusa whispered in Ashiya's ear and the woman nodded solemnly. The child went to the far side of the dwelling and then behind a curtain of emerald green. I caught a glimpse of the low-lying bed beyond, doubtless where our hostess slept and conducted her own business.

"You have a very comfortable home," Menethus said, looking around at the trinkets, some of which were gold, and well-kept furnishings.

Ashiya was prosperous.

"It has to be, to attract the clients," she said. "This place would usually be busy. We can comfortably fit seven or eight bodies and their women in here. Food, wine, song."

"No doubt all heaving and writhing like serpents," Menethus said with a knowing smile, his caution relaxed and bravado returned with the comfort of sustenance.

"Men from all over Greece have sought this very house of decadence, and paid well for the privilege. Whether they still will after the disease..." she trailed off with doubt in her voice.

Medusa returned. She carried a neatly-made box of wood with grey metal decorations, intricately patterned like woven fabric. At its centre was a small symbol of a rod with a single snake wrapped about it: in Libya, this emblem was a common mark of healing. The medicine vessel was old, passed down among generations like the wisdom it supported. It had belonged to her mother, I privately concluded. She looked at Ashiya for permission, who nodded to the girl.

"Medusa will dress your wounds," Ashiya said to Menethus. He looked immediately doubtful. "She is adept. Her mother taught her, when she was alive. A family inheritance. She is gifted in the skill. She can even stitch heavy cuts. She is like a seamstress mending a rip in fabric."

Menethus looked at Medusa with an uncertain stare. She gave the man a smile, sweet and slight.

Her eyes ensnared him with reassurance, but still Menethus asked me.

"Should I trust this child?"

I hesitated briefly. "Yes," I said.

Ashiya fetched hot water and Medusa set to work. I watched her healing craft, and was quietly stunned. She was more than adept: gentle and purposeful with her initial studying of Menethus' injuries; tidy and efficient with her tending to them. Even in rougher hands Menethus would not have yelped or made a scene. He listened attentively as Ashiya spoke, recounting the woe of the recent disease.

"The sickness came carried by the winds and the people venturing out from Mycenae and beyond. The first victim received good care from Baktria, Medusa's mother. We thought the illness would pass. Then another two became ill with the same and the first died. Baktria journeyed to Mycenae and consulted a reliable physician, and the small temple of Athena there. There were no remedies or answers. Some would be affected by it, others would not, as is the way. Praying for the winds to move the disease on was the only medicine."

"Nothing new to tell you," Menethus said.

"So it would seem. Baktria returned. Six more had fallen ill in her absence. Word had not yet spread, though we knew the physician in Mycenae would talk. Not out of corruption or spite, but from professional interest. It took just five passings of the moon for the eight to die and we built the pyre for the nine. There were over one hundred people who called Tanis home. Five of the nine had lived and worked here for many seasons, the other four were guests. As the first flames were lit, those of us who call ourselves leaders of Tanis convened, including myself and Baktria. We speculated on what to do if the sickness continued. We spoke of disbanding the village, but our livelihoods are ingrained here and the desire to leave was weak. We decided that remaining was a better risk than abandoning the lives we had built."

Medusa had cleaned Menethus' wounds and was about to begin the process of stitching the gash to his head. She dunked a thin needle into a vial of a foul-smelling substance. She giggled as I recoiled from the stench.

"I know that smell," said Menethus grimly. "Ethyl. I'm glad to see the child using it."

Medusa deftly threaded a horse-hair twine through the needle's eye, doubled it over and twisted it to thicken it and immediately set to work on the deep cut. Menethus only screwed his face once as the needle and thread bound the first of many stitches, and as the antiseptic ethyl aggravated the wound. I had witnessed such minor surgery before; but none so precise, or made to look so easy, as Medusa's effort. Her skill with a needle was as addictive to watch as her beauty.

Menethus distracted himself from the surgery. "You seem to know your business," he said to Ashiya. "I could vouch for you in Mycenae, though I have been away a long time."

"I do not doubt you would. But you should know that our business in Mycenae is now strictly governed, very difficult to make a living as newcomers. You must know the preference is to have places like Tanis. It would likely be ruinous for us, for the children, if we tried."

"What about Piraeus and the settlement beyond? It does not yet have the political will to match Mycenae for strict morals. You could establish yourself early. Easiest way to prosper."

Ashiya seemed to consider the option, but had no answer. There was a brief silence, the only sound of Medusa sometimes shifting her position. She concentrated purely on her task, but a shadow of sadness had also passed her face. Most people would be made ugly by frowning, but not Medusa: her face took on a new symmetry, her beauty sharpened by the acute angles of her dark brows and the penumbra of her cheekbones.

Ashiya continued. "Baktria and I spoke privately of returning to Libya. We had the notion to reinvent ourselves as healers in Tobru. There is no shortage of need, what with the continuing war against the Haruj. Baktria's skill could be taught, Medusa lifted from this life. We both have blood relations there."

"But it did not come to pass," Menethus said.

"It did not come to pass," Ashiya repeated reflectively. "Within a week, before we could make any permanent plans, Baktria and others had succumbed to the sickness. Twenty-three more. Some died quickly. Baktria cared for them, even while she suffered from the disease herself. Her act of selflessness kept her alive the longest."

Medusa's face was now solemn as she finished the flesh stitch. I expected her to shed tears, her mother's death having been recounted, but she did not.

"Of the hundred who inhabited Tanis only fourteen days ago, thirty remain now. Thirty-two dead, thirty-eight departed. Some of the younger children left orphaned by the plague were taken. Who knows what will happen to them. I tried to keep them all here, but their value is too great. I managed to protect Medusa - look at her, she was in such demand. One of the departing families, themselves having shrugged off the disease, became insistent that I hand her over to them. They threatened me with violence, but were harried away. I would have put my own body in the way of that girl, for the friendship I had with her mother."

Medusa snipped errant horse-hair thread from

Menethus' face. She stood back and admired her work. A scar would form, but infection would be kept at bay. Menethus felt where the gash had been, slowly running his fingers along the ridged stitching. He beamed at Medusa gratefully.

"You shall be rewarded for this work, child," he said. "I shall bring you something special from my train."

"Maybe my reward will be that you take me with you," Medusa said brightly. "Ashiya has prayed for it. I have heard her at night."

Ashiya's face reddened, but she could not deny the honesty of the child. Menethus frowned, mildly embarrassed but contemplative. I felt immediately happy at the possibility. The girl was favoured by Athena. I knew this in a sensation: one similar to the beginnings of a ritual frenzy, when Olympian communion occurs under a full moon. This girl held some importance, and it fizzed with prospect.

"She has the hearing of a bat," Ashiya said, smiling. "I cannot deny what she says. Baktria and I prayed to Aphrodite for something better for the child. And I alone maintained the offerings at night, without Baktria knowing. The best sandalwood I could find, the altar kept with fresh myrtle and clover. Even turquoise, expensive and rare. I have been attending it at sunrise, sunset and moonrise since Baktria died. Then yesterday we learned of your market-train. A small party of men told us - trading scouts from

Piraeus. They stopped here for food and water as they made for Mycenae."

Recognition flashed across Menethus' face. "They passed us after the battering we took from the thieves," he said. "They did not stop. They probably thought *we* were thieves. Did you tell them of the fever-sickness?"

"We did not need to. They saw the pyre. It did not trouble them, they said they had each taken blessed medicines prepared by apothecaries. They believed themselves to be immune, and yet their stay was short."

Medusa went to her, tugged lightly at the sleeve of her robe. "Tell them," she said.

Menethus and I looked at Ashiya expectantly.

"I learned who you were from one of the trading scouts," Ashiya continued, wonder having crept into her voice. "He recognised the insignia on the side of your caravan. Two long-necked birds coming together, facing each other, but they are one. He said you had sustained an attack, he saw heads on spikes fixed to your rearmost carriage, fresh blood dripping from the severed gullets, a warning to other marauders."

"We made more a mess of the thieves than they did of us," Menethus said proudly.

"The man told me your name. And while he did not know you, he knew your reputation - trustworthy, and not so obsessed with trade as to make you unscrupulous. You should take Medusa into your care. You are something better for the child. You are what I prayed for."

Menethus did not immediately agree to take Medusa. He was sensibly careful: to him the proposition was too good to be true, too easy for a man who had built his reputation on profiting fairly from often difficult negotiations less valuable than a very beautiful, gifted girl of twelve years. Now he had stumbled, albeit at the behest of divine intervention and violence, into what could be the deal of his lifetime.

Normally so adept at identifying problems with seemingly straightforward business, he struggled to find any weaknesses. He had relied on my god-sense to warn him on occasions before. But I too had a clouded vision of what could be. I felt no air of deceit in Ashiya's words or actions; no element of unspoken, mendacious plans. Athena's prior warnings in other matters had been supplied to me in sudden moments, like a lightning strike; flashes of danger for me to realise. Nothing came then.

The convenience of Menethus having to return to his train to supervise rescued him from making any fast commitments. He would come back, he reassured, once he was satisfied the overnight camp was organised and the many carriages of the train secured.

"Stay here," he said to me as I went to leave

with him. Then he remembered his manners, and said to Ashiya: "May I leave Miranda here? Until sundown?"

"Of course. I insist you and Miranda stay under this roof tonight. There is enough room for you both. You and Miranda will be comfortable."

"I accept. A softer bed would be welcomed by the bruises on my back," Menethus said. "I will buy a round of that spiced bread to be shared among my workers and assets. Can you arrange enough for eight?"

"I will do it now, and bring it to your train. I'd like to see it for myself."

"You are welcome. But to leave them here alone?" Menethus nodded to Medusa and I.

"There are only good people left in Tanis. The small number of degenerates were either scourged by the fever-sickness or have left."

"Very well," Menethus said. "Let this be our second test of trust."

"The first being?"

"Your food and drink did not poison us. How much should I pay you for the bread?"

"Consider it a gift."

Menethus smiled. "A gesture to smooth the path of a deal for your child. It would be rude to refuse such generosity, but neither can I say yet whether I will take the girl."

Medusa and I were left alone. She briefly busied herself by putting her medical utensils away. She went behind the green curtain and re-appeared carrying a small metal tray. Upon it smoked a pyre the size of my fist, and I recognised the smell of rosemary and olive branch, sweet and earthy as they gently smouldered: Athena's botanics.

She placed the tray down carefully, with respect and consideration. The burning plants sat near the ornate hearth and the smoke spiralled and wisped upwards, captured by the breeze outside. I was reminded of the priestesses at temple in Gonia, their own handling of the ritual herbs dripped with more attention but with less confidence.

"You honour Athena in a place where Aphrodite might expect it," I said, breathing in the smell and grateful for its familiarity. "In this house of…pleasures."

"You can say the word '*whore*' and not cause offence," she said, loose but polite. "We honour both gods here and sometimes others, depending on our needs. Perhaps the fever-sickness was one of their jealousies. A punishment."

"Such a thing could easily be one of Aphrodite's," I said, and then regretted criticising the god. They can hear all if they wish, and may save reaction to a slight until a time when you forget you spoke it.

"I agree," Medusa said and sat opposite me,

stretching her legs out and using her arms for support. She had relaxed more since Ashiya and Menethus had gone. "She has less patience, more of a temper. It's her sea-nymph mother - the bitter ruin Zeus once caused her has trickled into their daughter."

"You speak very surely," I said fearfully.

Still Medusa smiled - not in malice or gameplay, but as a compatriot.

"Athena is no better, in her own way," she said. "She has both Zeus *and* her mother's pride. Her haughtiness is the same to Aphrodite's sensitivity."

She could see I was worried by her statement, as I looked into the smoking herb and branch and uttered a prayer of apology.

"Do not worry so much," she continued. "The gods may perceive *that* and think you ungrateful. You can't win. So speak your mind."

We sat in silence. She had startled me with her forthrightness, spoken without arrogance or elaboration. She had a confidence that I knew I could never replicate; she intimidated me without ever intending to.

"I hope Menethus agrees to take me," she said. "I could join you in Athena's new temple, in the new city beyond Piraeus. I would be an excellent acolyte."

"You are too beautiful for Athena's temple," I said. "Aphrodite's temples take girls like you."

Medusa did not smile coyly, or with any ill-fated pride at mention of her beauty. Contrarily, it deflated her: a puncture to her swollen confidence.

"Ashiya has the sickness," she said, changing the subject. "She does not show the symptoms yet, but I can smell it."

"The toll is complete at thirty-two," I said, sure that the god could not be wrong. "Athena never lies."

"And she does not now. By the time you leave here it will still be thirty-two. Ashiya will not die for some days. She will leave tomorrow too, with or without me, bound for Libya. Ashiya will not be in Tanis when she dies. Therefore Athena is correct."

"How do you know this? Have you communed?"

"I have no skill for that. I have an intuition. A magic thought that I cannot help but believe to be true."

She could be taught how to commune, I thought: the recognition of signs, how to intoxicate the self with the aid of the summons. She could improve her unexplored connection to Olympus.

"What does the fever-sickness smell of?" I asked.

"Metallic and smokey. Salty on the tongue. Like hot blood."

She shifted position and leaned forward to tend the small pyre. She gently disturbed the herb-pile to permit air in. It had lost its heat and the smoke was dying. She sharply blew its bottom to ignite it again, deftly shook the offering back to life.

"I can understand why you would prefer to travel with us," I said. "To be on the road and then your mistress dies days into the journey, leaving you at the mercy of the land. What did your mother want for you?"

"Not to return to Libya. She agreed with Ashiya to placate her. The sickness made my mother want peace. For her hard-won exit from that place to be confounded by her own daughter returning there...her shade would haunt my every step. She wanted me to be taken in by a good family, or a temple. She believed in education. Education is liberty, she would say."

"Convince Ashiya to go to Mycenae. Or Piraeus. Maybe the sickness could be cured. You and her could have a good life."

"Wherever she goes, she won't outrun the disease. Besides she is determined to return to Libya. She has convinced herself it is what she wants."

Medusa reached into a pocket of her robe and produced a handful of amaranth, a shade of dull red. She threw it on the pyre and a flame immediately took to it, scorching the plant and creating a sickly-sweet smell. It seemed to reignite the pyre, and the near-ashen leaves of rosemary and charred olive branch lit orange once more.

"At this moment I pray not to Athena but to you, Miranda," she said, staring into the smoke and low flames. "You might persuade Menethus to take me. You know the words to say, to include me in his train and take me to Mycenae. My potential is not to be wasted."

The botanical fire grew, its earlier weakness lost. Our silence drew me into the chasm of the communion trance again, partly driven by a desire to plumb the depths of Medusa's latent, untapped piety.

Chapter Four

From her private Olympian chamber, Athena watched Medusa and I. I had been put to sleep on a makeshift bed of cushions, within one of the curtained spaces of Ashiya's home. We lay close together; Medusa's position implied protection of me, which in turn suggested she had volunteered, rather than been asked, to bed down with me.

Perfectly circular and bright, Athena's room had been fashioned somewhere in the depths of the mountain. The origin of the light was unclear; brightness appeared to emanate from every crevice. Hollowed into the walls were rectangular recesses, which provided soothing corners: welcome breaks amidst the ever-rounded heights. These nooks were mostly empty, awaiting occupants. Some were filled with figurines: small ornaments of clay in varying colours, fashioned into the shape of mortal men and women. These models were caught in poses, frozen mid-gesture to show a trait of their character; immortalised as statues.

A basin of stone, sheer-white and as smoothly hewn as the vestibule, stood to the height of the god's broad, almost masculine waist. The vessel was a wide-rimmed bowl of no great depth, with a stem supporting it that seemed to naturally grow from the floor. This broad bowl had, impossibly by human standards, been carved from the original hollowing of the chamber.

My and Medusa's forms quivered in the basin's shimmering pool. The god stood over it, peering with unblinking umber irises into the liquid similar to what I had witnessed Poseidon and Aphrodite fuck and bathe in.

I compared my face with Medusa's: mine flat and slightly too wide, with a small nose and slightly open mouth, a homely face. And hers, joyfully alluring even while at rest: the bone structure of her skull gave her a longer face than my own, and was made slimmer by already high cheekbones; and her eyes, though closed then, had a symmetry between them that could only be matched when open-lidded. While I was clearly a child nearing the threshold of adulthood, she could have already crossed that precipice and was embracing those early years of womanly refinement.

Athena spoke rhetorically, though in suppressed anger.

"How dare you be put in the path of thieves and marauders. Poseidon and Aphrodite are limited to self-indulgence."

Of course I could not reply: my summons, like all mortals' to the gods, was conditional on my silence.

"Were it not for the familiarity with violence

that your trader-master has, or indeed his devoted care of you and his other property, it would be other heads on spikes. Yours, his. I can especially stomach war when it is fought to protect a greater purpose."

She turned her attention from the basin. The image of Medusa and I vanished, leaving a silky, cloudy ether about the liquid. The god produced a clay ball that was dark orange in colour. She began working it with both hands, expert motions that made the substance submit easily. She walked to an available recess and placed her finished product inside: it was a perfect imitation of Menethus, standing proud with arms loosely crossed. His sombre, serious face had been caught well, disguising his true kindness exactly as it did in life.

"I have a way to reward your master for defending your honour, and therefore mine. This method will be an exercise in my just pursuit of wisdom, trumping Aphrodite's relentless hounding of beauty. And it shall reward piety - that of yours, and that of Medusa's mother." She turned to face me and smiled slightly, her former anger abated. "You were marked as a baby, fresh in the womb. I recall your birth well enough, upon midsummer's day. The day of pure harmony in the mortal calendar, when good and evil are perfectly matched. Your mortal life as one of my vessels shall be filled with love and fear in precise balance. You accommodate me and, you will one day realise, Olympus itself."

Her gaze left mine and she slowly began to pace her chamber. There was a sorcery about her words that made me accept them without question or foreboding. The god did not want me to reject something formidable, and which would not be revealed to me for some time.

"Your new friend Medusa has power. Aphrodite has missed or ignored it. More fool her. She must be a slave to love to overlook Medusa so easily, she who would slot neatly into any of her temples."

The god paused and stopped, thinking, as if about to take a calculated risk.

"I cannot fathom it entirely," she said carefully, as if not to upset the opportunity. "Medusa is beautiful, certainly - perhaps profoundly so - but wholly mortal. Her mother prayed to Aphrodite, rightly considering her circumstances. And her mother prayed to me, rightly since she valued healing and education, and sought to share those honed skills with humility and courage. Medusa already shows great potential, though she will need taming and direction for her latency to be harnessed fully."

Athena returned to the basin. The pool shimmered and an image of an adult woman appeared. She knelt upon a stone floor, and was naked save for a garland of olive leaves and geraniums, woven into a tight halo atop her head of long, black hair. Her eyes were closed. Black ink had been painted over her eyelids and curved into a pattern upon her face, the dark markings neatly spread across her cheeks as if brushed from a bird's wing dipped in pitch. The woman shared the same harsh femininity as the god, but her features were more pleasing. Her body appeared equally athletic. Her right hand rested upon her left breast, and the other held a tall, golden spear. She was supplicant in the way of a High Priestess, ready for communion. Had she not been so prominent in religion, she would have produced many strong children.

"Ursula, the High Priestess who I have installed in my temple in what will become the new city, beyond Piraeus. Menethus takes you to her in Mycenae, where you and he will part. Then you will continue your journey with her."

Ursula slowly opened her eyes, a brilliant blue colour, like water in a cave caught by daylight.

Athena addressed her, speaking into the pool. "Ursula. Construction of the city beyond Piraeus is determined, underwritten by Zeus himself. The contest to deify the city, between Poseidon and myself, beckons."

"Pallas Athena," Ursula said, her gentle voice at odds with her commanding presence. It echoed softly around the chamber. She used the name 'Pallas', a sign of long-served endearment to the god. "The settlement evolves into the city it will become. Men and women toil day and night, inspired by the father-god. Never before has such a common goal been so clear. All are united in the cause. As are we, here in your growing temple."

"Soon you shall receive the young acolyte Miranda from the trader Menethus. He has performed a great service to us, selflessly and inadvertently. He will have a second girl with him - Medusa. It is my command that you also adopt her into temple. While Miranda is naturally suited to the temple disciplines, in the beginning Medusa will not be. I encourage patience with her, but spare no initiation. She may grow to be a powerful asset to our community. Pay the trader Menethus a fair price for Medusa, he deserves to be rewarded."

Even by the shallow waves of the liquid window through which Ursula could be observed, a slight flicker of defiance crossed those lagoon-blue eyes. To accept any girl into temple was subject to great scrutiny: to manage the flock was the primary concern for a High Priestess after ensuring the rites of worship. Gods did not make a habit of shoeing acolytes into temple; such behaviour bred distrust and complacency among their earthly guardians of the faith.

Athena smiled slightly, as if aware that her request for Medusa to join Ursula's ranks might rankle the High Priestess. Ursula could show dissent, but she could not deny the god.

"It is my wish that Miranda and Medusa are not separated," the god said.

Ursula confirmed Athena's wish. "Temple shall receive two new acolytes from the trader Menethus. They shall be initiated, and subject to the same rigours and standards."

"If Medusa fails to maintain the calibre, she may be released and her fate made her own."

"It will be done. And now, I have something for you to hear and judge. Maestra and I spoke of the contest, and what you might present to the people to win their favour."

Athena frowned. "Maestra. Rich that she should have a view on godly power. She who, though broad in her philosophies, waters down her belief in the gods with every year she continues to live."

"She would commune with you, if you permit it," Ursula said.

"She must do the asking," Athena said. "To do otherwise puts her above us."

"Maestra cannot help her great knowledge, inherited from her Stygian ancestors."

"But she can her stubbornness."

"We rely on her very much," Ursula said, with light finality. I was impressed with her defiance.

"May others witness your friendship and loyalty to her, and learn from it," Athena replied flatly, little warning in her tone.

"Maestra and I both agree that, when the time comes to present yourself to the people of the new city, an olive tree should be conjured from the ground of the citadel."

Ursula let the notion settle, but had more to say.

"Go on," said Athena.

"It will be realised as a symbol for peace, wisdom and longevity. The city should not have its destiny started and finished on the fickleness of war, as we fear Poseidon might try to entice the populous with. We believe that strong empires may not be built on violence."

"What should they be built on?"

"Alliances. Trade. Piety. Honour."

"Those things can be aspects of war. Those things can start as many disagreements as they might prevent."

"I have sent acolytes and priestesses out among the people, to use their ears discreetly. They say most have come here to escape slaughter and bloodshed, to flee from some marauding force or dispute that has escalated into war in corners of the world. There is an appetite to have a life well-lived, not cut short by the blood-ridden command of someone else's cause. Most people building this great city seek solace. They believe in it. The god who inspires consolation and peaceful prosperity will be the winner."

She spoke assuredly. Such trust in the god, I thought, that she can be so candid; like a pupil nearing the status of master.

Athena liked the idea. "Strong empires may not be built on violence," she said quietly, repeating Ursula's statement. "I know what Poseidon plots. He will offer the people of this great metropolis a subtle invitation to be that marauding force, to begin more disputes, to wreak more havoc. They will create by breaking, with Poseidon as their figurehead. And then, when there is nothing more to shatter with war, they will break themselves. A short-lived legacy. Instead I will offer them creation and survival by collaboration. They will be equipped in education first and in arsenal second, to withstand any violent forces and resolve disputes with honour, fairness and justice. The olive tree will stand firm as a symbol - deep roots and lasting foundations that support steady growth and that nurtures life, instead of self-destruction."

The favour emanated by the god caused a single teardrop to roll down Ursula's cheek. The trickle glinted like the precious stones Menethus coveted, mined from the lands south of Libya.

Chapter Five

I was late to wake the following morning. The space that Medusa had occupied beside me felt cool, with no trace of recent body heat. The cordoned area that formed our sleeping space smelt acrid, of burnt herbs and woodsmoke left too long in ember; the pyre had been lost to carelessness, the sweetness allowed to turn bitter.

I could hear movement outside the property: people in discussion, animals braying, the crunch of wooden wheel against dry ground. The noise was such that it assumed nobody slept; the sun had been up for some time. Through the curtain I heard Menethus' hearty laughter. Ashiya's too, which was light and genuine. Relations seemed warm between them, though whether a deal had been struck to acquire Medusa was unclear: their laughter could have been to replace awkwardness following Menethus' refusal, just as it could have symbolised an agreement.

I got up and felt the sickly force of the communion's aftermath. I wanted to lie down again, but I knew Menethus would be impatient to leave Tanis, with or without Medusa. I needed to bathe: I smelled of journey and had half-rubbed dirt marks from the ashen dead of the funeral pyre upon my skin and clothing. I wished for nothing more than a hot bath, and the thought of it spurred me from the lethargy. I straightened my robe, modest material which had kept me plain and unattractive to prying eyes. I sheepishly cast aside the curtain and stepped into the main room.

"She wakes," Menethus announced playfully.

Ashiya gestured to the floor-cushions next to Menethus. "Sit. Eat," she said.

A plate of dates and a small stack of sliced bread - the thick and rough stomach-filler made from the bottom of mill-catch - stood ready to be devoured on the low table.

"Thank you," I said, and meant it.

I stole discreet stares at the woman as I sat and bit into a chunk of bread, recalling what Medusa had said about Ashiya having the sickness. She moved to pour me more of the leaf brew, this time cold and flavoured with lemons. She wore a small smile, and I noticed a new, slightly yellow pallor to her skin, a creeping darkness beneath her eyes. She showed no fever upon her brow. I wondered how close Menethus had been to her; whether he could have contracted the disease.

"Medusa will come with us," Menethus announced to me. "We leave immediately after you have eaten. You and Medusa will travel in the same cart, to look after each other. We will move with speed and reach Mycenae tonight."

He looked me over, frowning. "You need to bathe. No time for it here. You shall both visit the scented baths in Mycenae."

I smiled at Medusa: Menethus' statement verified the god's intentions, and the Mycenaean baths promised thorough cleanliness. She looked at me gladly, and with a notion of wonder that I had seen before in others impressed by my divination - though I had not impressed my wishes upon the god.

"I admit I was conflicted whether to take the girl. It is a remarkable reason as to how my mind was made up," Menethus said. He never liked silence during a meal. "This will be the tale for this table, for you both. Long may you remember it."

He leaned forward for emphasis, and spoke slowly.

"Just as Ashiya and I had finished the tour of my train, my memory of this place occurred to me with such clarity. I *was* here before, in Tanis, briefly as a younger man, when I was learning my business under the tutelage of my father. We had been travelling and trading in Nubia for twenty seasons, based in the city of Kerma. That sweltering region so far south of Kemet is hostile to newcomers. Only the very determined and adventurous go there. But it is rewarding to those who persevere. We endured their barbarian hostility, we tolerated their blood-filled rites. Eventually we were accepted, eventually we found the people had softer forms of religion. By the time we left, our carts were laden with gold and other metals unfound in Greece, and with fabrics and rare witchcraft, and with workers of high skill and moderate temperament. Even our philosophy in business and in life had changed, become more mellow and forgiving, having overcome new hardships and having witnessed wonders few this side of the sea may know. We made the long journey back to Greece - to Patras on the north coast, where my father intended to stay and retire, just as I intend to one day."

He paused to drink, slurping his brew. Ashiya had already heard this story, but still listened as if she had not.

"I became ill. I contracted an ague during the sea-crossing from Libya. I was taken to the edge of death. My father planned for me to see a good physician in Mycenae and the moment we disembarked, me confined to a cart, he spurred the horses on. My condition worsened. My father believed me, his sole heir to our prospering trade, to be near death. At this very moment, when I was ready to cross the narrow chasm that separates life and what comes next, we came across Tanis - and Baktria, Medusa's mother. She was a young woman back then. Newly-arrived. No sign of you yet, child." Menethus gestured to Medusa.

"But her expertise in curing the sick was already potent. She knew what ailed me - a lesser ague left too long to fester in my body. It took most of the winter season for me to be nursed to health. I have not taken ill since. Her skill must have been bestowed by Athena herself. As soon as I saw you, child," he widened his eyes at Medusa, "there was something I recognised. A familiarity that time and events had eroded, but which held a spark to ignite the fire of nostalgia. I have an excellent memory for business - ask me what I paid for a single piece of quartz on a particular day a hundred seasons ago, and I will tell you. But I have unbidden skill at forgetting my own troubles."

"When you saw me yesterday, you saw my mother," Medusa said.

"Yes," he replied sadly, and studied her for a moment. Pity crossed his broad face. "Perhaps the god saw fit to remind me that there is no such thing as too much thanks. For me to now be diverted by sudden violence to Tanis, to meet the child of the woman who once saved my life. I cannot help Baktria, but I can help her daughter. And so it is that I have agreed to take Medusa with us to Mycenae."

"Miranda asked Athena for this," Medusa said happily, but incorrectly: I had made no such request. "She is loved by the god. There may be a place for me in temple."

I looked at her uneasily, but did nothing to rescind her joy: she spoke truer than she could know, but the god does not like her favours, even those she announces herself, to be assumed as being done before they come to pass.

"Temple is not possible," Menethus said, laughing mildly. "It is a careful negotiation to sell a girl or boy into the club of acolyte. A delicate business that takes place over a number of seasons, agreements toughly formed and seldom broken."

Medusa's face fell. "Then what will become of me?"

"Don't look so glum! I will find you a good family who will see your education complete, your safety assured and your honour intact. I have promised Ashiya that you will not suffer." He sat up proudly and jerked one of his great thumbs towards himself. "Menethus does not promise what he cannot deliver."

Ashiya reached a hand over and clasped Medusa's. "Your life begins today," she said earnestly. "It is not with me, or in this place."

We departed with little delay. Medusa's possessions, confined to a modest wooden box of simple design and no decoration, were placed into the cart we alone would share. Menethus' aversion to emotion made him gruff and impatient. He permitted Ashiya and Medusa embrace, but did not let it linger. He guided her to the cart, the penultimate in the train, and took his place at the front-most vehicle. The horses were whipped and all twenty carts creaked forward.

Ashiya's figure gradually disappeared behind us. Her coughs heralding infection had started suddenly, as if triggered by our departure. The neat arrangement of huts shrank with every crack of the drivers' whips as Menethus' carts groaned onward. Medusa stared after them, the look on her face not one of longing, but of content.

"Does the word *Tanis* mean anything?" I said, cautiously breaking the silence. "Is it the name of the first person who established the place?"

Without breaking her stare from her birthplace and Ashiya, both fast-disappearing into the distance, she said, "It means *Serpent Lady*. The place where the women charm the men."

"Are there snakes? Aside from the men?"

She laughed mildly. "Some. Only the vipers are poisonous. When the men are away the floor could be awash with them. They are gentle to women. Men aggravate them. Snakes don't like competition. I remember one man - a soldier, drunk and brash - took three women into a tent. He paid them well. They all had to fuck him at once. But he did not see the viper lying beneath the cushions. The moment he withdrew, spraying his seed everywhere like a burst sack of cream, the snake sprang and bit him on his erect cock. It drew blood that spurted high in the air and reached the tent's fabric ceiling. We could hear the man bellowing, though everyone believed it to be in pleasure. Within an hour the soldier was pinned down, soaked in liquor and his manhood sliced half off to stop the spread of poison. They used a brazier to seal the wound."

I felt sick with disgust and curiosity.

"How do you know all this?" I said.

"My mother. She loved such stories."

"What happened to the soldier?"

"He paid a surgeon to fit him with a prosthetic cock made from leather and pig gut. Apparently he endured the pain without the sleep-draught. His absence from Tanis was brief. And he always searched the tent before parting with coin."

I was gobsmacked, barely managing '*oh*' as she turned away from her past. She faced the uncertain distance ahead, smiling slightly and unafraid, as the train of carts and animals formed a path that trundled onward to our future. She told me about her mother.

Baktria had had her education administered in Libya. For centuries civil war had plagued the landscape of Cyrenaica, spilling into her birthplace of Tobru. Local mystics claimed it was an earthly reflection of a hellish battle between feuding demons; philosophers debated that it was a timely, natural resetting of mortal values;

and politicians insisted the struggle was about the ownership of vast gold reserves buried deep in the desert lands between the inland Haruj mountains and the coast. All believed themselves to be right, and none would be swayed otherwise.

The warring populations could cope with a confrontation that could last for a thousand seasons: the coastal cities had armies; the mountains had tribes. The long-standing war had periods of truce, when either side waited for soldiers to mature. It was in these intervals that young women like Medusa's mother were clandestinely shipped across the sea to Greece. They were removed to prevent them from being kidnapped by the tribal enemy and forced to reproduce bastard fighters who would wage war against their mothers' old masters. Instead the women were sent to foreign lands to provide leisure for the thousands of workers of cities like Mycenae, Thebes and Argus. Bastards of another, less murderous, sort would be born.

Baktria, bound and shipped to Greek hosts amid a halt in bloodshed, was rare among her peers. A great many gifts had been bestowed upon her to soften the blow of her predicament and surroundings: she had knowledge in literature, medicine and religion that many lacked; and she had a humour. Her most natural expertise was in healing and, so Medusa told me, she would be present at other women's births, or to extract a tooth, or be willing to concoct a remedy for infection. The woman even pulled Medusa from her own widened cervix, self-mid-wifing through clenched screams and hypertension. She was respected and needed; and in Tanis she was safe from the Haruj. In Tanis she was somebody, an excess to expectation.

In Tobru there had been deities prescribed by the local mystics and soothsayers, who claimed themselves to be deified: bastardised cults that competed with the true Olympian authority. If Baktria was to be a keeper of vice and a medicine-woman in Greece, then her reasoning was to honour the appropriate powers. Prayers for the preservation of desire were made to Aphrodite. Prayers for wisdom in survival and functioning poultices were whispered to Athena.

Medusa told me of her mother's mirror, and of her distant memory of first understanding her own troubling beauty. Of her sensitive hearing and the types of men who frequented Tanis. Of her life-long gift of nimble footedness, and her ability to embrace silence.

"I inherited my mother's mirror, among other things," she said. "I have it here, in my box of possessions. Would you like to see it?"

"No," I said curtly. I had not meant to speak so sharply, but since I had learned that the god found the mirror distasteful, my own revulsion for it overruled my empathy.

A prolonged pause followed. The train of carts had stopped. Grey clouds had gathered as the day waned.

I asked with care, and to break the heavy atmosphere: "Did you ever know your father?"

Menethus' workers were hurriedly sealing the wagons, expecting hard rain. Thick sheets of ox hide, which smelled strongly of the grain liquor used to treat the skins, were draped and nailed over the metal bars that enclosed us. These hides blocked out most of the scant light, but would prevent the impending soak from diseasing the organic factions of Menethus' hard-gathered wares.

Finally she replied, in a quiet voice. He was a rare and troubling subject for her.

"I used to keep watch for my father while my mother was at business," she said. "From the shadows I would look closely at the men she brought to our tent."

She cast her intoxicating eyes up to the sky, her view of it limited to a shafted gap in the hide covering. The rain had started. Droplets, fat and heavy, hit the skin shields like small stones on a drum.

"I would try to work out if one was my father. If any looked like me. I stared at some for so long, my knees and back ached from crouching behind the wine barrels."

"What did your mother tell you about him?"

"She told me he was a Trojan. He had spent time in Miletus before coming here. She said he was an engineer. A clever man. He was kind, and free-spirited. She told me he made her laugh. She said on their one night together they had been akin to old lovers rather than partners in a transaction. She believed she had found love in him, instantaneous and unexpected. But she was only provided a glimpse of it. Then she returned to serving lust, just as he returned to what he knew."

"I hear a glimpse of love is enough," I said, hoping to placate her. "That is what Aphrodite believes. Your mother was spared love's cruelty."

"That may be so, but my mother said Aphrodite can grant love for entire lifetimes."

"That is why the god is not to be trusted," I replied, low-voiced but confident. "Her mind changes. She is unstable."

We fell silent. The market-train creaked into motion again. The sound of the heavy rain outside became our companion. I felt the sensation that precedes the summons for communion. I wanted to lie down, and she insisted I use her lap as a pillow. She rested one hand on my head soothingly, and the sickness became mild. The rocking of the cart lulled me to sleep.

Chapter Six

In her chamber Athena worked more clay, one round in each of her muscular hands. The colour of the substance was pale grey: dull compared to the sumptuous, burnt orange shade of Menethus' statue, which I could see positioned within its recess.

Gradually, she created two more figurines. She held each aloft, ensuring that I saw them. They were models of myself and Medusa. Her beauty and my homely looks had been expertly realised. My pose was one of vague authority, my hands clasped behind my back; I resembled a too-young teacher. A robe had been carved smooth and clung well-fitted to my clay body, more so than how my current clothing hung loosely about my real flesh. What the god had made seemed more luxurious, and had a stripe of colour running across the length of the clay-fabric, starting at my right shoulder and finishing on the left side of my waist. The shade of the stripe was purple, to denote acolyte status within Athena's temple. Medusa's head had been turned slightly, as if listening to my instruction. Her hands were clasped in front of her, an apt pupil. She too had been carved a new robe, identical in its close fit and insignia. The god placed the clay models beside each other within separate recesses. Medusa's pose indicated dependence on me.

Athena gave me a sidelong look and her face relaxed into a rare, motherly smile. And then her eyes widened and her smile became brighter, exposing good teeth as white as her chamber. She had seen Zeus behind me: the father-god had appeared in the dark archway that led to other regions of the mountain's bowels. He had returned.

"That is a pastime that you don't indulge in often enough, daughter," Zeus said, entering the room.

He embraced Athena, who clung to him gladly. Her posture was childlike, harking back to some ancient time when perhaps, in a child's mortal form, she had gripped Zeus for paternal comfort.

"You have returned sooner than any of us expected," she said happily.

They disconnected and Zeus looked around the chamber, at the recesses scarcely filled along the rounded walls.

"I am pleased to be back," Zeus said, distracted by his interest in the room. There was an edge of tiredness in his smooth voice. "I found myself yearning for this place while away - the mortals with their joys and cruelties. My previous stay was too fleeting, too brief. I was determined that my most recent absence - while necessary - was equally so."

Athena nodded in acceptance and agreement. "They have an addictive quality about them, despite their frailties. We cannot help but watch them in fascination. An unexpected benefit of your creation, or a hindrance to our own *moirai*?"

Zeus smiled ruefully. He stared upwards into the never-ending chasm of white that crowned Athena's chamber.

"Our own *moirai*," he repeated solemnly, distracted by the concept, "our own destiny. Our own fate." He returned his attention to Athena. "I have chosen to visit you first, my competing daughter. Poseidon and Aphrodite do not know I have returned."

"Then I am twice happy," Athena said.

Zeus continued. "If you want to win my new city, you must understand the people. And you must go beyond that - you must retain them to your cause."

"I want to win the city," Athena said with finality.

Zeus walked slowly to the basin that housed the viewing pool. He did not have Poseidon's height, but his stout mortal frame gave him a breadth of dominance over it. He leant on it and stared ahead in deep thought, delaying whatever else he wanted to say.

"I have rarely come to this room, your private arena," he said. "My own is not as simple as yours. And yet I feel more comfortable here."

"It suits me well enough. Was your expedition worthwhile?"

"Fruitful, and barren. Like all things. No matter where I go, or where you may go in the future, there is balance. It is the first common aspect."

"And what of time? Where there is life there is measurement of it. The second common aspect."

"Time," Zeus said richly. "Yes, you are correct, wise daughter. From where I have just returned, they will have that invention too soon enough. Not as these mortals have conceived it or perceive it, but time nonetheless. The two figurines you just made," he gestured to my and Medusa's images in our recesses, "who are they? I see one standing here in communion with you." He looked at me and I stared back, feeling a wave of terror and ecstasy. His glance was enough for him to know me entirely: my past and my present, and what was to come.

"This child shares your stern brow. But the other," he returned his gaze to the model of Medusa, "she is striking." He narrowed his eyes, as if suspicious of something. "Is she the product of one of our affairs? She has an Olympian beauty."

"She is mortal spawn from head to foot."

"Remarkable," said Zeus, impressed. "They never cease to amaze me. I foresee her beauty to become sensational as she ages. She will be renowned across the mortal world, and here on Olympus. Are they new acolytes?"

"Both bound for my temple in the new city beyond Piraeus. Miranda," Athena nodded to me, "is one of my most powerful and adept followers. Perhaps one day she will be High Priestess. Medusa is the other, plucked from the obscurity of a village near Mycenae. Despite the recent loss of her mother and absence of her adventuring father, she is not cowed by the disadvantage. I admire that. And she has shown an aptitude for healing. Perhaps other traits will be uncovered with a temple education."

Zeus beheld the god with a mischievous half-smile.

"Does Aphrodite know that you have commandeered such a beautiful girl? Your sister may have wanted Medusa for herself. Such a prize would reinforce any of her temples."

Athena spoke carefully, never losing sight of the father-god's face.

"Aphrodite had an opportunity to harbour the girl. Besides, for their own schemes Aphrodite and Poseidon put Miranda - certainly one of *my* potent acolytes - in danger. In the path of violent thieves. She survived thanks to the skill and courage of her current master, a trader. Medusa's mother worshipped Aphrodite to sustain her provision of sexual pleasures, and me to sustain her ability to heal - what she truly cared about and what led to her death. She sacrificed herself upon my altar, metaphorically speaking. My acquisition of the girl is fair."

Zeus nodded thoughtfully. "Aphrodite is making a habit of missing chances. She did with competing for the new city, she has done now with Medusa. She'll not lie back and accept what you have done, whatever opportunity she may have declined, whatever is just."

"She should have acted more decisively. There are other beautiful girls in the world she could recruit to her cause."

"None like Medusa," Zeus said strongly. "Mark my words, her beauty will bewitch. Mortals always want what they cannot have, and as a virgin acolyte she will be totally inaccessible. She will be *craved*."

"Then I shall ensure that she is properly protected," Athena said defiantly. "She will be a unique jewel in the crown of my temple. She will broaden our appeal. The arrow of beauty will fit neatly in the quiver of wisdom, justice and healing."

"And what of war? You may not like it, but it is partly yours to govern. Can beauty sit alongside that?"

"Room will be made. My sister's coveting of beauty may trigger a war between us."

Zeus considered his answer. "Siblings fight," he said plainly. "I have decided on when the contest between you and Poseidon will take place. I have already seen the progress made in the city's construction. I am pleased, but I want to wait. I want the city to reach a point in its development to make it the most suitable prize - a standard to befit the winner of it. I want the mighty Acropolis completed, I want the population to swell even more."

Athena seemed disappointed. "I expected it to be sooner," the god said. "I am currently in a position of strength. Delay can only fortify Poseidon, if not weaken me too."

"I cannot show to be supporting you, Athena. This will be a fair contest. You and Poseidon will both stand level. It will be in no more than ten years, as they count time. For us, a blink of the mortal-form eye." Zeus touched one of his own eyelids, with mockery.

"You exaggerate," Athena said, humoured.

"Perhaps not a blink," Zeus admitted. "But I shall take mortal time and bend it to my will. Neither you, nor Poseidon, shall have to wait long to stake your claims."

Chapter Seven

I awoke feeling nervous and uncertain. A storm was raging, and yet the market-train had not stopped. I thought it foolish of Menethus to have attempted progress in a downpour, but his urgency to reach Mycenae had prevailed.

He eventually admitted defeat: soon the terrain turned to sludge, a viscous and unattractive yellow-brown mud. The wheels of our cart were dragged for a time before the other sets at the front stopped rolling, and the horses became unwilling. The rain hit the ox-skin tarpaulin in a low tenor, and against the ground outside in a sharp rattle like beads shaken in a pot.

For a time, there was nothing but the voices of Menethus and his workers calling to each other as they trudged the length of the train. Medusa and I sat alert, both afraid to speak and willing to allow the tension that the rainstorm had created to break naturally.

Suddenly our hide-cover was swept aside and Menethus appeared at the barred door to our cart. He was lashed with rain water, his own robe heavy with the soak.

He shouted, addressing me. "This tempest is going to keep us here for the night. Food will be passed down once we've secured the train."

He rattled the cart door, checking that its lock held fast. He did this not to satisfy himself that we could not escape, but that others could not get in. The train was vulnerable stuck in the mud, and Menethus had legitimate fears.

The afternoon passed into evening. The hard rain did not abate. Food was still yet to reach us. The carts, however, did not sink further into the mud, for which Menethus must have been thankful. The thick, rocky ground beneath the sludge made pools of the water, and permitted the carts to stabilise.

Our wary silence gradually dissolved; Medusa wanted to talk. She was polite and not too eager; she sensed the trepidation in me, which had matured since the setback of the storm. She wanted to know something of the other inhabitants of Menethus' train. She had only glimpsed the other human residents as we were hurried past the other carts to board our own.

"The first three carts are the driving train, Menethus' quarters and where he keeps the food, wine, water and precious artefacts," I said quietly.

"Precious artefacts?"

"Shining stones of different colours. Rare herbs and plants that the apothecaries covet, and cannot easily find in Greece. Fine wool, clothing decorated in the hair and skins of large cats and lizards. The wives and concubines of rich men crave those. Strange statues of the gods carved from dark wood that smells of dung. Metal trinkets and jewellery. And gold - lots of gold. Small bars and nuggets. I have seen the pile Menethus has carefully gathered - I admit it captivates me."

Medusa laughed joyfully. "I have known you for a day and I already know you carry too much shame. Too much for a girl of barely fifty seasons. It is no bad thing to think things wondrous aside from the god. I believe they like the competition."

Her intuition was astute; she was entirely correct. Her smile, easy and forgiving, quashed any retaliation from me.

"The next three carts contain slaves like us, and animals."

"We are not slaves," Medusa said, correcting me. "We will not be sold into slavery, so how can we be slaves?"

"We are not slaves, but we are assets," I said, correcting myself. "Menethus' overall aim is to profit from us all."

"What are the other *assets* like?" She said, mildly disgruntled.

"In one cart are three Nubians - a woman and a man, and their child. They are bound for a rich family in Mycenae. The man is skilled in weap-

111

onry, and will teach the patriarch's sons how to fight. The woman is skilled in music, and will teach and entertain. They will be given a home and a stipend. The child will receive an education, perhaps in Apollo's temple. They will be treated well."

"What animals has Menethus captured? I have only ever seen snakes, rats, dogs and horses. Some of the men that came to Tanis used to speak of great cats roaming wild in the desert."

"The Kemet and the people in the eastern lands think they belong to Hades. Menethus has two," I said proudly, as if they were my own.

Her eyes widened and I found myself staring at them, my mouth slightly open, drunk-dumb on the way they shined in the fading light.

"Can I see them?" She said, awestruck.

"Maybe," I said, still gawping at her. "Menethus will trade quickly when we reach Mycenae. They are not friendly being cooped up since Libya."

"Are there others aside from the three Nubians?"

"Yes," I said. My stomach churned, partly out of hunger. "Aramis and Tuk. Deserters from the army of Cydonia on the island of Crete. They are in the fourth cart, closest to the three Menethus himself guards. He doesn't trust them and wants them near. Menethus has no contract of sale for them, which he unwisely told them. He tells me they are deceitful, greedy men, but strong and capable in war."

"Have you spoken with them?"

"Once, in passing. Tuk has sincere manners, and both have cruel intentions. They looked at me with violent eyes. If they dared, then the god would make them regret it."

"Athena would get in line behind me. *I* would make them regret it."

A rough voice suddenly grunted "*Food!*" from outside our cart. Ravenous, Medusa leapt across the cart to the door, expecting something to be passed through the bars. Instead the skin covering was swept aside and a sturdy arm shot through. With military precision the hand at the end of it seized her by the throat. She immediately struggled, but the attacker squeezed harder, rendering the girl obedient.

The same voice, now smooth and confident with threat, spoke again, directed at me. "Make a sound and I'll crush the breath out of her, little witch."

I said nothing, more shocked by the swiftness of the ambush than the instruction. The lock to our door rattled and then it swung open. Through the tarpaulin sprang Aramis, his quick and athletic pounce into our cart at odds with his round and unattractive frame. He was like a hairless pig, with a large and crooked nose, broken and improperly healed, forming the only sharp angle about his barrel-like body.

He immediately took over duty from Tuk,

who had first manhandled Medusa. They exchanged roles, and I did not doubt that Aramis would snap her neck if I opened my mouth. Now Tuk slithered through the open cart door and closed it behind him, as if entering his own private quarters. He was taller and thinner than Aramis, wire-framed. Tuk might have been handsome had it not been for his leering smile showing bad teeth, offset by kind eyes that concealed heinous carnal appetites. Aramis positioned himself behind Medusa, she silent in his chubby clutches.

Aramis grimaced as he sniffed Medusa's hair. "This one's prettiest, but she smells like a barn," he said. Unlike the lean-tongued Tuk, Aramis bore a peasant's accent and rough manner, probably born from the very south of Greece.

Tuk advanced on me, a determined and sinister grin splitting his narrow face. He held out a hand to me, as if trying to calm an animal, and whispered: "I don't like the way the pretty ones look at me. Like there's something wrong with me. I much prefer the ugly ones. They are more forgiving, and I do my duty by showing someone cares. This will be quick, little witch." His Cretan accent was musical and disarming. "I will be so careful. Your temple mistress will never know that I have been inside you. I know how to do this without spoiling you. For all their knowledge you shall still be a virgin."

I tearfully backed away, but he was too quick.

He leapt forward and wrapped one arm around my waist and the other across my chest, his hand covering my mouth. The other immediately crept down my robe, brushing over my barely-formed breasts. His own robe was soaked from the rain, and I felt my own becoming damp. I let out a sound of distress as his wandering hand untied the bind of my robe with worrying skill. He slid his hand inside and caressed my belly. With every reptilian stroke I summoned no power from my piety; the god was absent from my plight, leaving me immediately vulnerable, hateful and disgraced.

"Quiet, or I will be less kind to you and permit Aramis indulge in his most preferred sport. He's a necrophiliac, you should know. Do you know what that means?"

The word "*no*" quivered from my lips, my anxious tongue tripping over the word.

"*N...n...no!*" Said Tuk, mocking me. "It means he will do to your friend's *corpse* what I am about to do to you. But not so gently. He's from farming stock - what should we expect?"

I began crying, wholly mortal weakness consuming me as I tried and failed to pray. One of his spindly fingers went shallow into my quim. His breathing intensified and he pressed himself against me. His phallus swelled and stabbed one of my buttocks. He withdrew his finger and sniffed it.

Into my ear he hissed, near gasping. "You smell

like a grown woman."

I looked at Aramis, who now had an expression of entranced perversion across his face. He had become distracted by what Tuk was doing to me, and inadvertently relaxed his grip on Medusa. She knew this and, in a manner even more swift and expert than those beasts had gained access to our cart, she whipped a small blade from somewhere amid her robe and stabbed Aramis in the groin.

His first reaction was to let go of her. Blood quickly pooled from where she had struck him, the area of his dirty white robe quickly turning scarlet. The small knife protruded where his cock would be; she had stabbed him with precision and strength. Medusa took no hesitation in withdrawing it, triggering Aramis' first scream.

Tuk snapped from his revelling in my musk. Aramis bellowed a war-cry and launched himself at Medusa, but his injury was too severe and he collapsed to the floor, curled up with pain.

Medusa pointed the blade at Tuk, and spoke assuredly. "His shouts will draw attention. Let her go and you might be shown some mercy."

Aramis, bent-double on the floor, let out a howl. Tuk relaxed his grip and I froze, my ordeal rooting me to the floor.

But Tuk had a final trick to play. Unwilling to submit easily, he produced a tube of metal from within his own filthy robe - a short bar broken from the door of his own cart. In a flash he struck my right leg, hitting the bone above the ankle. Now it was my turn to scream, the pain of it delayed by that numbness that precedes a heavy blow. I collapsed, slapping the floor with a hand in a bid to placate the shock.

Medusa let out an aggressive yell and charged on Tuk. He must have been expecting her to rush to my aid, enabling his escape; he was unprepared to have to face her wrath himself. She was quicker than him, and she darted left and right. His training as a soldier was not completed in mind of being attacked by an unpredictable young girl, and he lacked the skill to defend himself when she slipped past him and half-turned, garnering enough momentum to sink the blade into his groin with more severity than what she had served Aramis.

Tuk choked and fell to the floor, bowed over. Aramis still lay curled up, also alive and suffering. My damaged leg throbbed with slow pulses of pain and numbness, and I feared it broken.

Suddenly Menethus swept back the tarpaulin, and bellowed. "What in the name of Zeus is happening here?"

Two of his workers stood behind him, the three of them drenched. There was only whimpering from we the injured. Medusa said nothing and surveyed the carnage. Menethus and his men let themselves into the cart.

"Aramis and Tuk. You heathen bastards," he said loudly. "Miranda, what has happened?"

My tears stopped me from answering him: they were sourced from the radiating pain of my leg, the shame of Tuk's assault and the lack of help from the god during the ordeal.

"She may have a broken bone," Medusa said calmly. "I can see to it, but it must be done quickly. And these men have bloody wounds where their cocks are. Forgive me if they die."

Menethus beheld her with fearful awe. "Your mother's skill?"

Now Medusa withdrew her knife from Tuk's nether regions. He wailed as she did. Wet and red with his blood, she held it up for Menethus to see.

"The rapist's nemesis. One of her parting gifts to me."

Menethus bent down to Aramis. "You dare try to ruin these girls," he growled.

Aramis whimpered unintelligible words. Menethus shifted his attention to Tuk.

Menethus continued. "You dare take advantage of my goodwill. You would have both been food for the pets of minor households if it wasn't for me." He turned to his workers. "Shackle them. Return them to their own cart. Double the locks. If they die, they will still fetch a fair price as cadavers for the apothecaries in Mycenae. If they live, I'll sell them to Hades' disciples."

The rain stopped as Aramis and Tuk were taken away. The clouds shifted quickly, revealing a sky of deep blue bejewelled with shining stars.

Menethus authorised a small amount of poppy milk be given to me to numb the discomfort of Medusa's surgery. As the drug took hold, Medusa applied pressure to my leg to detect the extent of the damage.

"You are lucky. It's a clean break. I know by its swelling. It must be bound tightly, and splinted between two pieces of wood. Then you must rest it when you can."

"Yes," I said dreamily.

"The brace must be kept on for more than a season. From today until the cold air blows. If the broken bone shifts, it will cause more damage."

The comforting influence of the poppy made the painful prospect acceptable.

"Have you done this before?" I murmured.

"I have seen my mother perform it. Once on a young man who fell while drunk, and once on a mare. It's quite simple. These bodies the gods saw fit to provide us with heal best with precise, but sparse, intervention."

I heard the sawing of wood as Menethus himself fashioned the brace that would hold my leg in place and set the bone. I fought to stay awake; fought to tell Medusa how thankful I was for her and how she need not worry for her future. I whispered to her urgently, eager to speak before the poppy rendered me unable. I spoke the truth, but my speech was slurred and she could have rightfully disbelieved me.

"You and I are going to temple. Menethus doesn't know it yet, but Athena has decreed it. You will be an acolyte like me, eventually a priestess. Healing, wisdom, justice - you have shown command of the things the god holds dear. You even wage war well. She was right about you."

Medusa had saved us both from an unholy future. She deserved the reward of reassurance. I drifted into a narcotic sleep.

Chapter Eight

Poseidon had arrived in Athena's chamber just as Zeus had done: uninvited and seeking a confidential meeting. Zeus himself was no longer present; whether Poseidon knew his brother had returned from his latest off-earth charter was impossible to say.

This was an unexpected gathering of the two competing gods: a summit before their determination to win Zeus' new city was laid bare for the people of it to elect.

Through her viewing pool, Athena reviewed the ordeal that Medusa and I had endured, after the event had happened. She replayed it repeatedly, a single finger being dipped into the liquid to reset the tribulation. The sea-god sidled up to her silently as she seethed, and watched it with her.

"Incredibly beautiful *and* adept at your traits, Athena," said Poseidon knowingly, referring to Medusa. "Whatever is to be done with a mortal like that?"

Athena paid him no attention. Nothing but the near-violation of Medusa and I mattered to her then. The event made her grip the perfectly round edges of the basin and, at the height of the trauma, her knuckles were as white as the substance forming it.

Poseidon took a cautious, sideways look at Athena, at the exact moment Tuk prepared me for his cock. The sea-god respected the bitter mantra Athena had adopted, but would not be put off his business. Few mortal events were truly significant to him; he was only truly interested in deeds in which he had a stake. This stance produced infrequent disappointments, but great expectations. The sea-god had compelled himself to invest shrewdly in the mortal cause.

"You are more attractive when you are angry," he said. His tone was playful and yet sincere. In any other circumstance where there had been a lesser distraction, I was sure he would not have spoken with any provocation.

Poseidon stepped away, no longer encroaching on the god. Athena cleared the viewing pool, having seen Medusa successfully splint my broken leg, and it settled into flat, imageless calm.

"Pity you would not protect her yourself," Poseidon continued. "Such an intervention would have been a sight to behold. We would have all gathered around your little spy-pool, to watch you unleash your wrath. That wrath you keep so firmly in control. You use it so rarely, it must be purest of all things. I am generally happy to have enemies, but I would be uncomfortable with you as mine."

She looked at him and smiled slightly, pleased with the double-edged compliment.

"If I had intervened," she said, "I would have denied the trader Menethus his profits - what could he do with two puddles of melted flesh? And there would have been no opportunity for Medusa to show the extent of her skill."

"True," Poseidon said thoughtfully, conceding. "And my brother would have disapproved. He would have constantly reminded us of the time when Athena wasted her power to conjure herself, to merely destroy two degenerate, deserting Cretan soldiers. A tactless display to the mortals that would have become a mere fireside tale among them, its truth terribly diluted."

The idea of real Olympian power being distorted into uncertainty and ignorance appalled him, but he had not come to Athena to debate this.

"What can I do for you?" Athena said flatly.

"I only came," Poseidon began carefully, "to appeal to you one final time. To give you the opportunity to withdraw from the contest for Zeus' city. We could agree it now, privately. We have such a better relationship when Aphrodite is absent. She follows me around like a shadow, and you and her create friction that takes too much tact to navigate."

"She is in love with you," Athena said, as if Poseidon was unaware. "She has become victim of her greatest fear, of her greatest displeasure. The same could be said if I went to war and wed myself to the battlefield."

Poseidon persisted. "If you withdraw, then I will not labour the matter. I will support you in front of Zeus when you tell him there will be no contest." He suddenly narrowed his eyes into a half-scowl, newly aware of something, and turned to face me. He studied me briefly, like a customer assessing vegetables at market.

"The less attractive girl, but the first target for the rapists." He turned back to Athena. "You may wish to end your communion with her now."

"I have no objection to Miranda staying. She deserves the comfort of Olympus while Medusa mends her."

"Very well," the sea-god said dubiously. "What do you say? Let me have the city beyond Piraeus, and I will ensure you do not regret it."

I knew Athena's answer. She pretended to think on her response, and walked to her wall of clay models. She took Medusa from her alcove and studied the piece.

"I thank you for your generous consideration - feuds are best avoided. But I will not agree to withdraw. If the city is so important to you, then you will make the necessary efforts to convince its people that you should be the figurehead. The city is important to me, our legacy on earth more so. And so I intend to do what is necessary. I am not your enemy, Poseidon. I am your competitor."

Poseidon's eyes flashed icily in disappointment. "Then may the best Olympian win," he said frankly.

Athena then spoke brightly, avoiding an awkward pause and mitigating any immediate backlash she feared from Poseidon.

"Zeus has returned," she said. "He has already seen me here."

Poseidon wandered the few paces to the viewing pool. He rested his arms, tough and brown as oak, on the basin. He looked into the liquid and soon dipped a finger into it, stirring it gently.

"I knew he had arrived back," Poseidon said. Whether he did or not would not be questioned; to be out-done for information by Athena would not do. "I admit, I expected my brother to be away for longer. He seems to have found his enthusiasm again for these mortals, and for our affairs."

"Please, do not disrupt the pool," Athena said, like a tired parent gently addressing a troublesome child.

Poseidon grinned at her and obeyed. He withdrew his finger and flicked droplets back into it.

"That girl you favour, the keepsake in your mortal hand. Perhaps Aphrodite should have her in her temple in Mycenae. Or in her temple in the new city. Such a beauty there, in what will be the centre of the world, would be more apt. It might smooth relations between you two, if you made a gift to her of Medusa instead of keeping her for yourself. And she would be safe from any seductions - more safe with Aphrodite than any creature on earth."

Athena looked at him coyly. "Even from you?"

"Even from me."

"Medusa is another mortal who shows promise. Many do at a young age. Aphrodite is capricious. I would not have the girl be rejected if, in adulthood, her current allure did not blossom and meet the high standards she insists upon. Beauty is a thin foundation to build a future on, upon which to base a legacy. Her other skills may eventually outweigh her looks."

Poseidon scoffed. "That chance is slim. Look at her. She will re-shape mortal beauty. And then what will *you* do with her? Your priestesses will not say it openly, but she will be scorned. In their cliques they will whisper that she belongs elsewhere. That she embarrasses the noble house of Athena. That she attracts too many approaches from men, and too many stares from jealous women. She distracts from the true purpose of your temple's work. What will you do with her when your priestesses entreat upon their god to act?"

Poseidon did not wait for an answer, and left the chamber. He wished to save his temper, and was determined to have the final word in this exchange.

Athena watched after him. Her face wore an expression that was either sheer confidence, or the concealment of fear. The chamber dissolved about me, fading into blackness as my essence was cast out of Olympus again.

Chapter Nine

At the peak of the mound upon which the great city of Mycenae was built, the palace of the Perseid dynasty sat. Zeus' famous temple, the most important building and snug alongside the palace, had twin pillars that rose above all else. Incense burned day and night in honour of the father-god, a constant message of honour from the city's founding, ruling family. A smoke-cloud hovered about those most prominent homes on the upper part of the hill, reminding those most wealthy of who to thank for their fortune. The haze clogged and drifted with the mood of the wind.

From afar, the approaching traveller would have seen these features first, before getting close enough for the vast cyclopean walls to block all views and enemies. Before those gigantic stones silently asked for a statement of business from the traveller, and imposed an honest declaration from them.

I awoke from my impromptu surgery with a dull headache. I lay propped up against one of the wooden walls of the juddering cart. Sun beams warmed my face and the air was cool, rewarding my hardship with a blended comfort of good climate and renewed security.

By the position of the sun I could determine that it was morning. The blood from Aramis and Tuk's wounds had been cleaned from the floor; two patches remained, left to dry into faintly pink stains. Someone, I assumed it had been Medusa, had lit rosemary. The herb smoked in a small brazier. I watched the plume gather and be ushered away by the passing breeze that came through the bars. It was pleasant, but as Aphrodite's herb I wondered why it had been lit when Athena should be honoured. But this thought was quickly made idle by my crapulence: there was no monopoly on piety in the cart we shared.

My leg, tightly bound with rope and the wooden brace Menethus had made, was raised to rest on a small chest with a curved lid. I recognised this temporary support as belonging to Menethus: it was a clothes chest and, despite its unremarkable decoration, I stared at it for some time. My wound throbbed with a slow, pulsating rhythm. I wanted to move my leg, to test the threshold of pain, but Medusa, who lay by me and watched me as an owl does a field-mouse, shook her head. *'No, keep it still'*, she gestured.

The grassless landscape that we had travelled since Tanis had become green, fertile ground. We were close to Mycenae, for this farmland surrounded the approach to the city in all directions. For leagues this arable land spread, and the earth was tilled and harvested to feed and trade with the busy population.

A market-train of fewer carts than Menethus' cruised alongside, intent on overtaking. Foreign faces decorated with patterns of bright red ink stared at us through the bars of the second wagon. I counted six people in a cart half the size of what Medusa and I shared. Their skins were pale tan, and their narrow eyes showed worry; their approach to Mycenae brought the possibly poor change in their lives closer with every turn of their cart's wheels.

Medusa waved, staring at them with curiosity. On seeing her, some conferred warily; some changed their expressions to astonishment. They were captured by Medusa's looks, twofold prisoners either believing she was an agent of Olympian splendour gifted to mortal earth, or a harbinger of ill-fate.

A horn was sounded from its driving carriage, indicating its presence. The friendly warning was heeded, and our own horn was blown. The smaller train accelerated onward.

Medusa became excited. "Did you see those people? Where are they from?"

"The eastern lands. I recognise the wide faces and thin eyelids. The painted markings show their abilities, and therefore their value."

"One had pointed tips beneath both eyes."

"Indicating they can hunt. I have seen it before, on Libyan slaves. They looked at you intently."

Allusion to her allure, her quality that was as enchanting as it was pernicious, made her smile slowly drop and disappear.

"Tell me about Mycenae," she said, dismissing talk of her beauty.

I took a breath and flexed the toes of my damaged leg, anything to satisfy my need to move. A burning soreness shot through.

"Did your mother never tell you about it?"

"A little. I heard things about its politics, its wealth and disputes. But I want to know its origins. My mother distrusted the place. She said it was a wolf wrapped in a golden fleece. She said it was not for me."

I had never seen Mycenae for myself and could not verify Baktria's fears, but I had received a detailed education on its beginnings from Menethus.

"Can you see the city yet?" I asked.

She angled her neck to see through the bars.

"I see a hill in the distance. No walls, no buildings. Just a hill."

"Mycenae should be to the west of that hill the way we approach it, on a mound of its own. You won't see it until we reach the foothills. We will gain access via the main gate - the Lion Gate, named in remembrance of the founding king's favourite pet, a great cat with a golden mane. Then we will make the slow ascent up the winding ramp, to the very top of the mound where the palace and the temple of Zeus are built. Menethus must announce himself at the palace before we settle."

"Why?"

"It is the law," I said. "The Perseid family govern. Mycenae is a merchant's city. It is rich in gold. Its founder was a man called Pers, who announced himself as the son of Zeus and renamed himself Perseus in honour of the god. *Perseus* - part Pers, part Zeus."

"Was it true, was he the son of Zeus?"

"It would be unwise to claim such a thing if not. But he was never challenged on it - until his death."

Medusa's eyes widened and waited for me to continue.

"Determined to cast aside the bonds of his humble beginnings, as a young man Pers came across the mound where the city now sits. At the bottom he found a fresh water spring, and at the top edible mushrooms. He took these things as a sign that he was favoured by the father-god himself. He convinced himself that he was actually a demigod, and that his wholly mortal origins had been a lie. He joined his name with that of Zeus and his prosperity continued. Gold in abundance was found amid the water stream. People gradually flocked to him, believing his demigod story. The population and trade swelled. The city was established. Perseus had many children, his dynasty founded. The palace was built on the peak of the mound, and beside it the temple to Zeus. Such prominence was given to the temple that its pillars are taller than the palace towers. Attention turned to defending the city from invaders, protecting its wealth and the livelihoods of thousands of families."

I paused to allow a wave of sickness to pass over me: aftermath of the poppy. Medusa stared at me, impatient for me to carry on.

"It has very high walls," she said, prompting me.

"Yes," I said, taking a deep breath. "It is said King Perseus himself sought out and bargained with the cyclops."

"The one-eyed giants," she said with fascination.

"I have never seen one. Not even Menethus has. Regardless, the king succeeded and the cyclops laid the enormous blocks to form the outer walls of Mycenae. Too heavy for men to lift, they were expertly stacked and bonded with clay. The walls are near-impenetrable. No army has attempted to attack it. If Mycenae were ever to be destroyed, it would come from within its walls. It would consume itself. Everything is therefore tightly controlled."

"Perhaps he *was* the son of Zeus, to build such a city. But you say he was never challenged on this until his death."

"When King Perseus was very old, he awoke one day and felt compelled to visit the city forum, built at the exact middle point of the mound's peak, between the palace and Zeus' temple. People soon gathered, expecting an announcement. What they witnessed was a performance. Out of his senses, King Perseus could not explain why he had gone to the forum. He blamed conjurers and dark sorcery. As he stood in front of concerned well-wishers, a lightning bolt struck him from the sky. He burst into flames. He knew his punisher was Zeus. As his body turned to ash, he raised his hands and pleaded with the god - he had meant no offence in claiming he was his son, he had been an imposter all his life, but look what he had managed to achieve with the lie."

"Why did the father-god punish him at that moment?"

"Perseus' demigod claim had sparked a feud between Zeus and his godly wife, Hera. She believed Zeus had seduced a mortal woman, which the father-god truthfully denied. But Hera persisted. To appease her and resolve the row, Zeus made an example of the founder-king of Mycenae. The death of a single mortal was a small price to pay to resolve such a persistent argument."

We fell briefly silent, with only the sound of the cart wheels rumbling against the grassy ground for company.

"Strange to me that Zeus did not punish the king sooner," Medusa said. "Zeus surely knew the man had been living a lie. Perhaps the father-god did not really want to damn the king. Perhaps the father-god admired him."

"Olympian punishment can be sudden, and for long-held grudges. Just as retribution can suddenly be turned to honour, to satisfy flashes of regret or if they feel a sentence has been served."

"They all have a sense of the justice Athena loves," Medusa concluded.

"All the gods share aspects of the best and worst of each other. For King Perseus, Zeus could not refuse the insistence of his wife. He had suffered Hera's jealousy before, though she herself is no stranger to infidelity."

"He tired of the argument and saw the way to end it. Just like any man would do - eager for the easy life."

"You know the frailties of men better than me."

"Were King Perseus' family left unharmed?"

"His descendant rules to this day."

I had begun to feel sleepy and Medusa, ever-watchful, noticed. She let me rest in silence and turned to face the bars and the view, still trying to catch a first glimpse of the nearing city.

We gained permission to enter Mycenae without any fuss, Menethus being known and unseen for so long. The city's administrators knew he brought wealth, curiosities and stories: money and gold were things they were used to, but rare objects from remote parts of the world, and the tales that accompanied them, were of special value. He spent the afternoon inside the Perseid palace announcing himself with greetings to old acquaintances, and with small gifts and platitudes to key members of the court to ensure smooth passage for his business.

The market-train was rested in a broad courtyard. We and the rest of his property kept to our respective carts. We had food and water, and Menethus had reassured himself that my injury was stable. His rule was that the carts be covered by the same animal skin tarpaulins that had protected us from the rain. They were tied down, secured - even the cart holding the disposable Aramis and Tuk. This was necessary for business: Menethus did not want any of his stock to be on show, to give buyers the opportunity to develop bargaining strategies. And he did not want to attract opportunist thieves, who were few in Mycenae due to the barbaric punishments imposed: but Menethus knew the most foolish were also the most determined.

It was nightfall when Medusa and I were finally granted access to the famed baths, as promised by Menethus. The stone edifice was blandly shaped and unremarkable, but the interior was glorious: a spectacularly simple array of floor-to-ceiling columns, themselves carved with birds and plants that had been brightly coloured. No god was honoured there: no incense burned, and no trinkets or animal blood were present in any corner for a shrine. Fire-torches had been cleverly fitted to be part of the avian and botanic decorations: flame burst from the open mouths of stone sparrows, and from the petals of carved hibiscus plants. The perfectly cuboid atrium was lit enough to find a way, and yet dark enough to award privacy.

The baths themselves were divided by a stone wall of irregular rocks, which had been fitted at the deeper end of either pool. One pool was for the men, the other for women. It was forbidden for both sexes to mix. This was not a prudish regulation, but a logical one: the herbs and oils added to either bath were tailored to the gender. The pool for men and boys had bergamot, narcissus and gardenia; the bath Medusa and I used had rose, jasmine and lavender.

Menethus paid a stern, elderly woman from the palace court to chaperone us. She possessed a stick of birch, which was as knobbled as she, and she held it with a latent ferocity, lest perverts made an attempt on our naked forms. Like thievery, such things were rare in Mycenaean society; Menethus had become wary since Aramis and Tuk's attack on us.

Through an ingenious system of plumbing, the waters were kept warm. Medusa, delighted to be free from her robe, swam the length and breadth of the heated pool. I was aghast at this, and watched her enviously as she moved and dived beneath the water like a salmon. I wondered how she had learned, having lived in land-locked Tanis all her life, but reasoned that her able mother had somehow taught her, just as she had done her in the art of self-defence.

I could not immerse my wounded leg in the water, and had to wait for Medusa to support me. She then held me in place as I lay back in the shallower end of the pool, my splinted leg raised out of the wet. I held my breath and let my entire head sink beneath the perfume, and felt the heat of the water cleanse my dirty hair and face. The memory of Tuk's thorny finger inside of me was eased, and the salt-tears that had long since dried upon my cheeks were washed away.

"Here," Menethus said to us, holding two fresh robes.

We had returned to our cart, clean and yet having to wear our unwashed garments: it was not permitted to wash clothing in the baths. I knew what the robes Menethus presented signified by the sheer whiteness and finer weaving of the cotton thread. Medusa looked to me with uncertainty, and I nodded for her to take them.

"I have met with your High Priestess," he said

with a tired sigh. "She arrived here yesterday, and has been keen to see me. She instructed the purchase of you, Medusa. She knew I had acquired you. I did not expect such good fortune, for all of us. Both of you are now in the contract of sale."

He waited for Medusa to exclaim with joy, his face expectant. Since I had already whispered this news to her amidst the poppy-haze as she tended my injury, she stared back at Menethus straight-faced. Her trust in me already ran deep.

"Those are from her. Acolyte robes," Menethus said awkwardly. "She will collect you in the morning at sunrise, so she tells me. Be sure you are wearing them, and they are not tarnished. She will transport you to Piraeus and its vast settlement. She has a team of horses. She will get you there before nightfall tomorrow. Your time with me is at an end."

"What of my injury?" I said quietly.

"I told her what happened on the journey. It changes nothing. Someone called Maestra will be responsible for your recovery in temple."

"What have you done with Aramis and Tuk?" Medusa said.

"Aramis died. The wound you gave him did not help his ageing heart. Tuk still lives. The head of the apothecaries took them both in a deal I only concluded this evening. A good day's work."

He nodded and left us.

Medusa handed me one of the new robes. "Collected at sunrise...is that the rite?"

I felt the garment's quality and smoothed its neatly folded breast.

"New acolytes for temple should only be acquired on the dawn of a new day," I said. "It promises favourable service to the god."

Mycenae was quiet at night, as organised in its restful state as its dealings were in the daylight. Whether a nighttime economy functioned at all was unclear to us, since we were held secure within our cart. We curled up together for warmth and used our new acolyte robes as pillows, unwilling to wear them lest we crease them. Sleep, deep and replenishing, came quickly.

Chapter Ten

I stood in Zeus' throne room, where they gathered around a large sphere of light conjured by the father-god himself. My new, white acolyte robe fitted me perfectly. Its thin, dyed stripe of purple fizzed with clarity, brought on by my closeness to Athena. My leg-brace was absent and I stood freely: trivial mortal ailments were not reflected on Olympus.

Changing imagery of Piraeus and the settlement beyond the port flashed and shifted within the shining globe: men and women heaved blocks of stone; artisans consulted written plans; irrigation channels were dug; mass feeding and bathing of thousands of people; streams of new arrivals entered the growing metropolis, happy and hopeful faces eager to be a part of something profound and tangible, and venerated by Olympian authority.

Athena and Poseidon stood watching with unwavering interest, hypnotised by the prize that would belong to one of them. Aphrodite looked on as a courtesy. Zeus returned to his enormous white throne, and took greater interest in observing his family. The sphere soon dissolved into the air.

Poseidon was the first to speak, his tone impressed. "A feverish display of construction and piety," he said. "You really know how to motivate the mortals, brother."

"Thank you," Zeus said, pleased. "But flattery will get you nowhere. You and Athena are entirely even competitors."

"That beautiful girl you have just acquired, Athena, will fit in so well once the city is built," Poseidon said, too innocently.

Aphrodite was roused from her apathy. "What beautiful girl? The whore's child? Who we arranged rescue for?"

"The very same," said Poseidon. "Athena snapped her up, quicker than a hungry wolf would a stranded sheep."

Before Aphrodite could protest, Athena spoke: "And I am delighted to have done so. My High Priestess acted quickly and decisively, in accordance with my wishes. We have broadened our usual pool of acolytes. We have branched out with beauty."

Athena waited for the backlash. Aphrodite's sharp, pretty face had grown redder as she dwelled on what was, to her, an act of betrayal. She owned beauty, she owned lust; she should own Medusa.

Poseidon watched her, amusement and mischief growing in his eyes; he applied some effort to withhold a wild smile. As Aphrodite grew silently livid, he could not help but provoke it.

"I cannot wait to see her when she reaches

womanhood," the sea-god said with exaggerated awe. "Walking those avenues as a priestess, her training as an acolyte successful, parading herself at the public rites. She will be a beacon, a light that draws men and women to her like insects to honey. And she will be utterly unobtainable."

He paused to let his words settle, and then continued emphatically. "Medusa will be the most beautiful mortal woman that ever lived. The best of it will be that nobody can have her, not even touch her. She will be more stunning than the city, another reason to come to it. If I win it I may name it after her."

He beamed gloriously. Poseidon had his faults, but no other god celebrated more genuinely than he.

Aphrodite glared at him. "Have you finished?"

His grin dropped slightly, but he maintained an enchanted look. She narrowed her eyes at Athena.

"What you have done is a slight against me, Athena. Purposeful and cutting."

"You have shown little interest in acquiring any new acolytes," Athena said factually. "You had the chance to coax Medusa into your temple. 'Chance' and 'coax' are too kind - you had a clear opportunity to seize her. Instead you spurned it, just as you did the chance to compete for our father's city. This is a habit of yours, Aphrodite, to reject opportunities and then complain when the benefits are made more obvious. Or when your fickle mind is changed."

Aphrodite glared at her. "Beauty, sister, belongs to *me*. You would feel aggrieved if I went out of my way to acquire a girl with a head for perfect justice, or a naturally gifted healer, or even a warrior. I can only conclude that you covet beauty. A worrying habit of the plain-faced."

"Ridiculous," Athena scoffed. "My temples have been no haven for beauty, or the vanity and obsession that it brings. There are no mirrors permitted, just as there are none in yours. Though I think you banned them for a different reason."

"And yet you invite Medusa into your fold! You have allowed envy to grow inside you," Aphrodite said combatively. "You see the way my mortal women and I are desired. We inspire men and women to breed. As the mother of beauty and desire, therefore, I *am* the mortal cause. You have always wanted what you cannot have, Athena."

Aphrodite turned to Zeus, entreating him for support. There was nothing she could do to acquire Medusa now, unless the father-god intervened or if Athena willingly handed her over.

"Medusa must belong to me," Aphrodite said. "Athena rejects her own authority over justice and loyalty, and dishonours me by taking her as an acolyte. For all her wisdom, she secretly knows that beauty is the essential component. She has discovered, and fears, that without it all else is crude and pointless."

Zeus initially beheld Aphrodite with interest, having a regard for her argument. But her passion, inherited from her nymph mother, had overruled reason and Aphrodite had gone too far. Zeus chose wise silence, but his face dropped grimly in response to her arrogance.

Athena addressed Poseidon, and spoke neutrally. "You make her feel this way. You have purposefully antagonised her to stoke an argument. I can only imagine you have done this to try and weaken my position as your competitor. It certainly won't strengthen yours."

Poseidon went to respond, his expression as placid as Athena's, when Zeus interjected.

"I feel I have made this clear before, but I will repeat a final time - if only to calm this stormy sea of dispute." The father-god paused for effect, not for opportunity to challenge him. Zeus appreciated drama, particularly when he controlled it.

"There will be enough room for all your attributes - and those of your absent kin - in the new city. Rest assured, temples will be sustained to honour you all. Stone icons that will still stand long after the mortals have stopped looking upwards to us, long after they have ceased to hold us in greater reverence than themselves. But only one of you, Athena or Poseidon, can have the glory of winning it, of being its figure-head evermore."

He searched each of them for an opinion, and none were forthcoming.

"Athena - your plain and functional looks will never be celebrated as beauty..." Zeus continued, breaking the silence.

"But..." she protested, and Zeus looked at her sharply. The god was silenced.

"...your skills in wisdom, healing, justice and - whether you like it or not - war, will propel mankind onward. And you, Aphrodite - beauty, desire, procreation and - whether you like it or not - love, will allow the mortals to *be* at all. There is *being* in the sense of being *born*, and there is *being* in the sense of *living*. In this way two destinies are forged: the mortals', and our own. We synchronise, we coexist - we are destinies adjoined." Zeus smiled, revelling in his own words. "Along with love and fear, the mortals will learn to carry each other. And so must we."

The father-god rose from his throne. He filled his lungs and his ample chest expanded; he stretched and straightened his back, as if preparing for exercise.

"Now, I grow tired of sitting on the throne. Don't you misinterpret that, Poseidon!" He laughed, booming. "Now, Aphrodite will walk with me on earth. We will disguise ourselves, and breathe air that is not so feudal."

Aphrodite obeyed and joined her father, taking one of his hands. They vanished, becoming one with the stark whiteness of the Olympian hall.

"*'Destinies adjoined'*," said Poseidon mockingly, turning to Athena. "Either dear Zeus doesn't understand the mortal cause or he does with a depth that I can't fathom. If I were compelled to gamble on it, I would place my bet on the former."

Athena stared into the blank, bright space where the sphere of light had been. She was oblivious to what Poseidon had said, to his irritation.

"You're not dwelling on his *'plain and functional'* remark, are you?" The sea-god said. "There is nothing more sad and unbecoming than a god, or mortal for that matter, sinking under the weight of self-pity."

Now Athena looked at him, as if struck by his wisdom. "I have not known the feeling before now," she said. "I don't know what to do with it."

"Destroy it," Poseidon said simply. "Treat it like an enemy in war. Zeus certainly meant the comment, you can mean the retaliation."

"You give me such an answer because you have experience of it."

Poseidon spoke with an air of counsel, taking the role of advisor. "As Zeus' brother, how could I not? I learned long ago to overcome despondency. Action takes its place. *Doing* something, instead of dwelling."

I doubted the sea-god's act, and suspected cunning. Athena, also wise to a hidden motive, deployed a pretence of surrender.

"What action can I take?" The god said. "Aphrodite is right. Beauty holds a greater place in the mortal world than wisdom, justice and healing. Zeus implied as much. Even war is made exquisite by beauty, the reasons for the battle trumped by its bloody allure."

"Ignore what my brother has said - he is only really half-learned in mortal matters. Beauty is second to the sea. Take the city we vie for: water, wind and horse will bring people there. Procreation, sometimes love, will fill it. The mortals will dispense justice, become learned, eventually seek to expand their empire, either by chasing war or conquest. But these things are fickle, pushed ashore or drawn into the depths by the tide of mortal development. Aphrodite and I provide the essential components. You do not. If you win the city, you cannot rely on she and I to bolster your victory. The fire behind its construction may be quickly extinguished."

Athena peered at him, curiosity in her eyes. She moved towards the sea-god, pushing out her firm, athletic bosom and raising herself to be nearly as tall as him.

"The answer is for me to withdraw," Athena said. She did not mean it.

"That decision is yours," the sea-god said, raising a single eyebrow. He faced her and they were almost touching, a breath apart.

"It would risk harsher remarks from my father."

"Remarks I would help contain, and persuade into blessings."

I could see his mortal-form cock begin to swell. It did not escape Athena's notice.

"What about Aphrodite?" She said, and I thought her hand would reach down to touch the titan phallus.

"What about her?" Poseidon looked at Athena hungrily, and yet hesitated to act further.

"You would put me above her, if I withdrew. She would be relegated down the list of your favour."

This made Poseidon think carefully before answering. New wrath - that of Aphrodite - had to now be considered. New dimensions to his relationship with Zeus had to be forecast. Not to mention revised management of Athena, the one god, excluding Zeus, who could match Poseidon in words and, though she may not have known it yet, actions. He had seen a dishonesty in her eyes; he had smelled her rare seduction, which had triggered sudden caution. The sea-god was being exposed as caring less for beauty than the possibility of sex with a target he had only ever considered he could not, would not, have. Athena's deceit had nearly entrapped him.

Poseidon spoke guardedly. "It is not something I could promise here...unless we have an agreement. You have made it clear before that you have no intention of making one."

Athena stepped away, knowing her efforts had been uncovered. Poseidon now seemed sheepish.

"Then this moment is lost," she said.

"As are all moments," Poseidon replied. "They all become like sand grains in a desert. I think it wise that we call this our final meeting together, until we compete to decide the city."

"Agreed," Athena said.

The god turned her back to Poseidon and looked at me, my human essence fixed in Olympian stasis. She appraised me, and gave me a small, conspiratorial smile.

Chapter Eleven

The High Priestess did not collect us at dawn.

Medusa and I sat waiting for Ursula and her entourage, our new acolyte robes properly adorned, our skins clean and our meagre possessions neatly packaged beside us. The cart we had shared those past days and nights seemed foreign, as if we were now guests who had outstayed a welcome.

Unable to sit still for very long, Medusa opened her box of belongings and produced a comb, its teeth widely set apart. I caught sight of her inherited mother's mirror, glinting in capture of a sun-ray. She would have to be rid of it, I thought, but said nothing. She began to comb my dark bird's nest of hair, starting at the front of my head and gently working the tool back and down, smoothing out its knots. When it was her turn, her blonde-brown hair relented easily to the comb.

"We should use the mirror, before it is taken away," she said.

"Why?"

"To have a memory of what we look like now, before we become women. We may not see ourselves again. To look at ourselves in a mirror is forbidden where we are going. And what is forbidden is most desired."

She took the mirror from her box. I should have stopped her. She held it up, and both our faces fitted neatly into the rounded piece of shined metal and glass. I could not help but compare myself to her: my rounder face, with prominent chin but no sharp angle to my jaw; my eyebrows were thick and uneven, and my mouth pouted. I suppressed a shudder at the memory of Tuk's assault of me, made worse that I could only be attractive to a man so depraved as he.

Her reflection saved me from being immersed in self-disgust, which made her seem even more striking than in the flesh. Her cheekbones were already high, and her dark, olive skin was so perfectly inherited from her parentage; her facial features achieved a level of proportion unseen in other people. I inspected her face for a blemish or imperfection. I found none.

"You are going to be a pretty woman," she said quietly, as if reading the disappointment I had in my own looks. And then, realising she could be thought of as discourteous, quickly added: "Can you stand it, that you will never be able to love another but the god. That you won't marry, have children?"

"I can bear it," I said without hesitation, returning my stare to my own reflection in the mirror. "It is sacrilege for people in our position to want love from any other but the god.

Besides, I am not a beacon for attention from others."

She silently replaced the mirror and closed her box of belongings.

"Will you stand it?" I asked.

She did not look at me. Instead she stared at her box, perhaps mindful of her mother.

"I fear my beauty," she admitted, the shadow of a terror kept under control in her voice. "Temple will protect me from the evils it brings. For that I shall only love Athena."

"What evils can your beauty bring? It is surely a blessing," I said.

"Great blessings may also be great curses. While people look upon me and marvel, I will always be the object of great desire. Desire that may inspire obsession, or madness in others. I don't speak from arrogance - I speak from the vividness of my dreams, from premonition, and from logic. Without the sanctity of temple, I would corrupt and be corrupted."

My fractured leg had throbbed mercilessly with discomfort. Overnight, Menethus had constructed a pair of crutches for me to lean on, to aid my walking. I had taken them gratefully but with uncertainty. Menethus' face swelled with pleasure that he had been of use. He urged me to try them, and watched proudly as his parting gift was at first wrestled with, and then used properly.

Medusa told me to practice, to become familiar with steering them. We passed the time, me balancing and Medusa laughing as I used the crutches to walk the length of the cart and back again. This useful entertainment dissolved into worry as the sun continued to rise beyond the dawn, and Ursula still failed to appear. My expectations for the future were so close to being met, and I thought it cruel that the crucial handover of us from Menethus to temple was delayed. What bad omens I conceived as a result of the dawn rite not being observed were flattened by my belief that the High Priestess would appeal to Athena, and that the god would ignore any slight.

As the time for the midday meal neared, Menethus returned to us. Relief was in his voice.

"The High Priestess is coming now. She has been locked in a dispute with one of the court officials in charge of tax. Ridiculous - he has insisted on a premium from the temple, because two of you are now being sold instead of just one. I have never heard of such a thing."

"Did she pay it?" I said.

"Of course," he said. "But she did not pay immediately. She negotiated, as is proper in Mycenae. The respect a High Priestess commands here is erratic - unless they are part of Zeus' temple. But now she has proved herself competent in deal-making. A useful asset for the future, if she were to return here."

Just as he finished, Ursula appeared behind the trader-lord, honouring his summons. She and Menethus were matched by their tall height. Her athletic frame I had noted in communion with Athena was personified: of a female warrior past her youthful prime; mature, but still powerful. She wore a cloak of thin material - perfect for the summer heat. It showed no dirt from her journey from Piraeus. It had a golden shimmer, displaying a finer, yellowish substance woven between tight threads of white cotton. Her black hair was held back by a silver band resting into her scalp, exposing green eyes akin to the sea-herbs found on beach shores. Their colour was not the dark blue I could recall from the communion, and I stared open-mouthed in wonder at how this could be.

Menethus bowed to her. Her eyes never left Medusa and I. She appraised us, sizing the purchase she had suddenly had to work hard for. She neither smiled nor beheld us with hostility: her look was one of judgement, of our fears and weaknesses. She spoke to me first.

"I recognise you from a recent communion," she said. "Miranda, birth-aligned with the god. You are wondering why the colour of my eyes is different to what you remember. Their hue is affected when seen through Athena's viewing pool, as all things can be."

Now she addressed Medusa, who stared at the High Priestess as if she were Athena herself.

"And I would know you anywhere for your beauty. I doubted it, but for once the rumour-mongers speak no lies. Medusa, you will be safe in temple, where your other skills will be put to use. We honour more than the body there. Welcome, acolytes. Beloved sisters. I am Ursula, your High Priestess."

"Beloved High Priestess," I said, as is proper.

"Beloved High Priestess," Medusa uttered nervously, following my lead.

Ursula nodded once and smiled slightly, perhaps ingratiated by Medusa's innocence.

"We have already lost much time," she said. "And, in the interest of a quick separation from Menethus - this kind man who you must look upon as more than a master, having spent much time with him - I insist we leave this place immediately. We can still break the port of Piraeus and arrive in the new city by moonrise."

"What of the dawn rite?" I said, with even-voiced respect.

"We shall honour the god as we travel."

With Medusa's help, I rose and we left Menethus' cart. He ordered our possessions be carried by two of his workers. We walked downhill to a courtyard, directly beneath where Menethus had stayed his train. I supported myself on the crutches Menethus had made, and was happy I had become adept at using them. Ursula watched me keenly.

"I know the story of your leg. A horrific act to befall you both," she said, gesturing to the splint. "You have a strong mind, a strong will. But you must speak of it if the memory disturbs you. It is not a weakness to do so. Nobody is immune to the torture of such trauma."

"Medusa prevented worse from happening."

The High Priestess nodded once in acknowledgement. We reached Ursula's transport: a modest, large and sturdy-looking wagon pulled by a team of four horses, all mares. Two priestesses waited, their yellow robes wavering in the breeze. They took our possessions from the men, who cowered slightly in reverence to these calm and capable women. I wanted to study them, take in their faces, but Menethus spoke up.

"I might see you in the new city, one day," he said. "I bid you both good health, a good life."

He would have embraced us, but it was not permitted for acolytes. His large and thankful face, broad-bearded with a smile of fatherly sincerity, was enough.

"We will honour you in our prayers, for your kindness," I said.

"Yes," said Medusa. "Thank you."

The High Priestess called to us, firmly and not unkind.

"Miranda. Medusa."

"Go," Menethus said.

◆ ◆ ◆

Medusa and I spent the journey hungry, and in silence. The incense smoke that filled the wagon dazed us into a semi-slumber, a halfway house between reality and dream.

The priestesses were named Pella and Acantha. Pella was the younger and was faultlessly dark-skinned, with near-black irises set against brilliant whites. I wanted to ask about her bloodline, believing it Kemet, but knew better than to do so on first meeting. Acantha was older and gave the instruction. She was pale-skinned, certainly not from the southern lands. She had an almost sickly look, as if she did not eat enough. Her hair, showing some grey strands, was modestly kept; but her face was avian and symmetrical, curious and attractive. I wondered if she had been the source of great desire when younger.

"Observe the rite," Acantha said to us. Her voice, which I could tell was normally forceful, was kept guarded for the sake of our confined space. "We light myrrh and storax in thanks to the god for our safe journey, and to ask that our late acquisition of you be forgiven. The smoke will be thick, the odour something you are not used to and you will feel the need to sleep, but you must not."

Medusa spoke. "Will it offend the god if we

do?"

Acantha beheld her with a harsh look, though a question was not forbidden before the rite had started.

"It is not our way to submit," she said.

Ursula spoke, her voice enough for Acantha to stand aside so the High Priestess could properly address us. "The skill in being an acolyte is to identify and use every opportunity to learn. Athena knows this, and rewards effort the most. Effort usually leads to success. Trying to please the god at all times is ill-advised because to do so is impossible, and leads to the disgrace of fraud."

"Yes, High Priestess," said Medusa, fearful because she had caused Ursula to interject.

The horses were whipped into motion and the wagon began its departure from Mycenae.

Pella opened part of the wagon's roof, letting in daylight and air. Acantha began constructing a metal brazier. The device was like nothing I had seen before: unfolded from a simple flat square, it soon became an ornate and three-dimensional hexagon. It was polished to a golden sheen and yet not gold itself. Pella smiled, noticing my curiosity.

"We have skills with metalwork, ceramics and wood," she said, her accent similar to what I had heard in people from the south of Libya. "The likes of which you have never seen. You will learn about them, in time."

They arranged the incense and set it alight. Soon the brazier smouldered, an orange glow of heat at its bottom. Though the roof was partly open, the smoke spread and choked the wagon. I had smelt myrrh before, but never storax: it stung my nose with its sweetness. With the myrrh the odour was like burnt cream: deliciously acrid.

Medusa began coughing. I tried to withhold my own, but succumbed; my spluttering jerked my bad leg, reminding me of its physical dominance over me. After a time, our lungs became used to the thick air. Our eyes stopped streaming and we were able to regulate our breathing. With the carriage now free from our acolyte chokes, Ursula, Acantha and Pella began singing. They started in perfect unison, very slowly, their harmonies forming a soulful drone:

Hear me, O Goddess, when to you I pray,
With supplicating voice both night and day,
And in my latest moment, give peace and health,
Propitious times, and necessary wealth,
And, ever present, be your votaries' aid,
O, much implored, you our parent, blue-eyed maid.

The incense and their lullaby stretched time, and melted the rumbling wheels and the panting of the mares into a rush of indiscernible sound and vision. I saw the priestess' faces change amidst the foggy smoke plumes: they became like statues, like the figurines made by Athena within her chamber, solidifying in their piety and self-hypnosis. The High Priestess became enthroned: a spear in her right hand, helmet on her head, and round shield in her left, all shining gold. They were unreal, intangible, but our eyes were convinced otherwise.

Nothing more than sleep was wanted by Medusa and I, and yet nothing more was yearned for than to resist it.

Medusa and I were gently shaken from our trance by Pella. Night had fallen. The first sound I heard was voices: rough accents of men from outside the wagon, aggression in their tone, and language I did not understand.

"We have passed the port of Piraeus and have entered the settlement," the priestess whispered. "Stay silent. Workers, yellow-haired men from the far north, have stopped us to search and to take commission. They have no authority, but feel they are not paid enough. And they are drunk."

Suddenly Medusa sneezed, remnant incense smoke now dried in the backs of our throats. There was a brief pause in talks outside. Then more coarse voices, and Ursula's own voice rose above them.

"I challenge your strongest to a duel," the High

Priestess shouted, rallying. "If he wins, you may take your so-called tax. If I win, you will be collecting his bloody remains for the public pyre."

A murmur of male voices and laughter started, quickly escalating. One man's rose above the others and silenced them. There were cheers, the challenger having been found.

Ursula opened the door to the carriage, and gestured to us. "Come. Watch me decimate this heathen brute," she said to Medusa and I, her eyes unblinking and fired with strength. "Our temple does not advocate violence, unless threatened. Then all is fair."

We inside the carriage crowded by its door. She turned to face her adversary. Before seeing the man she faced, I saw the settlement that would become the city: the orange glow of flame torches by the thousand lit up the growing metropolis against the blackness of the night. The place was already at least double the size of Mycenae, and the nighttime did not stop construction. The torches spread like fireflies, a field of dotted blazes that led towards an enormous hill, upon which the Acropolis was being built. This citadel was fortified by an outer wall, itself lit left to right by controlled flame.

Ursula stood against a man shorter and stouter than her. He had removed his over-shirt to expose a muscular sternum that protruded like a drum, greased with the sweat of anticipation and drink. A small crowd had gathered, the

162

clinking of coins changing hands in wagers. No peacemaker or authority tried to stop the fight; the city was not yet mature enough for firm law and order to take hold.

The challenger spoke crisply and sincerely, despite his crude stance. "I'm going to rip your tits off, witch," he said, tying his long, blond hair back out of his face. In the flame-light I could see his skin was pink, reddened by the relentless sun of a Greek summer.

Medusa watched unblinking, absorbed by the event. Her eyes were wide, alert to what could happen if the High Priestess failed. I thought of her mother's knife: useful against degenerates like Aramis and Tuk, but futile against a gang of these thicker-skinned marauders. Pella stood lean and taut, stressed; while Acantha was the very opposite, nonchalantly leaning on the door's timber frame as if she already knew what the outcome would be.

Ursula removed her robe, letting it fall to the dusty floor. She wore no covering to her full, globular breasts, and only a cloth undergarment over her vagina and buttocks. Circling this was a belt of gold, buckled in the centre of her belly. Resting on her right hip, attached to the belt, was a thin, golden baton.

"You will try," she said, removing the baton with care.

Doubt flashed across the face of her adversary.

"We did not agree weapons," he said.

163

"So back down. You should have been clearer in the terms of your challenge. Withdraw, and pray to whichever heathen gods you people adore that they may spare you for your cowardice. Your punishment will not be easy, after you have bragged so much and startled my new acolytes."

The man looked at us standing inside the wagon, by its open door. He stared at Medusa. I knew such a look by now: the unblinking eyes; the slight opening of the mouth; dumbfounded interest. Someone from the crowd threw him a blade, a crudely curved sword, and his stare was broken. The fighter took a battle stance, now prepared to face Ursula.

"I'll match you," he said.

The High Priestess jerked the baton with an expert flick of the wrist and the device extended, spiralling to become pointed at both ends. She held the javelin in one hand at its midpoint, ready to thrust. Her muscles flexed, indicating the spear held some weight; her legs were apart and her knees bent if the option to use force was needed. There were murmurings of encouragement in the crowd, and a circle had formed around them.

The brute was the first to attack, his impatience over-boiling. He launched himself at Ursula, and was clearly soldier-trained but out-of-practice. His sword arm flailed in an attempt to land an early, decisive blow, which Ursula stepped aside to avoid. He nearly collided with the wagon, but caught himself. Using the momentum he had gathered, he struck again: he swept his blade to her feet, left, right, while also trying to grab at her with his free hand. The High Priestess impaled the javelin into the ground and swung herself around him. She had the chance to hit him, but did not. The brute deftly spun on his heel and seized the javelin, and came away the worse for it: the spear was razor-sharp, except where Ursula held it, and his free palm was painfully split open. Blood oozed as he clenched his injured hand, the red liquid dripping onto the floor.

But pain was easy to ignore for this man. Summoning all his experience and wrath, he swung his sword wildly: blows which Ursula had to defend with her weapon. He drove her back and she led him around the makeshift arena; his anger let him get so close he landed a punch on the High Priestess' right cheek. At this Pella gasped; even Acantha stood up, ready to involve herself. Medusa took a step forward, as if to join in the fight too, but I seized her arm and held her back.

The punch dazed Ursula. The brute sensed a change in his fortunes and took aim with his blade: it was not sharp or refined, but could hack at a neck and make a terrible mess of death. This was his fatal error: keen for a sudden victory, he took what he thought was his ultimate chance and leaped into the air, sword

165

swung high and directed at the High Priestess' head. Less bravado and more control may have injured Ursula to the point of her expiry, but the man's bubbling joy at the scent of bloody glory betrayed him. He overestimated the effect of his lucky punch and Ursula glided aside as he brought the sword down. Wrath now flashed in her eyes, and her body twisted in such a way that would be impossible for most people to replicate. Her razor javelin was whipped into a vortex: the brute's arms were the first to leave his torso, then his legs were dismembered. The cuts were clean, near-surgical. His stumped body fell to the floor and all the man could do was gasp as he quickly died. His sword-hand still held the blade. Acantha cackled joyfully.

Ursula stepped over the vast pool of blood she had created, collected her robe and wiped her javelin clean with it. She shrank the weapon with another wrist-flick and she donned the garment again. The crowd of onlookers cheered, bedazzled by bloodsport, as the brute's accomplices, themselves stunned, started gathering his body parts as Ursula had predicted.

Our carriage set off again, ourselves wordlessly overjoyed by the High Priestess' victory in violence. We trundled the remaining distance to temple uninterrupted.

Our temple lay deep in the settlement's confines. In some cities, temples clustered together to form a district. In this the unnamed city, no such area would exist: the Olympian houses would be like islands in the sea of other buildings, with none greater than the temple that would eventually appear within the Acropolis. This would be the flagship religious structure of the city, built to honour the figurehead god, and it would look down upon all the others from its hill: an everlasting symbol of their victory.

We stopped and were bidden to leave the carriage quickly. Our belongings stayed on board, to be brought by others to the temple's rear. Outside, the night air lingered with the smell of sweat and stone. Medusa stood close to me, shy and not wanting to break our bond of mutual reliance.

I saw we were near the foot of the hill, up which the citadel was mid-construction. Night-labourers ferried stone in a gradual, upward spiral to the apex, like ants carrying morsels to the mounded entry of their nest. No regard for the sleeping hours was given; the great build must continue.

As our wagon was driven away, temple was revealed. Its five thick columns supported a stone cross-beam with a shallow triangular roof atop. Beyond the columns was a floor-to-ceiling wall, in which a gap housed a heavy iron door, rich with neatly hammered decorations in each corner: an owl's head, a spear, a distaff and a shield. The quality of the building was emphasised by its simplicity: whoever had been commissioned to construct the temple had taken their task seriously. Nothing appeared misaligned, or lacking in proportion. Despite being relatively small compared to other Athenian temples, it still towered above its mortal users.

The metal door opened inwards, revealing an ancient priestess, leaning on a walking stick.

"Late!" She cried, scolding, and pointed her stick at us with venom.

Ursula led Medusa, Pella, Acantha and I across the threshold created by the columns. My crutches slowed me. The crone stood aside to allow us entry into the cool, fire-lit atrium. She beheld Medusa and I with gawping, silent enthusiasm. My splinted leg made her bushy grey eyebrows rise. The woman was certainly very old, but not hunched or decrepit; despite her walking stick she stood straight and capable. She looked a natural Greek, her skin brown from years in good sun, and she had the bone structure of similarly sturdy women once pointed out to me by Menethus as a tribe set apart from others. Her hair was plain white, brilliant in the candlelight of the temple's interior. The ignorant would have thought her the High Priestess, on age and domineering posture alone.

She closed the door after us. The iron door boomed as it settled, echoing security around the cuboid.

"Miranda, Medusa, I introduce Maestra," said Ursula, gesturing to the elderly priestess. "She will teach you the arts of archery and healing, and the philosophy of justice."

"She is a mad old witch, a cast-off from the Stygian sisters," said Acantha.

I expected Ursula to shame her, but instead the High Priestess laughed.

"Don't look so appalled," Maestra said, looking at me. "Acantha speaks true. I was the runt of the Stygian litter, those sick flesh-eaters smelled the god's favour in me. To their noses, it was like old meat is to us - inedible. What happened here?"

She used her walking cane to tap my splint. I looked at Ursula for permission to speak, but this infuriated Maestra.

"Do you not have a mind of your own, girl? Speak! She can't tell you when to or not. Only perhaps on holy days, and today is not one of those."

"Two men attacked us," I said. "One hit me, broke my leg. Medusa healed me."

Maestra bent down to inspect my injury and Medusa's repair of it more closely.

"Did she now. And did she also not spill the contents of their balls all over the floor of your trader's cart? Answer!"

"I did," said Medusa.

"Hmmm. Does Aphrodite know you're here,

pretty girl?" Maestra said this without looking up from her continued study of my leg. "My mind for the gods may be temperamental, but I still know things - more than any reasonable person might imagine, to look at me." Maestra stood up and beheld Medusa with understated awe. "You did well. It is a well-wrapped splint, done at the right time after the blow. It does not smell putrid, and your patient stands before us now, happy as a lamb. But I'm afraid the injury will not heal properly. Ever."

I felt sick. Ursula narrowed her eyes.

"What do you mean?" The High Priestess said. "You surely cannot tell just by looking at it so casually."

"I can and I do. You, girl, will forever limp," Maestra said, looking at me pointedly. "You will hobble along for the rest of your days. No matter - you are in the house of Athena now. We don't care about such deformities. Certainly not ac-quired in the field of battle. Speaking of which, what happened to *you*?"

The crone pointed her stick at Ursula, indi-cating her bloody robe. My leg twinged with pain, mourning its apparently perpetual loss of normal function. I wanted to cry, the diagnosed imperfection spoiling the vision I had for my fu-ture. To be told so casually by a supposed ex-pert; I felt crushed. Medusa subtly reached for my nearest hand in comfort, and I took it.

"First we were delayed at Mycenae, in a dispute over taxation for two acolytes rather than one. And then we were forcibly stopped beyond the port - drunkards, men from the far north with pale skins and fur boots in high-summer. Poor fools. I challenged their strongest."

"Poor fool," Maestra echoed. "Learn from this...why are you holding hands?" She pointed her stick at Medusa and I, and brought it down gently on our bodily connection, breaking it.

"You may not *hold hands*. Along that path lies dependence, and the god will punish you. As I was saying - learn from this. Your first lesson: some say acolytes should not bear arms. This is preposterous, as demonstrated by your High Priestess. Those who learn to defend themselves at a young age become experts in maturity. Ursula started when she had just ten seasons to her age. I know, I was there. We shall begin your training tomorrow, after the initiation. Bow, spear, shield. Even with your limp you shall be capable."

Ursula ended the discussion abruptly, wanting Medusa and I settled for the night. Pella ushered us away, leading the way across the atrium. The obscured far end of the large, square room became clearer. As we walked, hobbled in my case, a giant statue of Athena was revealed. She had been carved from pale stone and polished using the technique of the *Polada*, the people in the country nearest west from Greece, where vines and olives grow abundantly. The god sat enthroned, enrobed and with spear and shield in either hand. The helmet upon her head was plumed; the god seemed dressed for war, like a female general about to rise from her seat and follow her own orders. We stopped in front of the statue and looked up.

Pella spoke, her voice soothing. "The night ritual has passed, but you must bow to the god. Do as I do."

The priestess put her hands together in suppliance and slowly bowed her head down, eyes closed. Medusa and I did the same and, forgetting them, my crutches clattered to the floor. The noise echoed around the tomb-silent atrium, ensuring our arrival was even more disruptive. Medusa picked up my crutches and helped me regain balance.

"Come, you are both hungry and tired," Pella said.

She led us behind the great statue where broad, stone stairs descended. With Medusa's support, I shuffled down the flight. At the bottom, directly beneath the floor of the temple's atrium, a wide corridor beckoned. More iron doors, smaller imitations of the temple's main entrance, lined the passage.

"These are the private rooms of the priestesses, our library, Maestra's own quarters and those of the High Priestess," Pella said as we walked on. "You will never enter most of these rooms. You will share accommodation with the other acolytes, but the first night is usually spent alone. Since there are two of you and you have come here together, we have arranged that you both share a room tonight."

The priestess stopped outside a particular door, identical to the others, produced a small key and opened it inwards.

"You will be woken at first light for the dawn rite. And then you shall have your initiation."

Pella gestured for us to enter the room. We entered and she left us, closing the door quietly. The room was lit with an oil lamp, and had two simple wooden beds, cradles moreover, with straw mattresses. A table with a ewer of water, ceramic mugs that were not smoothed with slip, and two large chunks of wheat bread smeared with honey awaited us.

We wasted no time in pouring water and tearing into the bread. There were no windows, and were it not for the cleanliness and modest comfort of the room it could have easily been a prison, a dungeon deep beneath a holy house. A hidden ventilation system kept the room cool and fresh air drafted in, soured by the smell of burning oil and the odours of the busy settlement.

We soon lay on our beds in the dark, the oil lamp extinguished and our bellies full and thirsts contented.

"What will the initiation be?" Medusa said. I had been near sleep, and the question was unwelcome.

"First we will be tested for virginity. Then we will be presented to all the other acolytes and priestesses in temple. Our belongings will be shown off, and ceremonially removed from us. We enter temple with nothing but ourselves. Then we will be flogged - three strokes of a cane across our backsides in front of a naked man, to have us associate the male form with discomfort. Then we will be formally accepted, healed and bathed."

Whether it was my ratty tone, or the heralding of our new life, she was silenced.

Dawn sunlight streamed through a retractable piece of the temple's roof, shining down upon the statue of the god. Her structure was illuminated: though her composition was pure stone, she could have been partially mineral, even golden, the way the sun's rays sparkled and lingered upon her helmet and shield. Enrobed, Medusa and I and the High Priestess, faced the god. The other eighteen occupants of the temple behind us watched. We had already seen Maestra who, with surgical precision and politeness, had verified our innocence.

"Pallas Athena," exclaimed Ursula, hands held high, "we entreat you grant acceptance of these mortal girls. With your blessing and our guidance, they are your acolytes today and one dawn will become priestesses. May your traditions be carried forth, abreast with time and even after time itself ceases to be."

I had not been permitted my crutches for the initiation, assured that my suffering was necessary. I stood awkwardly, balancing on my good leg. The statue's eyes stared straight ahead and yet seemed to peer downward at all, we new and those tenured supplicants.

"No rejection is forthcoming," continued Ursula. We turned to face our audience. "Bring out their possessions."

Pella came forth carrying Medusa's small box and my sack of belongings. Already they seemed like foreign objects, souvenirs from another life. Without any ceremony, my bag was emptied first, the few clothes and worthless trinkets spilled out onto temple floor. The other acolytes and priestesses, Maestra and Ursula too, peered at them with scrutiny. They were searching for anything poignant, anything they could use as an opportunity to evangelise. I knew I had nothing; I was glad to be rid of the responsibility for meagre items that exposed me as anything but acolyte and priestess-to-be.

Next came Medusa's box. Pella opened it and immediately her eyes widened in horror: she held up the mirror, the parting gift of Medusa's dying mother. Medusa stared at it with a restrained longing; a yearning she knew was now impermissible. Gasps emanated from the audience; Ursula herself barely contained her surprise. Only Maestra remained silent.

"The most forbidden article," the High Priestess said, addressing the room in preparation for dealing with the object.

Pella continued to hold it up. Disgust was upon her face, and something else: desire.

"Give it to me," Ursula said.

The High Priestess approached Pella, who handed it over but now looked at it as longingly as Medusa had.

Ursula held it with distrust, as if the thing was cursed and holding it for too long would be infectious. She looked squarely at Medusa.

"You perhaps did not know our rule. Reflection of the self detracts from our purpose - it is a distraction that grows and grows, until vanity spoils."

"It was my mother's, a gift to me at her death," Medusa said cautiously, but truthfully.

Ursula thought for a moment, taking in her underlings and exchanging a brief, confirmatory look with Maestra, who nodded once in some unspoken agreement.

"It shall remain in temple. It shall be kept in the same box Medusa has brought, with no prevention to accessing it," she said, loud enough for all to hear. A collective gasp was exclaimed by the audience of priestesses and acolytes. "This shall be a test of our resolve to resist temptation. With this *musalu* but a short distance and so easily accessible for any of us in temple, we shall forever be mindful of it as something so ensnaring and so forbidden. To resist easy temptation is a hard and worthy lesson."

Murmurs of agreement echoed around the atrium. Ursula looked up at the statue behind her, half-expecting the god to stir and refuse the plan.

The High Priestess passed the mirror to Maestra, who hid it within her robe. Pella continued to empty Medusa's box: there were no clothing or trinket as curious as the mirror.

Ursula then addressed the audience. "We enter temple with nothing but ourselves," she announced.

They replied in unison. "Nothing but ourselves."

The High Priestess looked at Medusa and I. I knew what we must say, but I did not want Medusa to look the fool.

"Now you must say it," Ursula said.

Medusa and I spoke at once. "Nothing but ourselves."

"Bring forth the initiation guest," Ursula announced.

There was some commotion as a man was brought from the temple crypt. He was a Greek, deep-tanned with sun and handsome with hair cut short in the fashion of the better-paid. Naked as a babe, his muscular torso and legs were offset by a hesitant face as he was paraded in front of the all-female audience. His flaccid cock and testicles dangled between his legs like a dead chicken hung upside down at a market, and he made no effort to cover them.

"Silence!" Ursula commanded. "This is a man, the sort of man any of us could be attracted to, could have married, could have bred with had the god not had better use for us. He is known to be a good man, and is the son of a prospering builder."

Maestra cried: "Initiate him!"

This generated laughter. Ursula smiled and addressed me first. "Miranda, face this man."

I moved awkwardly to do as told. The man pivoted and we stood only several yards apart, Athena's statue the distance between us. Maestra appeared behind me, deft for one so old, and gently loosened my robe until it fell to the floor, fully exposing me, naked except for my accursed leg-brace. I knew what was to come, and prepared myself for a smarting pain across my backside.

The three strokes were administered quickly, and by Maestra herself. The first was harsh, and whipped both buttocks; surprising force from the arm of the aged priestess. I felt no pain until the third and final caning: a sore burning that I knew would soon be remedied.

"As long as you serve temple, he is not for you. His sex is not for you. May this serve to remind you," Ursula said, forcing me to endure the pain.

Maestra replaced my robe, the fabric brushing against the raw wound and forcing me to suck in my breath. I stood aside, and Medusa faced the handsome Greek. While he had beheld me with indifference, mild curiosity at best, his eyes were unblinking and his mouth agape as Medusa was stripped before him. The builder's son did not look the type to ravage a young girl; but Medusa's type was rare enough to inspire undreamt, unwholesome actions.

Her eyes became wet after the first stroke of Maestra's cane, which I could now see was a thin, whip-like piece of birch. She endured it and stood firm as the third landed.

"As long as you serve this temple, he is not for you. His sex is not for you. May this serve to remind you," Ursula repeated.

Medusa dressed again, sniffing away tears, and the man, his guesting over, was ushered back the way he came. He turned his head once to catch a last look at her.

"Miranda and Medusa have been accepted without restriction. Loyalty is rewarded, treachery is punished."

The High Priestess stood between Medusa and I, and turned us towards our audience: now our sisters in religion and our family in piety.

◆ ◆ ◆

Nine years followed, in which we gained our temple education and became women. It would be sacrilegious to share the wisdom in making and using weaponry; to lay bare the ingenuity of the mortal body; and to reveal how the philosophy of one's being is determined. It would be impious to tell the secrets of our temple.

Chapter Twelve

The procession of the bull started in the Agora, and ended in the Acropolis. The beast was enormous, sired from Theban stock that had once been brought to pasture on the grasslands east of the new city beyond the port of Piraeus. The person who had risked much to keep the livestock intact and thriving long enough to breed deserved to prosper: the early days of Zeus' great desire of stone and humanity had brought chaos to the region; cacophony and violence that had eventually settled into a rich rhythm, which had not gone unnoticed by foreign neighbours and Olympian intent.

The bull sweated from fear, rather than the early summer climate, and stamped its feet and snorted within its open-top wagon. The beast knew what awaited it at the top of the spiralled hill, beyond the citadel walls; before the altar that the augurs habitually sprayed with blood during *thusia* like this.

The bull's keepers tried to calm it, and adjusted the crown upon the beast's horned head: a neatly bound ring of hyssop and damiana, held together by oak and honey. The blood would mingle with the sweet flowers of the plants and nectar, making a rich sacrifice for the father-god.

Slow and gradual was the ascent up to the Acropolis. The bull's wagon was not pulled by horses, but by young men: able acolytes of Zeus' own temple, itself positioned within the Acropolis. They were clad in white loincloths and nothing else, their juvenile muscles being stretched and strained as the upward gradient began. Zeus admired teamwork and admonished laziness: attributes reflected by the wagon-pullers that would strengthen the offering even more.

Their work was made harder by the sheer public attention the procession created. A large segment of the population followed and surrounded the wagon, urging it on and chanting thanks and prayers to any and all of the twelve Olympians. The entrepreneurs and traders were also out in force: honouring Zeus meant good business. Sellers had set up stalls; entertainers spat fire and juggled trinkets; performers made audiences laugh. Dignitaries from Mycenae and Thebes observed the masses, muttering to each other; important men and women from overseas, dark-skinned like Pella and with beautiful headdresses and flamboyant clothing, beheld the circus with smiles and whispered in each other's bejewelled ears.

Those same foreign guests looked on in admiration at the rate at which the city had taken over the lands around the port of Piraeus. Merchant fleets continually moored with stone quarried from the Kemet lands; ships still ferried food and drink from around the known world; and travellers by the thousand still arrived on boats each day, intent on taking the road, the final piece of their journey, which connected the port and coastline to the city.

People were drawn there for stability. The embryonic period of the city, which had bred natural disorganisation and uncertainty, had within ten years blossomed into a new standard. Deep wells that had been plummeted into the earth now also housed man-made filtration devices, which provided water that could be drunk with little risk of disease. An underground sanitation system had been completed, revolutionising the management of human waste. Streets and avenues now sprawled neatly, sourced from either the Agora or the Acropolis, and most were kept proudly clean. Homes were not scarce, and built with simple function at the forefront of their design. But imperfection still existed, as it does in all things: the wondrous city could not tame the tastes and manners of everyone. Unscrupulous opportunists took their chances for quick wealth or power, just as in any other village, town or city. This unwholesome condition spawned a small number of districts that were plagued with criminality, where oppression could suck residents into a vortex that was difficult to escape.

There had never been an attack from an in-

vader. The defensive walls of the Acropolis had
been completed: an indication of impenetra-
bility, a near-warning to other nations perhaps
thinking of easy conquest, which could be seen
from a great distance. An outer wall had followed around the perimeter of the settlement,
excuding the port: this was no less effective at
protecting its citizens. The lack of invasion and
robust defences had made certain sections of
the population arrogant, and rumours of conquest and expansion abroad were growing: for
the new city to be the invader rather than the
plundered. Such a grand, well-functioning city
should be replicated, they argued: the city and
its population is a solution for peace, not war.
But the preference for education and philosophy, for medicine and justice that ran through
the city's veins had allowed it to mature and
settle. Worship and economic prosperity, rather
than simple conquest, had become the local and
intangible currency of progress and survival.

We dutifully followed behind the sacrificial bull
and its entourage. The public commotion was
not limited to the beast and entertainments: we
from the temples garnered plenty of attention,
mostly of a kind sort.

There were the boys and male priests belonging to Poseidon, the younger clad in proces-

sion robes coloured pale green, and the older in lapis blue. Their serious faces, too grim for the joy that surrounded them, resembled a small and mysterious army, marching to some distant battle. They were led by Hyperion, the young and able High Priest. He resembled a youthful version of Poseidon's own mortal-form, which I knew from communion: he could have been the sea-god's son, and some maintained that he was indeed demigod. Unlike others who have claimed so, such as the ill-fated King Perseus of Mycenae, Hyperion knew better than to encourage such rumours.

Aphrodite's court was next, a small and exclusive crowd of pretty girls and stunning women, dressed in lighter and darker shades of red. Men and women crowded to see them, their presence in the city on a typical day uncommon: their High Priestess' aloof aura made it so. She was Hydraphea, ageing and flooded with the authority of someone long-familiar with power. Hydraphea was not conventionally beautiful, but had a face that made one pause for thought: angular and leonine, her looks were an acquired taste. As a younger woman she probably attracted unwanted attention from people keen to broaden their carnal experience. Her sharp looks and eyes ensured public reverence of her acolytes and priestesses was limited to distanced, respectful wonder.

Then came we belonging to Pallas Athena.

In the nine years since Medusa and I had been sworn in as acolytes, the number of us in temple had increased slightly, in line with what our temple could reasonably accommodate. Ursula, in a golden-threaded garment that shimmered in the late morning light, the sun not yet at its peak, led our procession. The priestesses followed in their yellow robes, Acantha and Pella among them. Pella was a capable and honoured member of our community; delicate and pretty, her kindness was personified by her physique. Acantha had aged unkindly, her own stature edging her closer to crone-like, but her skills as a priestess had grown and she considered herself an applicant as successor to Ursula when the time came. Maestra was not present at the *thusia* sacrifice, preferring to use her very great age as an excuse for her distaste for it. Physically Maestra had changed little, the years having barely affected her.

Behind the priestesses came we acolytes, clad in our usual purple-striped robes. Others the same age as Medusa and I fronted this coterie, and the younger were behind us, leaving Medusa and I snug between the groups. This shielding was standard practice due to the attention Medusa always drew when out in public; she never walked anywhere alone outside of temple. Though the leg-brace Medusa had once applied to my injured leg had been removed years before, I could not walk properly without support.

I normally used a wooden stick, but that day I linked her arm, which slowed our progress and kept her close to me.

She hypnotised people with her savage and uncompromising beauty. She had been striking as a girl, and now aged twenty-one years she was a beacon of good and evil in all mortality, as she had once stated she would become. Men fell at her feet, praising whatever had conjured her, offering to marry her; women would offer her small gifts, tokens that she should take to guarantee the giver some unknown blessing that went beyond Olympian grace. And she compelled men to rush at her, overcome with a lust that could only be replicated in the mad-houses of uncivilised worlds; and some women spat at her, thinking her looks a curse sent from Hades meant to ensnare good people into having heinous thoughts and committing worse acts. To some Medusa was now an idol, a living god; to others she was despair, a living deceit. She had been unnervingly accurate when younger, when in fear of her beauty.

A sneering voice suddenly sounded in our ears.

"You can link my arm, pretty woman," said a man who had somehow gotten very close. His face was clean, respectable, and made livid by Medusa's unobtainable virgin beauty. "That cripple does you no justice," he hissed, referring to me.

Without hesitation Medusa seized her chance and whipped her free hand to strike the offender. The crowd about us fell silent, mouths agape. He withdrew, shocked, his hand barely covering the red slap-mark that was spreading like a rash.

"One can only truly know justice when one receives it," she said, aloud and spirited.

A cheer went up and support for Medusa immediately prevailed. The offender had no choice but to leave, shamed.

"Nicely put," I said.

She clung to me more closely. "You protect me, and I do the same for you," she kissed me lightly on the head, and I just felt the touch of her lips through my wiry, curly hair. The tingling sensation of joy followed, always felt in such unbidden moments of tenderness with her, beginning where she had laid her lips and ending in my toes. I smiled, elated, and felt invincible.

We were both devoted and respected acolytes, and not yet priestesses. Medusa had adopted the teachings of Ursula and Maestra with natural aptitude, producing loyalty and love for the temple and for the god that was unmatched by any other member. She was athletic, with a strong arm for archery and an aim that made Maestra herself take careful note of her bodily actions. What I lacked in sport I made up for in learning: my gifts were cerebral, and in the shaping of metalwork. In my maturity as an acolyte I had perfected the bronze-tipped arrow; designed a new locking system for temple's main door; and engineered new spears that could fold into the size of pine cones.

We had both privately agreed to become priestesses at the exact same time. If one of us was offered the role first, she would wait until the other could be promoted too. Ursula had made no indication of our ascent, but I knew the moment would come soon. The crescendo of the bull-sacrifice, of this *thusia* so long-awaited, meant that all other affairs and key decisions had paused.

We reached the Acropolis at the top of the hill. Zeus' acolytes who had pulled the carriage exchanged words of congratulation at achieving the feat. The bull had calmed, seeming to accept its honoured fate. Inside the citadel walls the members of the temples and the city officials gathered. The general public was not permitted beyond its gates.

Being Zeus' city until a figurehead was decided meant that Boreaxus, the High Priest to Zeus, conducted the ceremony. The Acropolis housed the great temple to Zeus, and the grand homes of state. The officials dwelled here, lording over the swelling populous. They were elected administrators, and had been instrumental in organising and settling the immense population. To begrudge them the luxury of prime position and public reverence akin to temple-masters would have been unfavourable: an unnecessary show of mortal pettiness and resentment towards human authority; stains that would have been hard to clean. The citadel also hosted a barren piece of land, ready for the construction of the grand temple awarded to the god who won the city.

The great temple to Zeus had four pieces to its external structure: two enormous blocks set opposite each other, connected lengthways by a third. An enormous recess was created by this architecture. Wide and shallow steps filled this gap, leading upward to where columns were arranged with precise regularity. Their positioning outlined the temple's semi-square shape, and beyond them was the shadowed mystery of the temple's interior. A flat roof of stone formed the fourth piece: it was the thickness of a grown man, and sat atop the columns. Hundreds of artisans had spent many seasons decorating the edge of the roof: wholesome images of men and women engaged in farming, teaching and prayer.

The bull was carefully released from its transport and led up the steps. We gathered at their foot, line-upon-line of us reflecting the rows of steps. Whether by godly command or not, the beast went willingly. Waiting at the top stood Boreaxus. He was an old and stern Greek from the north, entrenched in tradition. His pure white robe covered a deceptively strong and able body, himself having spent innumerable seasons toiling for the father-god in cities small and large all over Greece: he had pulled his share of bulls and other creatures to sacrifice. Upon one arm sat an enormous eagle, placid and vaguely interested in Boreaxus' generous beard that was as white as his robe. As the bull neared, the bird's focus was drawn to it instead - as ready as its master for the blood to come.

The bull disappeared beyond the columns with its coaxers and Boreaxus, into the cool shade granted by the immense roof, to the awaiting altar upon which its blood would be spilled. In the cloudless sky the sun reached its high-point. Echoed voices of the rite's prayer rang from within the temple. Then a pause, in which a breeze swept across us: a presence more substantial than a mere change in weather. The cries of the animal rejecting its death broke the silence. The knife wound would have been slickly done across the neck, but the braying snorts implied an unexpectedly violent end.

Boreaxus reappeared at the top of the steps. The eagle was drenched in bull's blood, which had spread up the arm of the High Priest. Boreaxus released it and the magnificent bird ascended, energetically shaking its blood-soaked wings, as if the gore granted new zeal. It did not fly high, enabling a red shower to pour down upon the temple steps and the High Priest. Soon Boreaxus was head-to-foot in bull's blood, all the while watching the eagle hover and play its role.

As the supply of blood thinned the eagle took greater flight, twisting head-first into the sky, screeching and soaring. Boreaxus, his beard spattered scarlet, beheld the bird's actions with such reverence as if were his first kill for the god. Soon five more priests joined him and between them they observed the scarlet spray left upon the steps by the beating of the eagle's wings. The six of them became omen-readers in those moments, transcending their roles as guardians of Zeus' holiness and zealots of his temperament. Few others had the power to decipher the gore.

Boreaxus suddenly bellowed. "It is said!"

He descended the temple steps and stared at us, the waiting crowd baking in the sun, with a frenzy in his eyes.

"Written upon these steps that tribute mighty Zeus," Boreaxus cried. He stopped at the bottom and raised his hands, emphasising his find. "Two shapes can be seen. Use your own eyes if you must. The trident of Poseidon, and the diamond-cross of Athena."

The sea-god's emblem was a three-pronged spear; and that of Athena was a cross protruding downwards from the corner of a lopsided square.

"The father-god's brother and daughter will present their offerings to the people on the last day of this season's heat. To vie for control as figurehead of this, the greatest city on earth. The new cornerstone of humanity. We shall vote for what path the city follows - that of Poseidon, or that of Athena. From this day forth we prepare - prepare to accept the greatest bequest!"

Chapter Thirteen

Womanhood signalled a change in the Olympian communion for me. What I had thought was a sacred affair, purely with Athena, was in fact preparation: a tenderising of my senses to be able to cope with the rigours of the free-summoning I could experience in adulthood. Now, as a child no more, any god could bring me to Olympus for any reason planned or unbidden.

Athena had been merciful; not every god would have been so considerate to their mortal conduits. Some live a life with no indication that they are favoured, with no awareness of their sensitivities, with no knowledge of communion; and when they are drawn to it for the first time - suddenly, as adults - the experience can be a brutal awakening. Thereafter some live in a limbo between mortality and the communion-trance. Some can never be roused: they become permanent Olympian guests, and are either held in sanctity on earth, used to harvest information and promote prayers; or they are treated as objects of fear, isolated and distrusted for the spontaneous and dramatic change in themselves.

◆ ◆ ◆

It had been some years since I had been in communion, before Poseidon abruptly brought me to the holy mountain as we observed the *thusia*.

His tone was depressed and wanting. "I have summoned you here for a purpose," the sea-god said plainly.

I stood mute and watched him. His private chamber was more a cave: darker than Athena's bright anteroom; rocky walls of raw mountain formed a queer shape around a hole in the ground. Poseidon stood over the watery abyss that this space housed; staring at the image of Medusa. Over and over, the god replayed the moment she had slapped and deterred the determined man during the bull-sacrifice. Light reflected and shimmered from the water, capturing obsession upon his brow; an autistic focus on Medusa, as if trying to manipulate some feeling in her.

"She is far more beautiful than Aphrodite," he said simply. "Terribly attractive. Aphrodite knows this. She is loathe to be suppressed, so easily replaced. She wants to know how this has come to pass. Has Zeus created Medusa as a test? Or as a cruel way of teasing? Or as a lesson? My brother could easily believe Aphrodite should be taught humility."

He paused and tore himself away from the pool and beheld me.

"And Medusa is still entirely unobtainable. I am a god, Medusa is mortal. She should obey my every command, and if I wish to seduce her, to taste that beauty unseen elsewhere anywhere on earth, I should not be stopped. And yet she is protected by Athena. That makes the conquest all the more desirable. We gods especially want what is denied - and we should be denied nothing."

He returned his attention to the pool.

"I do not wish to confide in my brother, and certainly not Aphrodite or Athena. So I admit to you that I have watched Medusa closely as she grew from childhood to womanhood. In secret, a carefully nurtured obsession. I want no further dealings of the coital nature - that disruptive and yet addictive mortal urge - with Aphrodite. I must have Medusa. Curse this yearning mortal form, it is as confounding as it is remarkable!"

He punched a rocky wall in passionate frustration. Grey shale splintered away, and a mark was left. He only used a tiny portion of his true strength, able to restrain his discontent. He calmed, and dropped to his knees and touched the pool, and the image of Medusa, the closest he could get to her at that moment.

"And so I tell you, her closest friend and confidant. You might choose to tell her. Medusa might find me a worthy proposition. She could reject the temple life. Many do, even if brought there under similarly desperate circumstances as she was. I would ensure Athena took no slight. I would offer Medusa new protection. She would be queen of the oceans, we would have children of profound power. I could love no other if she loved me in return."

I could not speak to reply or comment - that rule was left unchanged.

Zeus' voice suddenly echoed. "Careful, brother."

He spoke with too much authority, which would irritate Poseidon. The father-god had appeared at the dark, doorless entrance to the sea-god's chamber. As he entered he nodded to me slightly in greeting.

"I know what attractions the mortals can breed within us. I have even loved some of them myself, and in doing so have tamed *obsession* - a beastly mortal creation, unwittingly nurtured and released by them into the world. I can understand why Aphrodite treats love with distrust. Medusa is certainly the most beautiful mortal woman of the age. One mortal must be, and it is she. Her virginity and loyalty to Athena are the springs from which mortal, and now Olympian, obsession for her comes. She is unobtainable to man, woman *and* god."

"I know this," Poseidon said critically, rising to his feet. "Why do you tell me to be careful, as if I were your child or another to patronise?"

"Because obsession is delusion. Perfect plans are created when enchanted by fantasy. These are impossible schemes that never come to pass. Resentment and bitterness follow. I would not wish that for you, brother. These mortal forms we take are partly vessels for pleasure and pain. I suggest we apply ourselves to the former."

"Then what is the pleasure in denying myself Medusa?"

"The avoidance of pain."

"And what if I win your city? You have come from the rite. I can smell the bull's blood on you, spotless as you are."

"On the last day of this season's heat, by mortal reckoning of time, you and Athena shall perform, the city shall vote and we shall know which of you has won it. It is a prize greater than beauty or love. Win the city, and you win not just a single legacy - you would not only determine that of the mortals, but that of your own. Athena could be persuaded to make you a gift - a loser's gift of the winner's choosing. You would not abuse your power, I would not object and she would be obliged. This is the way you could satisfy your love for Medusa. The only way."

Zeus spoke persuasively, his words designed to galvanize the sea-god. At that moment Aphrodite entered, freezing the talk. Poseidon quickly waved a hand and Medusa disappeared from the pool, the liquid becoming imageless and crystalline. The sea-god ignored Aphrodite and departed, no ceremony observed. This saddened her and her eyes were cast down as she felt the sting of his wordless rejection.

Zeus manipulated the liquid, conjuring Medusa at prayer before Athena's modest altar in our humble temple. Aphrodite noticed me, not yet released from the communion though my summoner Poseidon had left. She narrowed her eyes in recognition, recalling my younger self in my adult body.

"Poseidon is in love," Zeus said, distracting his daughter.

"And not with me," she answered.

"With Medusa. Look."

Zeus gestured to her to join him at the pool. Aphrodite obeyed. Her face became as stony as the chamber walls. Zeus watched her carefully.

"Athena's girl," she said. "She has indeed become profoundly beautiful. Poseidon always did have good taste. I suppose it was he who summoned her ugly friend over there. Tried to compel her, gave her words to whisper into Medusa's ear. Well, hear this, whoever you are," she turned to face me and pointed, and I was afraid. "I have forgiven his past indiscretions, and I shall prepare myself to forgive this when he abandons her and returns to me, where he belongs. She will be just another conquest."

Zeus' voice became more grave, compelling Aphrodite's scrutiny away from me.

"Her beauty is not the only reason he obsesses over her," the father-god said. "Medusa is beyond his reach. She will not leave Athena's religion. Not voluntarily. And he will not dare overcome her by force. To antagonise Athena now, before the competition for my thriving city, would be a mistake. But none of you will be denied." The father-god suddenly barked out a laugh. "I would not be one to deny him, knowingly or not. He is so *enraged* with love. A wondrous thing."

Zeus departed the chamber, his laughter echoing until it disappeared, swallowed by the corners of the mountain. Aphrodite watched after him, ensuring he would not suddenly return. Satisfied, she turned to me again and looked at me with piercing eyes.

"I shall release you back to the care of Athena," Aphrodite said. "With a gift. One that even she will struggle to reveal."

I immediately felt an overwhelming sadness: a sense that I could forever regret all my actions past, present and to come. In my throat I tasted bitterness, as if I had chewed on lemon skin. Aphrodite looked upon me and smiled shrewdly, pleased her spell had affected me so bluntly.

"I admit I crave Medusa's beauty. I am not so proud that I deny my envy of her. She is loved by whom I love. She bests me for what I am worshipped for. No better way to belittle me. Let Medusa know my envy. Let her best that."

I could not withstand Aphrodite's poison. I accepted it; it was my shame to do so.

The god released me. I felt the horrific discontent disappear from my senses as quickly as it had started. But it had not vanished, and it had not been imagined: it was a seed planted deep within me that I would fail to prevent germinating.

Chapter Fourteen

I had collapsed after Boreaxus' announcement and had remained in the communion-trance for some time.

I had to be carried back to temple when the *thusia* was disbanded. I knew this task would have been met with discontent among the other acolytes, their grumblings made out of Ursula's earshot. The extra care needed because of my leg, the late afternoon heat, the masses returning to the city all at once: all things that would make carrying me inconvenient.

I woke upon my bed, lying flat on my back, in the dormitory shared with Medusa and five others. I thought I was alone: the five were younger than Medusa and I, and followed our lead; they would have known to leave me be. The sun was low and making way for keen night. The dormitory had skylights, which were open and letting a cool breeze in. These were an invention from one of the city's master builders, whereby obtusely angled rectangular recesses were installed into a ceiling. A mechanism opened and closed wooden shutters, blocking or permitting wind and light as needed.

Medusa's voice came from my bedside. "Ursula wants us all gathered," she said.

I turned and saw her, and I immediately felt at ease by her presence. She was using a small, fine blade to smooth an arrow shaft, carefully shaving the elm length into a perfectly tight cylinder. A point of heavy metal was already at the other end of the shaft, blunt and awaiting her attention. Another arrow that would find its target on first use.

"I'm sorry - you had to carry me back."

"Were you summoned by the god?"

"By Poseidon. He...," I hesitated. I knew the words to speak for the truth to be known to Medusa, the truth of Poseidon's obsession for her. And yet different words spilled from my thirsty mouth. "...He wanted to warn me. He wanted to tell me that Athena will not win this city, and he will see to it that we are enslaved when he does win it. We must prepare ourselves, he said."

"Pah!" Spat Medusa, as if she knew that what I said was utterly false. She rose and fetched water for me. I sat up and slurped it greedily, parched.

"Posturing Poseidon. He has courage, to seize you at Zeus' rite. He must be wary of defeat to make such threats. Will you tell Ursula? Or maybe Maestra?"

"Only if they ask. Did many complain for carrying me back?"

"They all did. Even me."

She smiled at me and I felt even better: those perfect lips, the neat teeth. At that moment, they all belonged to me.

"It must have been exhausting in this heat."

Medusa looked at me solemnly. "You are more gifted and favoured by Athena than any of us. They must learn to pay for the greatness of your presence. And they are envious. *I* am envious. Some of us still await our first communion."

She referred to herself: Medusa's firmly-rooted consciousness to earth was bittersweet. Apparent lack of Olympian interest in her had made her quietly wary of the temple life; hesitancy that had only recently surfaced and which she had only confided to me. In her maturity, each day that passed without Olympian summons to commune convinced her further that she lacked true holiness: that temple had served only as an education, a means to prepare her for the harshness of the outside world that she believed she was destined to eventually confront in some way. The truth I could have spoken then, honest warning that the sea-god worshipped her, would have changed her growing feelings. My tongue found no rhythm to speak of it.

Ursula stood before all of us.

"There are no secrets in temple," she announced. "We do not lie, we do not conceal. Openness and honesty form the foundation upon which justice, wisdom, healing and loyalty - and war, we must admit - are based. None of us have reason to fear truth."

We were stood in the main temple atrium. Nothing had changed since our youth but the faces of the priestesses and acolytes: some had come and gone, others had stayed and aged. The statue of the god was as perfect as when I had first seen it, only brushed by breath and breeze as the seasons and years had passed. The High Priestess, flanked by Maestra and Acantha, was resplendent in the same robe of white and gold she wore at the *thusia*. Our acolyte clothing was juvenile for Medusa and I; the yellow, dignified priestess robes would have better suited our adult frames.

Ursula's mentioning of loyalty had been a consistent inclusion in her recent sermons. The High Priestess maintained that the god craved it more than anything, believing it to be the key ingredient in the potion of success in life, and in the poison of deterrence to its ills. I thought of my communion, the memory of it sharp and real. I should have felt unsettled with Ursula having raised the subject of loyalty, and of truth: coincidence was rare in temple. And yet I felt calm and indifferent, even glad to be acting deviously by withholding truth from Medusa, my sister in all but those who had sired us.

"To mark the occasion of the contest between Athena and Poseidon, a new priestess shall be appointed. I wish to promote an acolyte. I shall hear your voices now, and decide the appointment once the winner, whether Athena or Poseidon, is announced."

Nobody spoke immediately. Acolytes must wait for priestesses to speak first when we were all addressed, the eldest given the honour after High Priestess. That was Maestra, who shifted uneasily on her wizened feet, her great mind working. This method of selection was rare, whereby all of temple was consulted in a forum of debate. It could only mean that Ursula was herself divided in her preference for the single role.

Medusa and I shared a sideways glance. One priestess would be made, and one or both of us had to be under consideration. We were the longest-serving and most able acolytes, though those facts were not the only rationale for promotion in any temple.

The strength of our private agreement to only become priestesses together would surely be tested. I wanted nothing more than to be promoted: it was my birthright, virtually promised by the god, and I had nothing else. Medusa had two paths opening up before her: to commit to temple for the rest of her days and seek the priestess life; or venture out into the world, with a good education. The latter path would critically lack the protection temple offered: armour her beauty would still need, if she was to survive the horde attention that was her own birthright.

Maestra suddenly announced her thoughts. "I say Medusa!" She cried, pounding the atrium floor with her worn stick. There was some immediate murmuring of approval. "She has shown the most aptitude for what I teach - lethal with a bow, even as a child, and her gift for healing is well-known. But her wisdom needs sharpening, she is not demure and is too confident. But is that not the point of the priestess, to learn yet more obedience and compliance? To reign in the temerity of youth. There is only so much good sense an acolyte can learn."

Urusla looked warmly at the wizened priestess. "Your voice counts for much," she said. "Who else? Speak now, or not at all."

"I say Miranda," called out Acantha. I was surprised: she and I had never been close. With the friendship Medusa and I had, it had been impossible to foster similar relationships with others. "She has borne her lifelong injury without complaint. She makes sound judgments. And she has the natural favour of the god. Her values and piety are not skin-deep."

There were more hushed voices. Medusa and I received appraising looks. There was division, and seemingly no other candidates to be voiced.

"Clearly," the High Priestess said, silencing the small crowd, "Medusa and Miranda are the obvious candidates. Their presence in temple brings nothing but honour and benefit. But length of service as acolyte should be disregarded. Consider Pella - she was but twenty seasons as an acolyte before she ascended. Are there no other nominations?"

The silence prevailed. Maestra cast a wary eye over us all.

"Perhaps, if Athena wins the city, two priestesses may be confirmed," Ursula said cautiously. "But the god is careful. To be made a priestess is a serious, wondrous thing. Not to be doled out like charity. It elevates a person to a status of true power. It marks the person out as an exception on earth - an island of greatness in a sea of mortality. To be a priestess, or priest, makes one part-god. Athena will expect one name from me, but it seems I should offer two."

The following day signalled a full moon. The silver orb began its rise in the late afternoon. By nightfall, the statue of the god was soaked in moonlight. We all bowed before it, staying still as predators on the brink of ambush, as Ursula recited the incantation. No garments covered our bodies, our nakedness bent double to touch the cold stone of the temple floor. Every arm was perfectly outstretched, every palm faced downwards.

At sunrise the worship climaxed. Acantha lit the dried scammony and galbanum resin, smothering the statue with smoke that was at first putrid and then sweet. We were permitted to relax from our prolonged period of intensity, to sit in front of the statue and recover. Many had bled onto the floor, Medusa and I included. A vaguely metallic odour emanated, which mingled with the herbs and drenched us all with a pleasant sickness. A younger acolyte vomited, overwhelmed by her first time to menstruate.

We bathed and dressed in our acolyte robes. Six of us, including Medusa and I, with Pella leading as priestess, were sent by Maestra to the herb market of Pelamon: the neighbourhood that accommodated the apothecaries and the city's medical school; citizens who shared wisdom and secrets only among themselves and us, the students and worshippers of cures and healing.

Temple's stocks had to be replenished and we carried a long list to fulfil, visiting a number of businesses. The stalls heaved with produce: flowers and plants of varying colours; exotic animal parts; offers of physical fixes to any known condition. People packed themselves closely, bartering with traders, debating practices, holding hands up in prayer for medical salvation.

The six of us formed a tight circle about Medusa, with her at our centre. Maestra liked to send her out of temple, believing it to be a good test of all our resolve and skills, to mark the temple and strengthen the god. Medusa was well-hidden enough to not attract attention for longer than a short moment. We were so well-drilled in the art of concealing her beauty, of protecting this unusual asset. Had she been acolyte to Aphrodite, she would have been kept behind those temple doors more often, seldom shown off to the public; and her beauty would have quickly slipped into legend, celebrated only in rare ritual.

All bonds may be broken. To sever ours around Medusa was to entirely eliminate one of the chain: Pella had no chance of avoiding the assassin's uncompromising brutality. He deftly bustled past, in the midst of the herb market crowd, and beheaded her in a single swoop. His actions were those of a warlord, a man skilled in seasoned combat. To him Pella was no priestess, she was sworn enemy.

Blood erupted skyward, ejected from her neck artery as her head fell backwards. The blood showered down upon us, like the blood-soaked eagle had done upon Boreaxus at the *thusia*. Pella's head dropped to the floor before her body.

Medusa was exposed. We near-stumbled over Pella's corpse, her yellow priestess robe already smothered scarlet. Pella's assassin fled and, quick and determined, a man who I recognised exploited the gap in our chain and seized Medusa, pulling her away from us with force. The shower of Pella's blood, the sudden doom, prevented any of us from acting. Their ambush had been well-executed, calculated with the venom of something wicked long-desired and well-planned.

A material bag covered Medusa's head. It was a simple, clever move to disguise her, the best-known woman in the entire city. She was dragged by two more men, who joined he who I knew: he from the *thusia*, who Medusa had slapped and shamed for his insolence.

As our wits returned, and noise of protest to the violence against a holy woman erupted, I heard Medusa shriek from a direction that went towards the Labyr district: a maze of streets where people of few means lived.

I felt a familiar sinking in my belly, a feeling of euphoria followed by white blindness. The communion-summons was upon me again.

Chapter Fifteen

Poseidon was on his knees, bent over his chamber-pool in anger.

"Look!" He shouted into the pool, but appealed to me. "You have entirely failed to protect her. You are all supposed to be unified, a fortress to keep her safe. Her beauty comes at a price. She's being dragged by her golden hair into the backstreets, due east from where you stand stunned."

The sea-god calmed. His anger was usually first blasted like a sudden gale; and then laid low just as quickly, to then simmer and seethe beneath a calm surface, ready to erupt again.

"And that witch Maestra has much to answer for. Sending her out of temple on an errand only fit for slaves. Such misuse of what is precious. If there was any sense and fairness, Medusa would not *be* in temple at all. She would have married and produced children, her allure would have faded and been a cause for celebration in memory alone. I would have been spared this torment of addiction to her."

He pounded the cliff-stone floor with his fist. The imagery in the water flickered violently, save for flashes of Medusa's distressed face.

"They have her in an empty home. Four of

them. They have ripped off her robe. She is bare-breasted, bare-cunted, and petrified. By all the holy powers of Zeus and Hades, I shall rip those men to shreds. They shall be the oldest mortals kept alive - evaders of death, denied the pleasures of oblivion. Because they shall be serving me in pain for as long as eternity becomes. Epic poems will be written about their suffering. Songs will be written about my revenge."

Zeus' voice interrupted Poseidon's menace, the father-god having slipped into the chamber.

"Only if I permit it." He gave me a small frown, as if sniffing something in the air that I was the cause of. "Athena's girl. Back again," he said, looking at me.

"Medusa's shadow," Poseidon said, of me. "Always with her. They are inseparable. Beauty and her alter ego. You must allow my intervention, brother. Watch and rejoice at how lesser mortals are dealt with."

Zeus spoke with judicial precision, at odds with Poseidon's zeal. "If I allow it, and you save the glorious Medusa, then her virginity and her honour will be preserved. You will still be unable to have her for yourself. Her unavailability will be reinforced by your salvation of her. Your obsession will continue. You will only ever then love her from afar."

"And if you stop me?"

"The thugs will have their way. Medusa will lose her allure and your obsession with her will pass. She will live to tell the tale. But any place for her in mortal greatness will be forfeit. The wonder of Medusa will fade and cease. Your love for her will be memory alone - as long as you have this body as a vessel."

Poseidon beheld his brother for a short time, weighing the balance of his dilemma.

"Save her and condemn myself to be a prisoner of love. Leave her to the wolves and be a slave to regret," the sea-god said quietly.

"And there are Aphrodite and Athena to consider in your calculation," Zeus said, reminding Poseidon of further complications.

Poseidon looked at his brother as if a great secret had been revealed. "Entirely correct," he said. "Aphrodite would thank me for leaving her to these heathens, ridding her of competition. A violation against Medusa would return me to Aphrodite, so she would assume. But Athena would punish Medusa and, virgin no more, banish the girl. If I *save* Medusa now, then Athena would thank me. Aphrodite's rage and envy would swell. She could become very capable."

"Athena's hand would be strengthened by her retaining Medusa with her virginity intact, you having saved her," Zeus said redolently. "It could tilt the balance in Athena's favour during the contest."

"No more than if Medusa had not been snatched at all."

"True, but your competitor would certainly

be weakened if you did nothing now. Such a scandal before the contest would be distracting."

"You doubt my ability to win?"

"No more or less than I doubt Athena's. It is fact that you now have a slight advantage - I am interested in knowing whether you recognise it and use it."

Something then occurred to Poseidon, and he narrowed his eyes in disbelief.

"Athena does not know about this attack, does she? She would have intervened. A priestess murdered in the street, a prized acolyte kidnapped."

"She knows," Zeus said. "Of course she knows. No god can ignore one of their priestesses being killed in cold blood - it is an abomination, sacrilege, blasphemy of the worst kind. Neither can any god ignore a rarity such as Medusa being compromised. Athena knows, but I have held her back. She is locked in her chamber, powerless by my command. She dare not break that, or the city is yours by default."

Poseidon laughed, a wild and cackling sound. "She may believe you *want* me to win your city."

Zeus smiled, but shook his head slowly.

"She also knows you are the only one I permit to act. This is an unexpected moment, unprecedented, one I have chosen as critical. Your actions, brother, may have a profound and resounding effect that touches the very essence of mankind aeons hence."

Poseidon beheld the father-god with apprehension across his face, like a man being revisited by a long-forgotten wrong. He turned to his floor-pool. Medusa was surrounded by her kidnappers. She did not attempt to cover her nakedness, and stood as if prepared to surrender to an onslaught. Her open vulnerability manifested her physical perfection to a conflicting apex: unattainable to the divine, accessible to the unholy.

"Of all things on earth," Poseidon said, his face reflected in the quivering pool, his image coming between Medusa and the men, "she should only be touched by one of us."

Chapter Sixteen

I awoke standing outside a lacklustre dwelling, a home abandoned and not yet taken by the city's administration. Through one of its shutterless openings I could see Medusa, her face and naked body occasionally revealed by the uncertain footing of her assailants circling her. They were moments away from violating her, from ruining the most precious beauty produced by purely mortal means.

I shouted and tried to advance forward, intent on saving her, but an invisible force held me in place. It was as if I was still in communion, but Olympus had been replaced by the city. No other person walked or loitered in the narrow street running left to right: the power that held me also deflected the movements of everyday life, and isolated this house of impending rape.

I heard her abductors shout and argue. There was dispute over who should go first. The force that controlled me dragged me forward, the soles of my sandalled feet brushing across the floor of dusty stone. My long-injured leg gave no obstacle, and I held my walking stick so it too skimmed the ground. I was brought close to where Medusa stood. I noticed a flicker of recognition in her face: of an unseen authority; a power familiar and yet not, which was lingering, charged, in the air.

I had a clear view of her attackers. The man I recognised, shamed by Medusa at the *thusia*, had long-unresolved disappointment in his face. Two of his accomplices reminded me of the brutish Northman whom Ursula had once dispatched with bloody death. The fourth was an uncertain, skinny man, not Greek and there to make up numbers. He would certainly be last in the chain of violation.

The familiar man won the argument and would be first, this entire affair being his plan. He slowly removed his lower garments revealing tanned legs with dark, bristling hairs. His cock was enormous, keen for the endgame, and stuck out at an angle that defied his cloth-shirt. Medusa stared at it, aware of what it was capable of. She had no fear in her eyes, but a realisation that one life could be about to end; and that she would still live another that would be birthed amid the aftermath of the first. Already she calculated her future, anticipating harshness. The man advanced slowly, savouring what he surely felt was a seminal moment. I looked on helplessly.

Medusa was within his grasp, when he suddenly stopped. He beheld her curiously, as if she had uttered a magic word to render him useless.

It started with a small cough, like he had swallowed water into his lungs rather than his gullet. Soon he could not stop spluttering: he held his hands to his throat as his accomplices watched on, perplexed. He began spitting water from his mouth. The volume of water within him increased; he began vomiting the liquid up, spraying it onto the floor of the humble home. His penis deflated. He dropped to his knees, unable to contain the foamy spew. The other men stood with wide-eyed horror, unwilling to help. The thin, underwhelming man made for the closed door, only to find it unyielding: bound by the same power that locked me in place outside. The Northmen dared not act.

The water-vomit stopped, and was replaced with the glistening, dark-coloured beginnings of a bulbous octopus mantle, brought forth from somewhere within the man's belly. The mantle was too large for any throat to force out easily, and the man's jaw was broken to accommodate the creature. The man's screams were entirely muffled and eventually the tentacled beast was ejected to the floor, squirming and writhing. The lower portion of the man's face hung horrifically disjointed. A final wave of water first filled his mouth and then lungs, turning him blue of face. He dropped to the floor at Medusa's dainty feet, drowned on dry land.

Medusa had watched the rapid, gross spectacle with more wonder than terror. She stood rooted to her spot, unwilling to take a chance to flee lest it ruin the sudden safeguard.

The slight man gasped. "Poseidon protects her!" He took the shoulder of the smaller Northman. "Help me break this stuck door! The god knows the temptation of a beautiful woman - he may forgive us!"

"Your gods are not my gods," said the larger Northman and stepped forward towards Medusa, arms outstretched like giant hams being offered at table.

He took two strides before levelling with the corpse of the familiar man and the regurgitated ocean brood. Medusa was within his grasp, but she did not look at her latest assailant; she stared ahead, unblinking, and perhaps now affected by the same force that held me.

"You had better not be so rigid, woman, for your sake," said the keen Northman.

But it was he who would have to battle stiffness. His footing became stuck to the floor: he struggled to lift either leg, and a wave of greyness spread over his whole body. Soon his feet *were* the dirty, hard floor. His arms, once pink and meaty, quickly became the same colour. He called for help, but his voice rapidly expired, as if all the moisture in his mouth had dried up. He moved his tongue wildly, and swallowed desperately, determined to reinvigorate saliva. The greyness unrolled rapidly, and before our eyes he was a statue. He used all his strength to writhe free, but his doom was certain. The enchantment did not stop: the stone seemed to age, as fast as a flower would in a fire. Cracks appeared, evidence of some extreme and invisible force, and soon the ill-fated Northman exploded into a pile of fine rubble.

The decrepit man and the smaller Northman tried to flee, but the door remained an obstacle. They put their shoulders to it, determined to break it down.

Medusa then performed a remarkable ritual. She bent down and wetted her hand in the pool of sea-water still dribbling from the mouth of the familiar man. Using the dusty remains of the statued Northman, she mixed a grey paste in her palm. She blended this crude substance and then marked herself with it below where her breasts sat firm and supple. The shape she hypnotically drew on her bare flesh was Poseidon's insignia, a trident: Ψ

The door was unfrozen from its binding and the fleeing men burst through it into the silent street, unpopulated save for me. Not yet liberated from my stasis, my eyes followed the men who were running towards a street perpendicular to where I stood. They were about to veer left and escape into the mazed neighbourhood, when an enormous horse reached the junction. The beast was magnificent, its coat sheer white. No rider sat atop it, no reins or markings suggested it was a tearaway. The men stopped before it, the horse blocking their progress.

Seeing the animal as an opportunity to enable their escape, the Northman tried to coax it. The horse turned its backside to them and stubbornly remained in their path. The men agreed to sidle either side of the beast, and for the Northman to establish quick trust with it. Within an arm's length of the hind legs, the horse leaned on its front set and kicked back. The men were each struck perfectly in the head and their decapitations were neat. The force applied was unlike anything I had ever witnessed: their heads rolled away from their slumped and bloodied bodies, returning along the street like balls rolled by children at play.

The horse returned the way it had come. I became free of the power that held me and I entered the home. Medusa had already dressed herself. She wore a petrified look as she stared at the wet debris of sea creatures, blood and dust upon the floor; she seemed ignorant of what had passed since being forced into the dwelling, despite being so complicit in the consequences; despite marking herself.

Neither she nor I spoke. I took her by the hand to lead her away.

We returned to temple quickly and quietly, the

sun in the beginnings of its descent. This was the *chrysi epochi* of the city: daily periods in the summer season when every street and building was emblazoned with the hue of auburn gold brought about by the setting sun.

Whether still honoured by Poseidon, or through our steadfast determination to return to the sanctity of temple, to Athena's bosom, we attracted little attention. Medusa had enough wit to make a hood from the sack the kidnappers had used to disguise her. I lead the way, my blood up from the Olympian intervention.

We found silent, profound grief at temple. From Acantha I learned that Ursula knew of Medusa's kidnap and my Olympian-graced pursuit of her. Neither Medusa nor I were summoned to the High Priestess, which came as a surprise to me. She had presumably learned much from the god, but her silence regarding the ordeal either indicated that the true extent of Poseidon's covetous intentions with Medusa had been withheld; or that Ursula knew all and had been compelled into complicity for a great and secret purpose.

I made no mention of Medusa's arcane behaviour, in adorning herself with the remnants of Poseidon's victims. Medusa asked for permission to bathe, and Acantha granted it. Acantha explained to me that Pella's body had been carted back to temple by our three acolyte sisters. In their shock of the attack, Medusa's kidnapping and my sudden disappearance, they had tearfully enlisted the help of citizens and left the herb list unfulfilled. Maestra had scolded them for this, and for lacking the strength in dealing with sudden death. The old priestess ignored Pella's corpse and departed for the Pelamon quarter herself. Her actions were not callous: almond oil and peppermint were on the list and, aside from their disinfectant properties, were necessary in the blessing of Athenian corpses. Not anointing Pella's body in good time would displease Pella's errant spirit if her body was burned without.

We gathered in temple's courtyard, where a pyre had been hastily built. Ursula led the rite: small garlands of lavender, cedar and rose adorned Pella's head, heart, hands and feet. Amid the twilight, the body was lit. We returned inside and did not observe her become ashes: the god believed it unseemly to intrude on the private moments of transition from this mortal life.

That night Medusa slept deeply. I watched her until my eyes could take no more.

Chapter Seventeen

Poseidon's murky chamber was even darker than before. The scant light refracted off the cliff-slate walls; they were moist and glistened with the evaporation of the ground-pool. The sea-god rose from hulking over it, the liquid cooling. Steam escaped through unseen holes and the god's naked body dripped as if he had been immersed in the pool. He let out a joyous sigh and roared, arms and hands held skyward. The walls shook and the god breathed in deeply, inhaling the turbulence and vapour.

A stillness followed. The light that I was familiar with returned, and I noticed the last ripples of fluid quickly seeping into the rocks. Zeus' voice emanated, but the father-god was unseen.

"Your actions were uncompromising," he said, neither angered nor impressed.

Poseidon turned to search for him; he had not expected company other than my own from his recent summons. Zeus emerged from his hiding place, camouflaged by the rock walls. His body disengaged from the crevice, spilling fragments of cliff. The conjured, rocky effect upon the father-god's skin faded away. His bright eyes stared expectantly at Poseidon.

"Uncompromising, glorious and richly deserved," Poseidon said boldly. "An awesome display. May the mortals not forget our scrutiny so easily."

"Nor you ours," came Athena's voice, and she and Aphrodite broke free of the rocky wall just as Zeus had.

"Welcome, hallowed guests," Poseidon said with sincerity, though he seemed concerned that his intervention to save Medusa had not been as private as he had assumed. "I was so focussed and devoted to my task that I didn't notice you. Quite rude of you all, in fact, to conceal yourselves, spying."

Zeus spoke. "I told my daughters not to reveal themselves. I am to blame."

Poseidon grinned, unable to incriminate the father-god or interrogate more information.

"I can have no bother with your intentions," the sea-god said to Zeus. "I am thrilled you witnessed Medusa accept my subtle offering. She marked herself with my symbol. The first man drowned, and the second man, the bold Northman, had become drought itself. She drew the trident near her perfect breasts. Another test was born: how far could my influence penetrate her layers of devotion to you, Athena. The result is encouraging."

"Your actions were uncompromising," Zeus repeated, still unmoved by his brother's exuberance. "You chose to save Medusa, and now she will continue her holy journey deeper into the legacy of Athena's temple."

"I know," Poseidon said, defensively. "You need not remind me. I will savour what I have done."

"And so you should," said Athena, her tone supportive. "I thank you for acting to protect one of my prized acolytes. Zeus restricted me from intervening myself, and I feared you would take the chance to spoil her yourself. I misjudged you. But I say this - our vying for my father's city will not change. Your protection of Medusa will win you no favours from me when that day comes. I still intend to win that city."

Poseidon bowed gracefully, pleased, and yet his smile was such, so broad and happy with himself, that it concealed something perhaps only truly mortal eyes could fathom: pretence.

"I thank you too," Aphrodite said stiffly. Her voice seemed to betray rare submission, as if she had been compelled to reject her true feelings on the matter. "You preserved precious beauty."

Aphrodite did not wait for Poseidon to retort and left his chamber with a coy swaying of her shapely hips. Athena followed, the god resting her unblinking eyes to me as she passed: a knowing look shared as if between mother and daughter. I witnessed no more. Zeus himself cast me away.

Chapter Eighteen

The hot season continued with no further communion for me. Medusa did not speak of her ordeal, or of the profound and violent deaths of her attackers. I noticed no change in her appearance or habits: the event could never have happened, save for my witnessing of it, and no effort was made to wring a recollection of it from her, either publicly or privately. Her marking of her own body with the detritus of Poseidon's protection was left unconfirmed: it was either an unconcious reaction to the sea-god's bewitchment, or one that Medusa was fully in control of.

I maintained my silence, to her or any other member of temple, of what I had witnessed Poseidon do to save Medusa, or of what she had done to herself. The memory, once satisfying by the hideous deaths of her attackers, had been tarnished with a horror I had not felt during the sea-god's onslaught. Vivid thoughts attacked me at random: of Medusa drawing Poseidon's trident beneath her bare breasts, the death-paste now, in my imagination, a sickening greenish colour. My throat would tighten, and I would feel my stomach heave as I swallowed down my disgust and fought to rid the imagery.

The kernel of envy planted in me by Aphrodite was nestled in my being, quietly weaving its way amid my Athenian fibres. The seed's roots grew longer and stiffer with every rising sun. Moments of introspection budded: moments spent in an emotional abyss, an endless vortex that spun as I entertained thoughts of self-pity and distrust of others. Those notions were irrational, and yet wholly acceptable to me: I deviously fixated on them and accepted the seed's growing influence as a natural path I must follow and embrace. Deep in my subconscious I knew the kernel was desperately close to flowering poisonous petals; and I had convinced myself that I could do nothing to stop the cursed bloom.

To me, Pella's death meant a second priestess vacancy. It was obvious to me that two priestess roles would now be available, and that Medusa and I should fill them. Ursula was unapproachable to discuss it: she was perplexed and vexed from a summer of near-muteness from Athena, frustration which she had shared with us all to perhaps motivate the god. Even Maestra, usually forthcoming and flippant, was guardedly uncommunicative and not herself. The High Priestess' manner seemed to infect the whole of temple, to compel its occupants into a steady and repetitive mantra that bordered on discontent. Her pre-occupation with preparations for the great contest was the excuse, and the season rolled on with a rare drudgery.

◆ ◆ ◆

On the last day of season's heat, as augured by Boreaxus during the *thusia*, the entire city turned out to vote for either Poseidon or Athena to be the godly figurehead. The sun was strong, but clouds drifted across the sky providing occasional, soothing cover from its glare.

A tight line of people stretched from the Agora to the foot of the Acropolis hill, and continued upwards, snaking around and up to within the walls of the citadel. Even children were expected to cast their vote, for the decision would echo more so through their lives and those of their offspring. Water-givers and fruit sellers wandered the long line. They were the only trades permitted: this was an orderly, sombre queue on a day that was neither joyous nor dour. Only when a victor had been decided would there be any cause for celebration: Boreaxus had decreed it so, in what was likely his last wish taken with any authority over the city.

The grounds of the Acropolis were awash with priests, priestesses and acolytes. The city's administrators were gathered before the temple to Zeus and joined by dignitaries from Mycenae, Argus, Tiryns, Pilos and Thebes: an organised and non-voting flock of observers to this singular ritual. I also recognised Trojan men, clad in black leather skirts and with swords strapped to their backs. Medusa's father had been one. They seemed tense and uncomfortable, disquieted to be away from their beloved Troy. Their women wore plain robes, and exotic crowns: plumage from birds unseen in Greece exploded from the metal braces, and colourful jewels studded them.

Two cylindrical podiums of stone had been placed near the steps to the father-god's temple. They were identical, each waist-height to a man, and hewn with the grace of the city's finest artisans: they were the stages for Athena and Poseidon's offerings to be displayed.

Boreaxus stepped forth and raised his aged arms for silence.

"We are gathered here in front of mighty Zeus," the High Priest announced, clear and invoking. "Beneath his sun on this the last day of season's heat, long-awaited to contest the greatest prize. This Acropolis and all that it overlooks has sprung from the ashes of bygone ages. Eras when chaos ruled, when man and woman fumbled in the darkness searching for the light of peace."

Boreaxus paused and observed his audience, watching for how his words settled. The citizens and dignitaries, including the doubtful Trojans, were entranced. We of the temples stood in silent impatience, having heard the High Priest bleat many times before.

"Two stages have been set," Boreaxus gestured to the stone podiums, "one for each of the competing gods. Displays will be made - each god's power and promises to you, wonders that will be long-remembered shown on these stones. They will be written in poetry and prose, and retold to our descendants who, in time, will undoubtedly question whether they took place at all."

The High Priest raised a small and rueful smile, as if only he knew the full extent of a secret only partially revealed.

"High Priest Hyperion represents Poseidon's offering, and High Priestess Ursula for Athena. Step forward, show yourselves!"

The youthful and chiselled Hyperion stepped forth as commanded. At the *thusia* he had been dressed ornately in green robes; now he appeared more statesmanlike in a tunic of the same colour, a golden band wrapped around his waist. He had his hands clasped behind his back, steady and focussed on the impending wonder. He glanced at Medusa, his aquamarine eyes resting on her for a brief moment in what could have been recognition; a secret friendship, yet they had never met. She betrayed no acknowledgement of him: her expression was wholly neutral, and her eyes were softly focussed on the imminent marvel.

Ursula joined him, herself clad in her usual golden-threaded robe. She had worn no special decoration or ornament for the occasion and appeared tired, unspoken trouble worn in place of jewellery.

Hyperion and Ursula bowed slightly to each other. Boreaxus sensed something in the air, a message from Olympus through the ether, and he looked to the sky. The clouds had cleared and dissipated; not even a wisp remained and only the sun and its surrounding blue stared down upon us all.

"Behold!" Boreaxus cried. "Poseidon's offering comes first!"

The High Priest moved away from the podiums. His movement was well-timed, since a lightning bolt cracked from the sky above, striking one pillar. The structure splintered, spraying shards of stone, and yet was not split in two. The audience, including we of temple, gasped and collectively stood back in shock. Smoke rose from the affected pillar, before a wide column of water neatly exploded from the top.

The liquid went skyward, precisely vertical with incredible force. It was as if a surge came from beneath the pillar, the water pumped with such power that we all strained to see what apex it reached: the spectacle was like a waterfall cascading in reverse.

Hyperion stepped forward and presented the still-spewing pillar as if introducing a dear friend.

"A spring of sea-water from Poseidon," he proclaimed smoothly to his audience, his voice more advanced in years than his physique. "The god promises a future complimented by the power of the oceans. Ships. Easy trade with foreign lands. Naval defences. Conquest abroad that will quickly enrich the city, and mark us out as a force to be respected and feared. A force that not only governs Greece, but the world now and the world to come. Security and prosperity will be guaranteed for generations."

Despite her despondency, Ursula immediately stepped forward to take her right to challenge the pitch.

"War is the brother of pride, and pride is the destroyer of legacies," she said. "There are many nations skilled in battle, honoured by Olympus. The city could be lost to war and discovery. The sea can be tamed, and used to commercial advantage in time. Better to build and sustain from within, rather than rely on pillaging the world."

Boreaxus nodded anxiously, reservedly alarmed at the continuing vertical blast of water, as if he had not expected such constant magic.

Suddenly a second lightning bolt, equally powerful as the first, struck the second stone stage. Boreaxus near fell back, startled, its crack immediate and loud. Gasps rose from the dignified audience, expecting something greater than even the first spectacle.

The second podium remained steadfastly unaffected by the lightning bolt. The crowd was drenched in silence. Boreaxus approached it cautiously. No other power came from the cloudless sky. The High Priest peered at the stone stage, his nose near-touching the podium.

Hyperion spoke with underhand optimism. "Is nothing to be offered to the city by Athena?"

Several of his priests smirked. I took a restrained, sideways look at Medusa and saw that she too smiled slightly.

"Is nothing..." Hyperion continued too confidently, and was silenced by a thunderous noise emanating from Athena's stage.

The podium split neatly in two, its halves falling left and right. Boreaxus' earlier caution had prepared him well and he nimbly withdrew, watching all the while.

From the ground beneath where the podium had stood, a tiny green shoot was revealed. It did not remain a sapling for long: it immediately grew and stiffened, its once web-thin stalk thickening in width and increasing in height. The stalk rapidly became a tree-trunk, grey-brown in colour and nobbled like Maestra's hands. Branches spawned as the trunk exceeded the height of a full-grown man, and from these came leaves of emerald green, slender and shaped like large teardrops.

The phenomenon stopped, and planted before us was a full-grown olive tree. The leaves, real as any of us stood before it, rustled in a passing breeze and an earthy, pleasurable smell wafted over us all. The tree's authenticity was beyond question, just as Poseidon's column of sea water was so tangible.

Ursula spoke aloud and with confidence. "Athena offers the city sustenance, wisdom and, above all, peace. The olive tree has long been associated with these things. I let the wonder of it speak for itself."

It was brave of the High Priestess to be so brief, but the crowd seemed to respond. Murmurings began as the people made their own conclusions, comments which ascended into praiseworthy commentary. One of the Trojan dignitaries proceeded forward to touch the tree, and was held back by one of his women who muttered something in their own language. Her tone implied a warning.

"Peace," Hyperion said, his voice rising above the growing clamour, which quieted as he spoke, "leaves us exposed to war. Wisdom is for the few, not the many. And as for sustenance, the fish in the sea will never run dry, whereas lands are at the mercy of the seasons our Olympian masters see fit to permit. There, a response as blunt as what the learned High Priestess stated to you all."

Without delay, Boreaxus authorised the commencement of voting. Through a relay of whispered voices that bled along the immense queue leading from the Acropolis to the Agora, what had been seen upon the stone podiums, and what had been said, was soon common knowledge. Small squares of parchment were distributed, and the behemoth line of people began its shuffling motion towards the pillared stages. Individual votes were cast, the papers marked according to which god was preferred, by inscribing with charcoal either Poseidon's trident or Athena's diamond-cross, and dropped into a giant cauldron of black metal.

Boreaxus himself oversaw the voting. We who had seen the entire spectacle remained, our own votes made first. Any boredom we felt, ourselves now used to the spewing sea-water and the magnificent olive tree, was alleviated by watching a seemingly endless stream of people being hurried past the wonders, most gawking and with hand to face in amazement as they tried to stop and stare.

The day wore on. Finally the last vote was cast as the moon had fully risen. Boreaxus, satisfied that the contest was complete and that we had witnessed it so, save for counting the winner, permitted us all return down the hill. The count itself would be done in the privacy of Zeus' temple; none but Boreaxus and his priests had business with the tally. The victorious god would be announced at sunrise.

Waking for the morning rite was difficult for all, the rigours of the voting day not fully expelled from our bodies. With the prayer said and the incense smoking before the god, Ursula commanded us stand and listen.

"Athena is victorious," the High Priestess said, her neutral expression at odds with the news. "The vote was counted, and more than half the city was taken by the olive tree. The people want stability, they want prosperity - but not at the price of conflict, or the plundering of our neighbours, or the burning of the world."

She quieted to allow the news to settle. There were no wild celebrations, only placid realisation that we would be moving: our current temple, our meagre house of worship, would be replaced with something far more glorious.

"I am told construction of our new temple within the Acropolis begins immediately. There will be no overbearing and unmeasured announcements of the god's success. We shall move quietly and steadily, symbolic of the offering and how we mean to continue, as promised to the people."

Acantha called out, rare excitement in her voice. "What will the city now be called?"

"The city is called Athens, after the god," she said.

"What of the priestess positions?"

Acantha had not asked that question. I did not look to see who had been bold enough; I did not look, because it was I who asked it. Ursula looked at me as if I were on trial for a great wrong.

Maestra spoke first. "It is not like you, Miranda, to be so forthright and ambitious," she said aloud, scolding. "It is not a child's question, and yet you have asked it with the ill-timing of someone new to the world. What makes you ask?"

"I...I do not know...," I said, stammering and lying: I knew precisely what had made me speak so bluntly: the nestled and imposed seed bestowed by Aphrodite, weakly suppressed and now bitingly reminded, had compelled me to announce my great desire. I felt my skin grow hot and my cheeks flush. What had once been a worthy and refined aim had, in the work of a moment, become disreputable and vulgar.

"To not know why you ask a question is the mark of the very foolish, the very drunk or the very influenced," Maestra said, staring at me suspiciously and educating us all with me as the lesson.

"You say positions," said Ursula, regaining control of the digression. She looked at me coolly, and I felt my peers also begin to scrutinise me like a many-eyed spider observing its web-caught feed. "I was of the mind, should Athena win the city, to suggest a second name. Now I am unwilling to broach the god backed by such flagrant assumption. Pella's death has not yielded another vacancy. Perhaps not for some time to come. To think it would shows avarice."

I felt my heart sink and my intuition sang of tragedy. And then the seed regained control: to further my growing bitterness, a voice I had never before heard in my mind questioned whether Athena truly cherished me; that I was purely another instrument to further the god's own ambition.

Ursula continued. "Perhaps there is no better time than now to announce it, the decision having been tilted. To mark the inauguration of Athens, I hereby state that the acolyte Medusa is promoted to priestess. Step forth, Medusa!"

Jealousy rose quickly within me, like Poseidon's water surge from the stone podium. I had no awareness of me congratulating Medusa. She did not share her joy with me, or reject Ursula's command so as to honour our pact. She stepped forward as asked, and discarded her acolyte robe to the temple floor. In doing so she abandoned our promise of ascending to the role of priestess together, as if the agreement had been but a breath in the wind.

Inner conflict gripped me, questions throbbed about my entire body: had she ever truly believed our bond; or was her sudden ignorance of it divinely intervened? She who said she still awaited her first communion: Poseidon had protected her in unwavering fashion, and now she secured her own future. The apparently overlooked holy woman should receive attention most consecrated. Had she lied about her true closeness to Olympus all this time, she who once told me to never be afraid of speaking truth? Answers then were impossible, and confounded any effort to control my seething discontent.

Medusa, naked and the epitome of womanhood in the morning light, stood to face Athena's statue. All about me chanted the words of our beloved god. Its verses were nonsense to me then; a foreign tongue never studied. Ursula herself draped the yellow robe of the priestess upon Medusa's astounding body. The High Priestess guided her, turned her to face us, presenting her as if she were a new and profound command.

The power that had forced me to speak so openly now did the reverse and held my tongue behind sealed lips. She, a most stunning example of mortal beauty. And I, a most remarkable example of spiritual purity. We had been thrown together in exceptional circumstances when Menethus had stumbled upon Tanis for the second time in his life, at the behest of Aphrodite and Poseidon. Medusa's acceptance of the promotion signalled the first penetrative crack in our relationship; our ten-year bonding was instantly weakened.

Whatever Medusa may have felt, I knew then that she did not belong to me. I perceived her acceptance of the promotion to priestess as the worst kind of disloyalty. An angry fire began to burn within me: its fuel was Aphrodite's kernel of envy, housed within a furnace forged from its husk.

Chapter Nineteen

Z eus' vast, sheer-white Olympian hall of simple architecture hosted a complex argument. The father-god sat back on his throne of bone, listening intently to his brother and daughters' fluctuating degrees of joy and frustration. He had summoned me himself and I stood beside his royal seat like a loyal pet.

Without breaking his stare away from the feud, Zeus spoke to me in a low voice unheard by the others.

"They can't see you. A feature that I can initiate if I wish, and keep secret from them. A guilty pleasure."

He smiled slightly. I wanted to ask why he had brought me there, but that feature of speechlessness remained the same. Could it ever be undone, I thought, since the father-god exercised his power to manipulate the communion.

"I want them to speak freely," Zeus continued. "Mortal presence can influence what they say and do. Particularly yours, considering you have witnessed so much up here. And considering you are so close to *Me-du-sa*."

He spoke her name slowly, relishing every syllable, as if she represented great mystery and was critical to an elusive plan. The father-god surely knew that our friendship had just fractured, and yet he ignored it.

"Medusa," the father-god repeated gravely, "she is half my brother's rage."

Zeus indicated that I should pay attention to them. Poseidon held his head in both hands: the paragon of displeasure and frustration. Aphrodite stared at him, steadfast in the face of the sea-god's madness. Athena beheld him serenely, certainly comfortable with her recent victory; she gloated without crowing aloud.

Poseidon appealed to Zeus. "Brother I implore you - I lost Medusa and now I have lost your great city."

Zeus looked at him with mild astonishment. "Not my city - Athena's. For good or ill."

Poseidon exploded. "But I am *more* than her!"

"What would you have me do?"

"Revoke the result. Keep the city yourself, it has done so well under your control. Give it to neither of us. Let Athena understand that this existence we incorporate is *not fair*."

"One's fairness is another's dishonour."

Poseidon narrowed his eyes and thrust out a finger, jabbing the air towards his brother, and tried a more aggressive tactic.

"You implied that I would win the city. You hinted I would be victorious, that I would win my just rewards, compensation for being second to you. True legacy in the city, and a suitable mortal wife in Medusa with whom to spawn my own demigods. You owe me, brother."

"I recall exactly what was said," Zeus said, staring at Poseidon with a casual harshness. "I said you had a slight advantage with Medusa kidnapped. Whether you took the appropriate action to win the city - which would have won you Medusa too - was entirely your own doing. But it is true - you still have great power at your disposal. What will you do now?"

Poseidon returned his brother's long look with equally unblinking eyes, and spoke with controlled vehemence.

"I will take command of my oceans and winds. I shall control the water on this mortal earth in such a way unseen since its formation. I will make the natural abnormal, in a most turbulent way. I will flood Athens. Let us see how they cope when the tide is turned against them. Let us test Athenian resolve. Let us pit Athenian wisdom against the force of my destruction. Let us show the people what they could have chosen."

The sea-god departed the throne room unobstructed. As he passed Zeus, he stopped and glanced in my direction. He would have seen nothing, though his face flashed with suspicion. Athena went to follow Poseidon, but Zeus bade her stop. Pleased, Aphrodite was contented with the drama.

Now Athena appealed to Zeus. "You cannot permit this. You cannot allow him to have his way. His vengeance is petty - will you grant that such trivial losses be avenged with greater ones, with the decimation of my people?"

"They are not trivial to my brother, and I will not take sides," the father-god said innocently. "And I will not permit you to intervene, to prevent his rage. The greatest wonders on earth are, and will continue to be, built on the survival of disasters. On responding to destruction, not on godly intervention to stop it. This is why the people of your city chose *you*. Don't think ill of me - I cannot deny that you won the city, just as I cannot deny Poseidon's embitterment. Being the figurehead is not always filled with glory. A lesson best learnt sooner rather than later."

Athena stood chastised and helpless, her head bowed down. But it was not purely submission I saw in the god: her face, certainly more beautiful when angered as Poseidon had once stated, was calculating, her mind forming a plan. She left without another word. Zeus did nothing to stop her. He was lost in thought.

Aphrodite turned to him. "I support Poseidon's intentions," she said.

Zeus brought himself out of his reverie and looked at her, smiling.

"Why is that, my dear and beautiful daughter?"

"A great flood upon Athens could wash Medusa away, and restore Poseidon's attention to me. I am not ashamed to say my desires are selfish. I will watch with interest."

Zeus did not offer her a response, and instead looked at her sadly.

She looked at the father-god with care. "What's wrong?"

"I am what the philosophers of mortal earth call *melancholy*. Such a word. I have thoughts of pleasing sadness."

Aphrodite peered at him, her eyes scanning him in detection.

"You are in love," she said, without accusation.

Zeus shrugged, but the corners of his mouth rose into a small smile.

Aphrodite gave the father-god a look of shock. "With Medusa?"

"No, not with Medusa," Zeus said soothingly. "That ship is full."

I was not to learn, then, who the latest mortal subject of the father-god's affections was. In my mind Zeus put a compelling thought: to say nothing of Poseidon's wrath and the watery doom he intended upon Athens; to permit the event happen as a shock to all but me. My secret communion ended suddenly, and the white of the Olympian hall snapped to blackness.

Chapter Twenty

Men toiled to construct our new temple throughout the change in seasons, as the climate gradually changed from hot to warm, and from warm to cool. The relentless ferrying of stone up the winding road to the Acropolis resumed, just as it had when the city first rose from the ground. No expertise was lost through haste: our new temple's construction had attracted the best architects and designers for the prestige, and plenty of labourers for the premium coin paid.

By the start of winter our new home was complete. Over the course of a single day we and our belongings were carted from the foot of the hill to the top, into the citadel to take up residence in what was the most glorious sight any of us had ever witnessed. The grand temple of Athena was enormous, a true stamp of the god's authority and ownership over the city. Its shape was a perfect rectangle that exceeded the size of Zeus' neighbouring temple: seventeen columns lengthways and eight wide supported an enormous triangular roof of shallow depth. Unlike our smaller temple, locked and kept intact for future use, the new was sparse with decoration. There were no carvings depicting great deeds, or images of the god adorning the front panel of the pyramid roof. It was as vast as it was functional: glorious in its simplicity; a celebration of modesty. It served to remind us and the people of the olive tree that held the same virtues; the token through which the god had won the people, and the city.

The interior had been designed with the exact same layout as our previous abode. The scale was far larger; more acolytes would be recruited, though Ursula showed no sign of acting on this with the same speed that the temple had been built. While a virtuous exercise in plainness dominated the exterior, ostentation had been concentrated into a single idol on the inside: we had been granted a new statue of Athena. Made exclusively from gold, the god stood the height of seven men. There was still plenty of space between the tips of her pronged battle helmet and the roof. In her right hand was the spear and in her left, held sidewards to her body, was the shield: both now pure gold rather than stone, as they had been down the hill. Her likeness, absent of any garment, had been well-realised by the artisans; they had surely received a description of her from Ursula.

And I was not a priestess. What compounded my silent and abnormal resentment was that Medusa took up her promotion with grace and expertise. She slipped into the role effortlessly, her beauty seeming to respond to her elevated position with a permanent glow about her skin. Like our new temple within the Acropolis and our old temple at its foot, there was clear separation between us: she priestess and me acolyte, mistress and student. I had been informal teacher to her in the near ten years we had been clamped together, and now she had official authority to direct me if she wished it.

But she did not. Frustratingly, she was kindness and respect personified. In those months of her ascendence we were like people who had just met: the hiatus in our friendship was obvious to us both and yet only addressed through courtesy. I wished her to dominate me. I wished for a confrontation. I wished for some form of punishment for my easy acceptance of Aphrodite's bestowment of envy upon me. Anything to clarify our relationship, and force me to account for my suppressed sourness that was as bitter as the gentian and goldenseal herbs she now arranged and burned for the god, in accordance with the earlier moon risings of the cold season.

The view over the city from our new temple within the Acropolis was one of urban astonishment: thousands of roofs, most squared, for the masses to live and work under formed a sea of stone. Some roofs were rounded, marking out the wealthier inhabitants; and a small number triangular, broadly set apart, indicating the temples.

Smoke constantly rose from the Agora, the market and activity incessant. The wide avenues that led from the Agora fed into veiny streets, like a bodily organ distributing blood to extremities. And in the distance, on a clear day, from the western side of the citadel, the port of Piraeus could be seen: turquoise sea and ships' masts of the larger galleys, packed with goods and people, sustenance and dreams.

Newcomers would not have noticed the stark change in the city's atmosphere, as Poseidon prepared to unleash his resentment. The colder season generally attracted fine weather: cloud-cover was common, but rain was not and storms were rare. The dark skies that overhung Athens then were first thought to be a singular tempest. For days, however, the skies became a shade of grey close to black, and thunder continually rumbled from dawn until dusk. Catastrophe hung over the city, though its true extent was obscured by tension and by my silence as I obeyed Zeus' instruction.

Seeming to receive no wisdom from Athena, Ursula consulted Boreaxus. He had been quiet and elusive since the city had been won by Athena, holed up in his own temple within the citadel, obsessing over animal entrails and reading smoke while his new and powerful neighbours moved in.

"It is Poseidon's wrath," Ursula announced to us all, having spent nearly a full day with Zeus' High Priest.

She was flanked by her priestesses, Medusa separated from her only by Maestra. Mention of the sea-god's name made no change to Medusa's serenity. My sharp eyes noticed no flash of memory across her face; no reminder of when she had been compelled to mark herself with the victims of Poseidon's godly intervention.

The flames of the lit torches quivered in the wind that blew outside and vented in to the temple's enormous atrium. Ursula's voice wavered slightly, as if it too was affected by the breeze.

"A great storm is coming," she said. "Zeus himself has permitted his brother a quantity of vengeance for his loss of the city." She looked as if she could say more.

"Athena has been quiet," Maestra said loudly, addressing us all with the same enthusiasm as she did when teaching us, "because she has been silenced by the father-god. This is a good lesson in Olympian politics, which will influence our own in future. The god's ownership of the city is about to be tested, and *we* are the city. The god is not here, *we* are here. It is one thing to win the city, to name it Athens, and it is another thing to keep it."

The old priestess seemed to speak what Ursula could not.

◆ ◆ ◆

On the day the flood came, the meagre winter sun rose for its fleeting, daily appearance, showing itself through optimistic, wispy clouds. The blue sky around it was glorious, and briefly seen. Rain had poured, with only that curt pause, since the evening rite, the fumes of incense rising as the first drops fell from the sky.

We were eating a breakfast of honey-bread, apples, figs and the last of the pistachios from the autumn harvest when we heard the noise. It crept into the chasmic atrium as a low hum, countering the high pitch of the unstoppable wind and the lively patter of the building being carved out by countless raindrops striking it. Ursula encouraged us to finish our meal, to eat well; we would need our strength. Nobody was permitted to investigate, though I noticed a number of appetites slow as the noise outside grew.

We finished and Ursula urged us to exit the temple. Outside, the rain immediately soaked us all, and the wind stung our cheeks. I stood uneasily, leaning on my walking stick in such a way as to put too much pressure on my injury. I winced and had to constantly shift my weight. The brunt of the noise hit us: it was the sound of thousands of voices rising up in a unison of terror from the city below. By the immense and controlled force assured by Poseidon, the skies drenched us from above and, from below, the seas around eastern Greece had been roused. The port of Piraeus and the road to Athens had already been swallowed; the fluid titan had already consumed that organ and artery. As it had edged closer to the city itself, growing in partnership with the sound of public dread, a mountain of water had been formed: a tidal wave had been summoned, which satisfied his criteria of making the natural abnormal. The immeasurable volume loomed over the city, casting a shadow that the daylight struggled to compete with. The winding road uphill to the Acropolis was empty: the wave would strike the citadel with the brunt of its incredible, wrathful force; up there would be no safer than the streets.

Boreaxus suddenly appeared, and shouted at us through the rain. "Come to my temple!" The High Priest had appeared to find all of us staring open-jawed and helpless at the impending doom. "Yours will not survive - the wave's crest is destined for it. Look!"

He was correct. We looked up, straining our eyes to see through the intense rain and spitting water from our mouths. Far above our heads, the edge of the wave curled and foamed and stared back at us like the summit of a mountain. The main body of the water was curved into shape to ensure its peak would lash our temple with all its doom-laden power, before crashing down on the city below.

Ursula bellowed to Boreaxus. "Yours is protected?"

"As well as Poseidon's, as well as Aphrodite's and others down the hill. The sea-god dare not bite the hand that feeds him. It is the *city and its people* he wants to destroy, not us! Quickly..."

Wasting no time to retrieve belongings, we all followed Boreaxus. As if aware of our escape the tidal wave was released and struck all of its immense weight down upon the Acropolis, as the last of us were hurried inside the haven of Zeus' temple. The mass, fearful cry of terror from the populous below was cut short, replaced with the sounds of clashing stones, clapping louder than the thunder in the sky, and of water rushing in a torrent.

True to Boreaxus' word, the temple of Zeus stood firm and intact. Our own great temple, fairly won in accordance with the father-god's rules, was brushed aside as if made of parchment. The homes of the city's leading citizens and administrators had been flattened. The city at the foot of the Acropolis became a river. The roofs of buildings were used by some to escape the flood, but debris from the Acropolis fell freely and struck these makeshift islands, sweeping people into the liquid onslaught.

I felt a soft, familiar hand take mine and grip it fearfully. I did not decline it. Despite the smell of earth and water generated by the storm, I knew the scent of rose and sweet mint that seemed to naturally pore from Medusa.

She spoke quietly, her voice shaken. "When will it stop?"

"When the city is destroyed, and all the men, women and children have been drowned," I said softly. "Or when Zeus compels the sea-god to stop."

"He is so angered to lose to Athena," she said, as if she knew Poseidon intimately and had sympathetically shared his bitter woes. "His expectations have been shattered. He cannot control himself."

"His loss of the city is not the only reason for his revenge," I said, sensing an unshackling of my tongue, which I had not felt since before the summer season. I turned to her, intending to interrogate her as to how far she truly understood and accepted Poseidon's infatuation for her; to plead with her to use all her efforts to dissuade any attraction she had to the sea-god. She seized my arm, stopping me.

"Look!" She said, excited, and she beckoned others to do the same.

Through the rain, glinting in stray sunlight that had escaped the clutches of the clouds, stood the great, golden statue of Athena. The shell of the temple was gone, but the golden god remained: impervious to the wave and defiant to Poseidon's terrible temper.

Chapter Twenty-One

I n Athena's chamber, I could not take my eyes from the miniature statues that dotted her curved walls. More had been added since my last communion there, but many recesses still remained empty: opportunities for the god to collect those she did not want to forget, for reasons friendly or not.

The figurines of Medusa and myself had been reworked to show our maturity: Medusa had been formed to include priestess robes; my likeness stood awkwardly. Unlike my mortal essence in communion, my long-injured leg and walking aid were depicted by my own statue. It was not the future depiction of us I had imagined in the first days of our sisterhood.

The god stood at her basin. She stared sadly into it. I watched her carefully, expecting an eruption of fury. But it did not come: she was either so livid as to be rendered incapable, or stoically accepting that there was little point in raging.

Poseidon joined her. His lean, vulpine face showed no satisfaction for what he had conjured on earth.

"Thank you for allowing my priestesses and acolytes to escape," Athena said looking and facing the sea-god.

Poseidon nodded slightly, acknowledging the gratitude.

"You should thank Zeus, he wished it. I merely obeyed his desire. As always." He filled his lungs and exhaled deeply, as if expelling discontent from his body. "Perhaps your glorious temple will one day be rebuilt. The port certainly will be - Zeus wants that. And he wants its original name of Piraeus to stand. He would not allow me to name after myself. *Piraeus* has part of his own name in it, he would never lose such a chance."

The sea-god laughed slightly, but on seeing he was alone in mirth his tone darkened.

"Zeus humours me, but I will not stop. Once your Athens is fully sunk and it is just priests and priestesses and acolytes left, scrabbling for dry land, I will move to the next city. Unless Zeus compels me to stop. Or..." The sea-god hesitated and smiled demurely. "...No, it will not be possible. It could never be agreed."

"What? What will it take for you to stop the destruction? Aside from Zeus who does not seem likely to act." Athena sounded tired, impatient. She disliked games, particularly those she could not easily play.

Poseidon looked at her wolfishly, his earlier modesty dissolved and reformed into urgency: a doggedness of someone who could smell a near and profound victory.

"Medusa. I will spare Athens from total annihilation if you release Medusa from your temple. I cannot love her in the way I crave to while she is a priestess. Once free, she will be the most honoured woman on earth. I will be the most attentive lover, and more besides."

A flash of realisation crossed Athena's mortal-form face: something had to be handled with utmost care.

"You wish for Medusa to be released from my temple," Athena said slowly.

Poseidon nodded, pre-occupied with the prospect of finally acquiring his long-obsessed and unobtainable prize, sparing no thought to elaborate on his terms. He went to leave the chamber.

"Consider it," the sea-god said. "I will stay my hand until you give me a decision. Once the sun is set today on earth I'll have your answer."

After he had gone, Athena was silent and contemplative. The god inspected her figurines. She selected Medusa and studied her.

"Poseidon has offered me terms and left my chamber," the god said quietly, without looking to me. "His proposal is binding. If he came back now wanting to amend the deal, I would have enough cause to go to my father for aid. Zeus would not be happy, but he would not refuse me."

At that moment Aphrodite entered, giving me a look of mild disgust. Athena replaced Medusa's figurine and turned to her sister expectantly.

"Poseidon's wrath is in hiatus," Aphrodite said. "When we were lovers it was the same - he always had such restraint, he would keep so much in, only for it to eventually explode. Then he would settle. Briefly. There is no steady stream with him. Only storms or serenity."

Athena spoke carefully. "He wants me to re-lease Medusa. To free her from my temple. Then he will leave Athens as it is - mostly destroyed, but not entirely."

Aphrodite frowned, displeased but thought-ful.

"Neither of us want Medusa spoiled," Athena continued. "Athens would be left part-intact, but my honour would be demolished. Poseidon would forever remind me of the time I submit-ted to him."

"I cannot face it if his love for the girl was al-lowed to be realised," Aphrodite said sadly. "He would be forever lost to me. What would be-come of me, lonely spinster goddess, beautiful herself and yet impossible to love?"

Athena answered, quiet and serious. "There is a way to navigate this like the best sailors do Poseidon's waters. I will release Medusa as Po-seidon's terms state, implying that she will be free from her holy obligations and available for Poseidon to ravish. But she will not be free - she will be taken in by your temple. Her release will actually be a transfer between us - from my tem-ple and protection, to yours."

Aphrodite's eyes widened as she calculated the extent of Athena's plan.

"It is no trick," Aphrodite said. "Poseidon should have been more explicit with his terms. The prospect of acquiring Medusa must have clouded his judgement. Perhaps it is she who is meant to succeed my ageing High Priestess, Hydraphea - beloved, loyal Hydraphea. There would be no gap in Medusa's protection, and Poseidon's deal would be satisfied. Just not in the way he expects."

"Such a beautiful creature surely belongs with others like her," Athena said, flattering Aphrodite. "But listen further: as I am the architect of this arrangement, I ask a favour from you. A condition."

Aphrodite looked at her dubiously. "Which is?"

"I would not want Medusa and Miranda split up. Their relationship is fractured, like my city, and I wish it repaired. By acquiring Medusa, you gain the eyes of the world. By acquiring Miranda, you gain eyes *to* the world. Their presence in your temple will elevate your status among the mortals. Their power would be yours to shape."

Aphrodite looked over to me and then faced Athena again, pointing me out as if Athena had not known me there.

"Your condition is for me to also take that ugly thing?"

"And to take her as a priestess, not as an acolyte," Athena said. "Miranda is not beautiful, but she has other assets. She has served me well, all her life. She would temper enthusiasm for Medusa, balance your ranks."

"You make a bold proposal," Aphrodite said, shaking her head in disbelief.

"Medusa would be yours, and with her the chance for Poseidon to forget her and return to you. In exchange for my fairly won city not to be totally obliterated, and for Miranda and Medusa's sisterhood to be healed."

Aphrodite looked at me once more, searching for something she could appreciate in my form.

"I will agree to your terms," Aphrodite said. "But if Miranda does not fit in, I have the right to eject her."

"Only after reasonable time has passed - time as the mortals know it. Let us say four seasons from when she sets foot in your temple. One year. Consider her a loan. If you find she *does* fit in, I will not stop you keeping her."

Aphrodite nodded her acceptance and departed, giving me no further look. Athena approached me.

"Say nothing of what you have heard us agree. Protect Medusa as you have always done, and she will return the favour as you both enter Aphrodite's temple. I thank you for this - I only give my best the most difficult tasks. I shall not forget it."

The god moved closer to me.

"I can sense that seed of envy Aphrodite once

planted in you," she said. "I cannot remove it without an argument, and I need my sister's forbearance now."

Athena studied me like a mother would an unhappy child: her concern was only matched by a look of determination that I should trust her.

Chapter Twenty-Two

The rain stopped as the sun set. The sky cleared, and was no longer grey and looming but a dark shade of blue.

Within Zeus' temple, bread, honey and water were laid on in great quantity. We ate, and in the starlight beheld the glittering golden statue of the god still standing in place, the lone remnant of our new temple.

Ursula ate little and then disappeared beneath the atrium. She was unseen until sunrise, when she emerged looking ill-rested and wary. I caught her staring at me from afar, and yet she did not approach me.

A warm wind beckoned us leave Zeus' temple. We looked out over the city: the sea had begun its retreat back to where it belonged beyond the port. As the waterline dropped in the flooded streets, the devastation was revealed building by building, corpse by corpse. The scathing sound of hungry gulls filled the air, passing a squawked message among their countless flocks of the rich, fleshy pickings below.

Boreaxus studied the sky thoughtfully. "Zeus himself has disciplined the sea-god," he said. "How else would this devastation stopped?"

Even the High Priest seemed unaware of the

Olympian bargaining; only I seemed to know what had been negotiated to stop the watery assault, to placate Poseidon's anger.

"Poseidon is not so easily restrained," Maestra said. "Zeus indulges his brother - he would not have been so quick to control him."

Boreaxus did not like being second-guessed as to Zeus' motives, and gave the old priestess a waspish look.

"This is an agreement of terms," said Ursula tiredly. "I was told so by the god, though no detail was shared. Our great statue still stands - Poseidon held himself back, perhaps hoping for the deal that has been reached."

Boreaxus studied Ursula, his grim eyes searching the High Priestess for answers. "What will you do now?" He said.

The High Priestess stared at the golden vision of Athena's statue. It was not a look of reverence, but one of suspicion.

"Honour the god. Burn the dead. Rebuild the city," she said.

We performed the morning rite. Neither all of temple's stocks nor all our possessions had been swept away: on the muddy floor lay occasional chests and bundles of sodden cloth. There was enough incense and dried lavender to light, and a heavy plume of smoke smothered the golden statue, held by a gentle breeze as we raised our hands in completion of the chant:

Obeisance to Athena
Who is pure being, consciousness, bliss.
As power,
Who exists in the forms of time and space
And all that is therein,
Who is the divine light in all beings.

With the help of Boreaxus' acolytes, we gathered what was left of our lives onto a cart lent us by the High Priest. Among the debris, the small box containing Medusa's belongings was found. We had not seen it for many years, not since it had been stored away when we first entered temple. It was intact, immune to the sea-god's wrath.

"I would like to look inside, to see that nothing is broken," Medusa said to me. She spoke quietly, her mind on her inherited mirror; the device long unseen and an unexpected survivor of the disaster.

Maestra, however, had heard her. "This is not the time to be dwelling on the past," the old priestess said. She seized the box from her and tucked it among the other salvage on the cart.

The day continued to be unseasonably warm. We slowly descended the Acropolis, the cart leading the way. No member of the public came to us, or stopped us; the city was hushed by death. An odious smell had begun to sting our nostrils: of stagnant seawater and old fish; and the ripe beginnings of mortal decay.

At the bottom of the hill Ursula strode forward, directing the cart and its line of followers towards our original, humble temple. We found the structure as we had left it: locked and empty. The tidal wave had let it be, though the surrounding buildings were ruined.

Boreaxus' acolytes emptied the cart of our rescued possessions, piling them neatly amidst the shelter of the familiar columns. They then returned up the hill to the citadel, no doubt keen to observe the fallout of the flood from their eyrie. Led by Maestra, a group including Medusa remained to organise the return into the old temple; the rest of us, including myself and led by Ursula, ventured into the ruins of the city.

We made for where the public funeral pyre had been, in the Apote district north of the Agora. Ursula thought it prudent to ensure a fire was lit for the burning of the dead and to reduce the risk of disease spreading. No better place than where the site had been before, and perhaps other survivors would congregate there for the same purpose. Smoke habitually rose high from there: a large city always had someone to cremate, but no black wisps formed their usual fog then.

We were vigilant for living bodies as we trod carefully through the ruins. None were forthcoming. Drowned men, women and children, and sodden, half-destroyed walls obstructed a clear path. Desolation normally associated with the desert lands, where sandstorms eroded all to dust, took the form of its liquid relation in Athens.

We reached Apote, and found the pyre washed away. A large, grey-black stain on the ground remained: the mark left by thousands of burnings was too stubborn for even Poseidon's wave to wash away.

A female voice, moderately aged and sensual, emanated from behind where we gathered.

"It seems great minds think alike," she said. It was not an accusatory tone, more an old friend goading another.

Ursula turned and found Hydraphea, High Priestess to Aphrodite, facing her. From one of the streets that splayed off from the pyre-square came a troop of her own priestesses and acolytes. Some were Greek, others were from exotic lands: their faces were either gently pretty or harshly striking; their skins were all smooth and each had faces painted like dolls. They were a procession of beauty contrasting the ruins. None bettered exquisite Medusa.

Several more carts emerged, driven by acolytes belonging to the temple of Poseidon. The vehicles were laden with the dead. The youthful High Priest Hyperion sat atop one cart. He steered around the square to the former pyre in a solemn parade, but his face was not one of arrogance at his master's successful fury; moreover he seemed focussed and concerned, conscious of not wanting to upset a delicate balance that hung in the atmosphere.

"This will be the first of many visits with loaded carts," Hydraphea said. "This has been a culling."

"A slaughter is more apt," Ursula said. "The sea-god's bitterness is inexcusable."

"Come now, dear Ursula," Hydraphea said smoothly. "What attachment did you really have to these people? Only the recently born could be called true *Athenians* - if any remain. Everybody else, only by association of simply being here in this city when Athena won their favour."

"I shall be sure to point out the same sentiments to you in the future, if something you hold dear is ruined," Ursula replied bitterly.

Hydraphea laughed lightly. "Let's not be at each other's throats. We have been friends all our lives. Our past will forever keep us intact. Our gods are sisters, after all, and so are we."

Aphrodite's High Priestess looked away from Ursula and noticed me. She narrowed her eyes in recognition, though we had never met.

"Not literally of course, but in spirit," she said to me, appraising me and searching for something to find attractive in my stocky, crippled, unappealing frame. "Your High Priestess and I were thrown together, became fast friends in difficult times and were then put on our separate holy paths. Much like you and Medusa *should* be, but are not it seems. Fear not, we will make you both welcome in temple."

"What are you talking about?" Ursula said.

Hydraphea knew who she was about to inherit: one desired in Medusa and one not in me. Truth had not been withheld from her by Aphrodite.

"Oh dear," Hydraphea said, not without pleasure. "You are unaware. I cannot imagine that you have not communed with Athena since this chaos. And yet it seems the god has withheld all the facts from you."

Ursula's face hardened, and her normally serene posture became tense. "Terms were reached to save what was left of our city," she said.

"But the deal not fully explained to you?" Hydraphea pressed.

Ursula spoke harshly with sudden frustration. "Tell me!"

"Temper, sister! Consider my position - I know a great thing that you clearly do not, while you are in the grip of a destruction aimed at Athena. You are vulnerable, and I would not seek to damage you further. Maybe it's best that your acolyte tells you. She is popular for the communion, I am told." She turned to face me. "In the temple of Aphrodite, we are not afraid to hide things. Just as it usually is in Athena's temple. We speak openly, and bluntly if need be - the god loathes subtlety."

"The wise speak when there is something to say, not because they have to say something," I said. I feared Hydraphea would admonish me, but instead she joyfully clapped her hands.

"Very good! We may be able to take the girl from Athena, but will we be able to take Athena from the girl?"

I felt myself go crimson red, and looked at the sodden floor.

"Tell me, Hydraphea," Ursula said softly. "Tell me what more I must face."

Hydraphea sighed. "*My* god will not care if I tell you, but *yours* might - let it be known that you are insisting on it."

Ursula nodded once. Hydraphea continued, low-voiced so only we could hear.

"It has been agreed between Athena and Aphrodite that Medusa be transferred from your temple to mine. This so-called release has tricked Poseidon into halting his destruction of your city. The sea-god is obsessed with Medusa, with her unobtainable beauty. He is using all his strength and cunning for his desires to be appeased. With this deal having been struck, he expects her to be utterly free. And yet she will be as protected in my temple as well as she is in

271

yours. If not more so - you must know how Aphrodite covets Poseidon as a lover. Though I think I would be too much for young Hyperion, energetic as he seems." Hydraphea laughed to herself, entertained. Ursula's stony face bade her continue. "Medusa will be released, and yet not. To agree to such a thing Poseidon must have been love-drunk! No fool like a fool in love."

Ursula said nothing.

"Clearly," Hydraphea said, continuing, "the acquisition of Medusa - widely regarded as the most profound beauty on mortal earth - is a boon to us. The condition imposed by Athena is that this young woman," she gestured to me, "Medusa's dear friend, be transferred too. To keep the beauty company, so I am told - though I doubt that is the *whole* truth. And both as priestesses to Aphrodite, no less! I have girls who have been touched by gorgeousness in lands that we will never see, who bring joy to the hearts and lusts of men and women, who all their lives have desired nothing more than to be in my priestess ranks, and have shown loyalty and ability to the god. And I must refuse *them*, to make way for *her*."

I did not want Medusa to be taken into Aphrodite's temple; and Aphrodite's temple did not want me to go with her. I wondered if Ursula felt my indignity, and feared that she too was disgraced.

Finally Ursula spoke in a defeated. "This is

surprising news. Medusa has been coveted all her life, more so as a woman. I should have foreseen that she would be beyond purely mortal desire. I shan't second-guess the god's motives for not telling me herself. I shall trust Athena's prudence. Miranda, you are getting your wish to be a priestess. Don't stare at the floor in that downtrodden way - you did not learn discourtesy under my roof. This is your new High Priestess."

My strongest desires had been granted in wretched ways. I did as told and looked squarely at Hydraphea, straightening my back and causing a painful spasm in my crippled leg. Tears welled from my discomfort, wrongly giving the impression that I was upset.

"She and Medusa are not mine quite yet," Hydraphea said. "Commune with your god again. You will learn when the transfer is due."

Ursula ignored the patronising direction. "We shall build the pyre. You bring the bodies. The sooner the dead can become ashes, the sooner the city can rise from them."

The winter remained largely dry, with only bursts of seasonal rain from the sky. No great temperatures of heat or cold affected the city: a microclimate had been bestowed upon us, and very slowly Athens forged the beginnings of a path to recovery. Over half the population had died, swept away by Poseidon's freak manipulation of the seas. None who dwelled within Olympian temples perished; it was us who banded together and cleared the drowned, we who lit a funeral pyre that burned from dawn until dusk and through the night until the late winter sun came again. It was a season of mourning, and of giving thanks by those who survived.

Athens began to flirt with its former glory as the millions lost to the water began to be replaced by new refugees, fortune-hunters, peacemakers and educators. The port of Piraeus was rebuilt with speed: evidence of Zeus' will, the mouth of trade was rapidly re-established to not disjoint the nation's prosperity, or to be cowed by the anger of a single god. Even the surviving edifices in Athens, most still dishevelled and drying, had earned a golden lustre reminiscent of a time now consigned to history.

The great flood was once crisis, and in the space of a season it had become opportunity. Athens may have no longer belonged to Zeus, but the father-god's pragmatic influence ran through the city's veins like strong blood does in prized stock.

"This will be temporary, at least for you," Medusa whispered to me.

She spoke kindly, to ease my discomfort.

We were enshrouded in near-darkness, inside a covered wagon. I had been quietly weeping, and Medusa had a comforting arm about my shoulders. We were dressed in the priestess robes of Aphrodite's temple: crimson red and of a smooth fabric the eastern traders called *siwa*. Medusa's fitted her perfectly, as if she were born to wear it. My own was ill-fitting and its tied fastening kept becoming loose.

Our official transfer between temples was imminent, and reminded me of when we had travelled together as girls, as part of Menethus' retinue. The memory of that uncertain but comfortable time enhanced my sadness for this certain and unwelcome event.

"*Temporary* is a cruel word," I said, summoning a courage to make my emotion obedient. "When we are old and grey, and when Poseidon has cast his desires elsewhere, then we might be permitted back to Athena. Temporary could mean remaining in service to Aphrodite for a hundred seasons, just as it could one."

The sounds of the rejuvenated city called and chattered outside the wagon's timber walls.

"They will treat you differently to how they will treat me," she said suddenly. "You will be a curiosity to them, perhaps a subject of confusion and impolite interest. Like I was in Athena's temple. Like I have been all my life to everyone."

"Like you have been," I said, agreeing. "People gawking at you for sublime reason. In this place they will gawk at me because I am not like them, or you. I will be an outcast they are forced to welcome."

"And I will protect you from them. Just as you did me these many years. I will shield you from criticism, just as you shielded me from desire."

"We are abandoned by the god."

"Misery should not be a symptom of being in Athena's influence since your birth."

She spoke true, but I could not accept our position.

"Poseidon will not take well to being tricked," I said. "Athena has been too clever, maintaining your purity has become her priority."

We fell silent. In the days before we departed Athena's temple Ursula had confronted Medusa, gently and with me present. She had probed her for whether the sea-god's infatuation was reciprocated. Information still seemed to have been withheld, for the High Priestess made no mention of Poseidon's remarkable saving of Medusa in Labyr: an event surely of keen interest had it been known. I was again offered the subtle chance to reveal Medusa's drawing of Poseidon's trident upon her breasts; the chance for the act to be scrutinised and augured by Ursula. I said nothing of the matter and the privacy of it endured: ointment to mend the fracture in our friendship, as Athena had wished.

The wagon rumbled on. I pretended to stare ahead, meditating, but I had an eye on her.

She too thought deeply, turning something unspoken over and over in her mind. She was distracted by a great and secret conundrum, and with every passing moment of silence she picked at its lock in a bid to be free of it.

The vehicle jolted to a halt: we had arrived at Aphrodite's temple. Abruptly, she said: "I am not for Poseidon."

Her statement seemed final. She had announced it either as a verbal remedy to counter another incantation, or as a definitive disappointment. I could not easily believe either possibility.

The rear door opened and Ursula appeared. She had sat alongside the driver, taking the opportunity to survey the city's progress as they navigated the streets.

Medusa and I rose and emerged into the daylight like cattle about to be sold. She carried her familiar box of belongings, and I a poorer-looking sack containing what I had not lost to the flood. There would be no initiation beyond this official conveyance. Our possessions would be stored in the bowels of the temple and, unlike our initiation into Athena's temple years before, unscrutinised by others. Medusa's precious mirror would be left unseen.

Two rows of people greeted us, comprised of Aphrodite's priestesses and acolytes forming a human avenue, with Hydraphea at their head. I saw that we had entered via a tall set of stone doors, into a large, square courtyard. Plants and flowers I could not immediately identify marked out the space, and columns of perfectly rounded symmetry were evenly spaced, granting entrance to the inner temple. In one corner stood a statue of Aphrodite: face refined and angular and body lithe and feminine, which I knew too well from the communions. It was not ostentatious, and elegantly simple in its bland stone material: a layer of modesty to the god's usual showy character. Water sprang from various orifices about her, spraying and dancing upwards in an ingenious method, perhaps in homage to her affection for the sea-god.

Ursula slowly led us down the middle of the stunning mortal aisle. While Medusa already strode confidently among them, my limp and stick boldly stated my exception to their old and coveted rules of physical perfection. I had seldom seen these women and girls at close quarters, and then I could feel the power radiating from their allure.

Their eyes stared at Medusa in wonder, held in the grip of her beauty that exceeded their own. They grimaced at me in restrained disdain. Some whispered words of admiration for Medusa; others giggled mercilessly at me. They were unchallenged by Hydraphea. Ursula paid them no attention, determined to conclude this chaos that had besieged her temple, and which she had been forced to accept vicariously and without protest.

Chapter Twenty-Three

Poseidon stared hard at Athena and Aphrodite, who stood close together in sisterly unison. His face pointed downwards in concentrated fury, angling his brows into perfect evenness. The darkness of their hairs accentuated his green eyes to a wicked blaze.

Zeus was unseated, stood with his back to his immense white throne, conscious of possible retaliation from his brother and ready to intervene. I stood near the father-god, though it was Athena who had summoned me.

The sea-god addressed Aphrodite, his anger so intense it hushed his voice. "I trusted you, above all others. I have misjudged your jealousy of Medusa. I have underestimated my own obsession with her. I tell you now with no pretence and to cause you pain, as you have caused me, that I can think of nothing else but loving her. Your *imprisonment* of her makes me more determined, if that were possible."

"You will not get to her under the roof of my temple," Aphrodite said conclusively. "They already adore her, worship her as they do me. It would be another mistake for you to force your way, the first error being that you gave love the chance to spread. You are diseased, infected by a mortal strain."

Athena joined her sister in support. "You cannot blame my sister for your own negligence, Poseidon. You should have taken more care to get what you want."

Poseidon turned to Athena, spitting out his words. "And you, you vile, crazed liar. Your great wit will be your demise, and that of your city. Wisdom, justice, skill...I will use my own to resume the destruction of Athens. I shall summon such unholiness from the depths that all stone so much as brushed by Athenian hands will become Athenian dust."

"I will not allow it," Zeus said, stepping forward a pace. "You should not have allowed yourself to be tricked, Poseidon. You have all but said so yourself."

"Thank you, father..." Athena began, but her gratitude was waved aside by Zeus.

"I do not stay Poseidon's hand solely for your benefit, Athena," Zeus said reprovingly. "I have another task for him that is more important, one that requires his careful attention."

Poseidon's rage imposed on him such that his face fell grim, as if silently resisting a torrent of pain.

"But first I have an announcement," Zeus continued with steady pride. "A new addition to our family - my son, my mortal son. I fell in love with and impregnated Danae, adopted daughter of King Acrisius of Argus. As Poseidon knows, some mortal women are impossible to resist."

Aphrodite and Athena shared a look of polite shock. Poseidon, now distracted, narrowed his eyes, as if trying to recall who Danae was. Then he beheld Zeus with a curious look that bordered on respect.

"Congratulations," the sea-god said softly.

"Thank you. I see my daughters are hesitant in sharing our joy."

Athena spoke plainly. "We don't think it sets a good example. Not considering the trouble Medusa has caused."

"Hera will not welcome the news," Aphrodite said.

"That is true, she will not," Zeus said heavily. "But Hera must learn the value of the demigod. For the moment, mortals spawning our offspring is critical. To be done rarely, but critical. She cannot afford *not* to believe in the mortal cause. None of us can. We need them more than they need us - they simply do not know this yet. That awareness must not be rushed. We will have our time, just as they have theirs."

"What have you named your son?" Poseidon said.

"Perseus."

"I know that name..."

"It is the name assumed by that king of old, who founded Mycenae. I always had a spark of regret for crushing him. You may recall it was the price for settling a feud between Hera and I, gone on too long. I admired his audacity, in the end. Hopefully that courage will rub off on my son."

"Hopefully not in the same way. What is the task you would have me do?" Poseidon asked. He suddenly seemed tired and spent, exhausted by his anger and mania.

Zeus emitted a frustrated sigh. "King Acrisius believes Danae has sinned, and copulated out of wedlock with another man. He has banished her from his kingdom, exiled her out to sea, Perseus still suckling upon her gentle breasts. I will not intervene to set the matter straight. I lead by example." The father-god paused and filled his lungs. "Poseidon, I want you to grant safe passage to Danae and my son Perseus. A gentle task to off-set your recent temper. See that they drift to an island, where they will live quietly until Perseus becomes a man."

The sea-god paused before answering. His mood seemed to lift, the dark shadow of the betrayal he felt shifting from his face like storm clouds dissipating. He spoke more brightly.

"Nothing would bring me greater pleasure."

In his face I could see license; the deliberation of a brazen plan.

Chapter Twenty-Four

The first spring after the great flood brought a swell in numbers within all the temples of Athens. Fortunate children who had survived Poseidon's tempestuous wrath had been put into positions of safety either by their own volition, or at the cost of their parents' or masters' lives. As refugees, they had turned to the houses of religion for salvation as the city's recovery began. Temple rules were temporarily relaxed, and a commitment was made to accommodate the broad range of ages, dispositions and skills.

In the temple of Aphrodite the influx of new acolytes was a welcome distraction for me, but unpalatable for most of the girls and women with whom I now shared my new pious duties. They acted as observers, while I herded and organised the newcomers; arranged their beds and sanitation; taught them of the bizarre and slapdash rites, which I barely knew myself; and acted as nurse and mother while they spilled forth their emotional turmoil having lost everything to the great flood. As Hydraphea had said, I could be removed from Athena's temple, but Athena could not be removed from me.

I noticed occasional whisperings among the

intake, for it became clear to them that I was conspicuous by my lack of beauty. Some became ingratiated with the long-standing acolytes and priestesses, and soon my exceptional presence there was known and never openly discussed within my earshot.

I did hear that Ursula had taken an abundance of girls and young women into the small first temple, substitute for the washed-away great house of Athena within the Acropolis. This was a symbol of generosity and defiance, and wisely strengthened the Athenian ranks with an eye on the future: the notion was that the city would one day be as it was before the flood, and when this time came Athena's temple should be dominant in its followers. The city still belonged to the god, a sentiment never to be lost or forgotten.

By the start of the hot summer season, the homeless and aimless young had been largely appeased. Very few newcomers were arriving at Aphrodite's temple gates seeking aid. The unwavering principle of beauty was reinstated: any girls and young women who did not meet this exceptional standard were turned away.

On midsummer's night, the date in the calendar marking the very slow descent towards the colder seasons, the *Adonia* was celebrated. Medusa had been told extensive detail of the annual rite; I had simply been told to be present in the atrium when necessary.

Medusa shared the depth of her knowledge with me, of the procession. Long ago when the city of Troy had just settled into the hands and minds of kings, the *Adonia* had been founded. It was named such in honour of a Trojan man Aphrodite had once tested by way of his sexual aptitude. Adonis had been his name, the son of a farming family of little consequence; handsome and obscure enough for the god to satisfy her seething curiosity. She had watched Adonis through her own viewing pool, within her own chamber seldom-accessible to others. She had watched as he grew into manhood and assumed the life of a tenant farmer, as his father and mother had encouraged. But his simple existence bred a complexity of feelings in the god and, on a midsummer's night, she revealed herself to him. In a field they fucked, Adonis unsure of how or why such a beautiful young woman had been presented to him.

More mysterious than her arrival was her departure. Lying amid the barley crop and staring at the sky, the cool night breeze brushing their naked bodies and drying the sweet sweat produced, they talked quietly and at length: of the earth's seasons and nature; of the Trojan city leagues away and what marvels and terrors it may produce; of the stars and their celestial undertakings, and what marvels and terrors they represented. Mortal-form Aphrodite eventually stood and dressed herself. Adonis lay flat, intoxicated with his perceived love-fortune and aware that their tryst was to end, but he hoped continue. Adonis expected her to take him by the hand and promise to see him the next night, or day; he had started to entertain thoughts of family introductions and marriage. He lay smiling at the sky, blissfully unaware that she had vanished.

For a year he searched for her. For four full seasons he frequented Troy, exploring every alley, waiting outside every house whether host to poverty or wealth, in the hope of meeting her. He neglected his farming labours; his ageing parents shared in his melancholy, while he did not share its amorous reason with they who loved him unconditionally. Finally, on the next midsummer's night, the anniversary, Adonis' obsession climaxed. Now cowed and sleepless with his fruitless hunt for Aphrodite, and not unaware of his family's disappointment in him, Adonis walked into the sea that separates Troy and its eastern promise from Greece. Perhaps she was there amidst the deepening waves, the last place he had to look.

Since their unrepeated tryst, Aphrodite had monitored Adonis from her very private Olympian chamber, occasionally interrupting her other interests to look upon his earthly search for her. She had thought it amusing, even charming, that the man should be so fretful to find her; and proud that he should be so persistent. Thankfully Adonis could not know that his suicide quashed intentions the god had finally mustered to revisit him, as a reward for his particular piety. Aphrodite had once been happy to admit that care for Adonis was flourishing within her, and his determined search for her was teaching her love's most subtly sympathetic attributes. But she was too late to truly accept them.

Adonis' self-destruction tarnished what the god thought she understood, ruined what made her feel so wanted. She could not accept that her procrastination, her delay in presenting herself to Adonis again, had heavily contributed to the young man's demise. Love was concluded to be distrustful by the god who supposedly owned it. She perceived that love was something that Zeus himself had conjured: a trick for them all to become victim; for behind his amusement there was often subtle teaching; love was too unpredictable to guarantee reward for accepting or pursuing it. The distress of Adonis not being able to find her had not escaped the god, and she feared love's capacity to let her wrongly consider the tragedy a joke. She created the *Adonia* in a tribute to her tryst with Adonis, and his death because of it: to honour blind persistence and submission to the madness love causes; and in case Zeus secretly wanted new rites.

The ceremony itself involved the controlled prostitution of virgin acolytes who had reached a certain age. Though intact ourselves, Medusa and I were exempt as priestesses. The flood-intake had resulted in more than one hundred girls and young women gaining entry. Not all were virgins.

Medusa and I, and our peers who had previously experienced the ceremony, watched as a careful orgy was orchestrated by Hydraphea. Since the Athens temple of Aphrodite had been established, the number of acolytes subjected to the *Adonia* had never been more than three in a given year. Only those who had breached seventy seasons in age were chosen for the rite. The number of eligible young women did not exceed fifty, with bodies having been inspected by those skilled in telling years and innocence. These initiates were taken to be cleaned in the sumptuous baths deep in the bowels of the temple - baths that did not match those in Mycenae for scale, but did for scents and vitality.

Meanwhile, in their absence, a number of men of equal age or older to the initiates were brought forth. They numbered fewer than the virgin acolytes, and they had a master: a man who reminded me of Menethus but with an openly sly streak across his shaven face. This man's role was clearly defined and he did nothing to stop Hydraphea from conducting what was certainly her business. He had fulfilled his paid duty by recruiting and bringing the men. Some stared at us like startled animals: needy and alarmed, and surprised to be inside the temple. All of them, every single one, lingered their eyes upon Medusa: they were all beholden to she who stood but yards from them, closer to her now than they would be at any other time in their lives; she who was wholly inaccessible to them. The tension generated between their desire and the certainty that it would not be fulfilled with Medusa was unyielding.

They were lined up in rows and each handed a tiny piece of parchment; the more handsome men were given two. Upon each scrap had been written a number corresponding to the same number held by an initiate. The virgins were ushered back into the atrium and the matching commenced. Some men were cautious, unsure whether seizing the innocence of a godly girl would result in Olympian disfavour. Some, upon seeing that their match was less attractive than others, raised their voices to complain, as if the temple were a brothel. I noticed snide nods between them, compliments and curses as to their fortunes in beauty. But Hydraphea coaxed them impatiently and with some indifference: the process must be completed and the men had not come forced.

They were instructed to lie naked on their backs, on the temple floor that was smooth and cold, Aphrodite's giant statue peering at them all the while. Then the matched girls would ease themselves onto their erect cocks: some slipped on easily, others required slower stimulation. Gasps of sudden pain hissed and yelped and filled the atrium in a cacophony that could besmirch the rite, but in fact formed it. Cries of endurance were offset by those of near-pleasure; in few cases the acolytes discovered quick enjoyment and fucked their allocation wildly. I averted my eyes, not from prudishness, but from disinterest: this act was never something I ever expected, or *be* expected, to do with any man. My gaze naturally drifted to Medusa, who watched the sex with a silent fascination. Her own childhood in Tanis had likely desensitised her to the orgy, but she had a hunger in her eyes that was familiar to me. The same passion I had seen many times in the eyes of others, as they imagined their body enshrouded with hers.

By dusk, the men were exhausted and the initiates were no longer virgins. The men were dismissed, some looking back longingly at the women they would never again copulate with. The atrium floor was left dirtied by the mess of blood, sweat and semen. Carts were summoned to take the entire temple congregation to the coast.

On the beach near the port of Piraeus the deflowered acolytes were encouraged into the sea to wash themselves clean. This final stage of the

Adonia honoured the suicide of the Trojan peasant Adonis: in the shallow waves the acolytes washed away the invasion of man from their bodies, just as Adonis had drowned in his sorrow for losing Aphrodite. Poseidon's seas would be honoured with the bodily remnants of the ex-virgins. Aphrodite hoped that with every repeated *Adonia* her well-concealed despair of the tragedy of Adonis, her first mortal love, would further dissolve like salt into water.

The reek had been cleaned from the temple floor, the *Adonia* had been completed and we all stood before Hydraphea. The flickering flames from the fires affixed to the pillars danced about us, the god's stone face shadow-shifting from beauty to terror and back again. The honey liquor fed to each of us after returning from the beach kept us alert and awake.

"Medusa will succeed me," Hydraphea announced. "I name her as the next High Priestess of this temple. There is no love more natural than to love Medusa. She who was gifted to us under the gravest and most unforeseen circumstances. Her gradual ascent to my position starts tomorrow."

There was no challenge to her words. I ought to have recognised that something significant was about to affect Medusa, the way the others had fawned about her as they ran along the sandy shore during the final stage of the *Adonia*, as the newly-deflowered acolytes were encouraged into the surf. I could only hobble as I was spurred on to run with the others, near-crying with my leg stiff and painful from the soft and unsupportive surface of the sand. Medusa had initially stayed with me, since I had been soon-abandoned by those newcomers I had cared for, as they too embraced the beach. But then she too was whisked away and into the folds of the temple's long-serving dwellers.

"We should carry the pariah," someone had shouted, referring to me and half-serious.

"She's too heavy!" Another cried.

They carried Medusa away from me, forming a human sedan and raising her aloft so she might oversee the ocean cleansing of the acolytes. She was their sudden champion, plucked from obscurity like Adonis had been by their god. She looked back to me, happiness in her face: a sincere smile that was of both friendship and surrender; surrender to them, her followers. It was to them whom Medusa now belonged.

Beneath the surface of her looks, she was Athena's priestess. But the subtleties of wisdom, skill and justice had been dominated and overcome by the bluntness of sheer beauty. The instant reward that allure guaranteed had never been more confirmed since Medusa had, with equal roughness, been taken from

Athena's bosom and thrust into Aphrodite's. Nobody knew this more than Hydraphea: whether spurred on by the god or of her own will, she had seized the opportunity to augment her temple, and therefore the god. This was, however, of Athena's own making: Medusa and our sisterhood had been assets to trade for some greater realisation of power.

When we had first entered the temple of Aphrodite, Hydraphea had permitted Medusa and I share a room of our own to sleep in. This was more a kindness that I had benefitted from: to know that I had a retreat within temple, where the other girls and women could not subject me to petty torments, was relieving.

The arrangement allowed me to continue secret and careful honouring of Athena, always once Medusa was asleep in bed. She never had trouble sleeping, and could do so under any conditions: a useful side-effect of her boisterous upbringing. But her promotion to be the understudy to the High Priestess meant we would no longer share the room. It would be hers alone; I would move to share with a number of the flood-intake, a dormitory of the unwanted.

On our final night together, as I heard the familiar rhythm of her sleep-breath, I noiselessly crept from my bed. I knelt beneath the skylight that was similar to what we had in our first temple. Drenched in moonlight, I took a small collection of olive leaves between my hands and prayed to Athena for what may have been the final time beneath Aphrodite's roof; doing so with a hundred other bodies about me would be impossible. I whispered to the god that I should be released from Aphrodite soon, to be returned to where I really belonged.

I begged for communion from any of them; I wished the sickly sensation would wash over me, and transport me to plead a case I was not permitted to speak. I pressed the leaves hard into my palms, and the sweat allowed their earthily bitter odour to linger between my fingers. My simple devotion did not last long. Entreating any god is found to be distasteful if done for too long; there may be more potency in the discipline of restraint, rather than the desperation of persistence.

I hobbled back to my bed. As I passed Medusa she jerked, screamed once and sat up, startling me enough to yelp. I changed course and limped over to her, but said and did nothing to interfere: brash awakenings from the dream-state are ill-advised. After a time she calmed and looked to me, taking my hands for comfort.

I whispered to her. "What's wrong?"

She spoke lucidly, but fearfully. "My dream. So vivid."

"What did you see?"

"A vast ocean. Horses galloping across the waves. No riders on their backs. Hundreds of them, as if retreating from a lost battle. I could smell it all - the salty air, the horse shit and sweat. And then suddenly the ocean ended. The horses disappeared. There was land, drought-ridden land. In the distance I saw a temple - as large as Athena's was within the Acropolis. I approached it - it was in ruins and yes, it was a temple, but not Athena's. Older, greyer. The air around it was caught still. Nothing grew there - no shrubs, no creatures. Death itself had taken it long ago. I walked through its outer columns, into its decrepit atrium. There were ungodly statues, roughly-hewn, of people caught in states of shock. I found stairs leading underground and I used them, descending into blackness."

"Did you feel afraid?" I said.

"Not immediately. I felt comfortable, as if I belonged there. An unfamiliar home."

"What was beneath the broken atrium?"

"Firelight. My mother's mirror was there, in the middle of the space, resting flat on the stone floor. I rushed to retrieve it, my inheritance. I picked it up and looked at myself..." She stopped, now upset and squeezed my hand in terror.

"What did you see?"

"Yellow eyes. Skin that was not my own, not of any mortal. And I heard the long hiss of a snake

296

- a familiar sound from my childhood in Tanis and yet so terrible in the dream. It must have belonged to one angry and poisonous, and so close to my ears."

She wept, and used her bedclothes to dry her tears.

"That is what startled you awake," I said gently.

She nodded, and began caressing the area beneath her breast where she had once drawn Poseidon's trident with the remains of her attempted rapists.

I then spoke bluntly and intuitively; the old envy planted by Aphrodite did not forbid me.

"The sea-god lusts after you, and his intentions grow stronger. No good can come of it..."

With no warning she revealed her naked breasts. In the dim, blue-grey moonlight I could see a red mark, akin to a rash, forming exactly where she had once administered the death-paste. The trident shape soon appeared, like a branding on a horse.

"I should speak with Hydraphea," she said.

"No," I answered. Medusa looked at me with uncertainty. "While you are under this roof, Poseidon would not dare advance on you. And if he steps beyond his limits, if the god chooses to break the boundaries, you must refuse him yourself."

"Surely telling the High Priestess would give me more protection?"

"No," I repeated. "You will be seen as unable to deal with a test. And if you surrounded yourself with others, Poseidon may be spurred on. The god is clever, and the obvious thing he may expect you to do is call for help. A High Priestess governs and instructs, and is closer to the god than any other in temple. She is respected for her overcoming of hardships - these make her stronger. None more difficult than denying the seduction of a god. Aphrodite values desire and the refusal to give way to it, which makes desire most powerful. You alone must reject his advances when it comes."

She clothed herself, and I returned to my bed. We lay in silence in the gloom. She spoke piercing it, her voice commanding; the tone suited her.

"You must protect me," she said. "If he comes for me. If he enshrouds me and I am unable to stop him, you must help me reject him. I will not rely on the many, but the few. Only you, Miranda."

I made great effort to answer her, neither with an acceptance to her wishes nor a refusal.

"I will not always be with you," I said.

I felt the familiar, nauseating summons for communion, craved for and unexpected, as one aspect of my earlier prayers was answered.

Chapter Twenty-Five

Poseidon assessed me with interest, as if I should be another of his conquests. His rock-faced chamber sweated, and his floor-pool emitted a blueish light that faded as its potency rescinded.

I looked into his green, changeable eyes. I felt afraid, to be alone with the sea-god's unpredictable temperament.

"Clever girl. Wise girl. You are a good friend to her," Poseidon said softly. His menace needed no forthrightness. "We should admire and learn from the loyalty you mortals sometimes show each other. Especially you, even while you suffer a long dose of envy from Aphrodite. Never believe you have suppressed it - that is its trick. Beware the power of she who hates subtleties - it is subtlety itself that is her real power."

The sea-god turned away from me. He returned to his pool and conjured a stream of water upwards, a smaller cousin to his effort to secure Athens. Within the body of liquid came an image of Medusa, lying awake as I had left her. Poseidon stared up at her, as a supplicant before her, the queen of desire.

"If Medusa shows discipline when I come to take her," Poseidon said, "if she shows self-control as you advised her, then I shall withdraw. I shall admit defeat. Be assured that I shall come when the opportunity is there. It may be sooner than you can imagine."

Zeus' voice suddenly echoed around the chamber, heralding his entry to the cavern.

"You are pleased with your progress."

"No more than you were with that woman, King Acrisius' daughter," Poseidon said absently, still watching Medusa.

The water column suddenly collapsed, commanded by Zeus, and the sea-god was compelled to pay his brother attention.

"Danae," Zeus said carefully, warning. "The mother of my son."

Poseidon raised his hands in innocence. "They are safe, as you must be aware. No harm came to them on their journey across the waters. Perseus will have a good life on the island of Paxos. As good as his namesake - until his namesake was unmasked and his life became very difficult."

"It is to no benefit to have a wholly easy life," Zeus said. "Nothing learned through constant peace and kindness. How would the strong face terrors on behalf of the weak, having suffered no hardship themselves? Perseus will not be excluded."

Poseidon smirked, but did not want to debate further.

"With regards my *progress*, as you put it," the sea-god said, "I have you to thank, brother. Your seduction of Danae has been inspirational. And it seems you have no intention of stopping me from fulfilling my greatest desire."

"You are as clever and as wise as Medusa's friend," Zeus said, nodding towards me. "You are correct. I have no interest in denying you what you want. For good or ill. But I should warn you."

"I'm listening," Poseidon said, most interested.

"Intercourse between us and the mortals lacks the primal innocence it once had. The act has become more troublesome."

Poseidon screwed his face slightly, suppressing exasperation. "What do you mean?"

"You may be disappointed, or face an unexpected outcome from satisfying your great desire. Use my most recent example - I did not anticipate trouble from approaching Danae."

Poseidon considered the father-god's words, dissembled and calculated them.

"You once spoke of our detachment from them," the sea-god said carefully.

Zeus nodded once, knowingly. "I did. I said this divine venture will only be successful if we are disciplined enough to leave them be more often than we intervene."

"And you named time itself as the mortal's greatest invention. You said - *we have no concept for it but theirs. Divine interactions must become rarer and rarer. We will influence, but only at key moments. And then, when the time is right, our activities will cease altogether. We will detach our-selves fully from the mortals. In doing so we will pre-serve our timelessness."*

Zeus beheld his brother proudly. "I would trust none more than you to recall my words so fluently. To heed them so carefully. But don't distract me from my warning - *the act of inter-course between us and the mortals has become more troublesome.* The goddesses of Olympus have a vengeance in them that we gods simply do not. Consider Hades' wrath, and double it. They would use that retribution in targeted ways that would aim to sadden us. Depress us. Geld us. She may not be here, but I know Hera spoke poison into King Acrisius' ears. She learned of my and Danae's tryst and sought to damage me. To see that young woman rejected and banished in a most brutal way was sobering."

The sea-god appeared unmoved. "What's your point? That Hades' fury is nothing to that of a goddess scorned? That should not stop us - any of us. We would not complain if they satisfied their own desires. Indeed, they *have* satisfied their own desires and we have *not* complained! That is the difference between those who call themselves goddess, and us. They feel deceit, and we feel progress. We choose to *celebrate* our time."

Zeus thought on this, and gave his brother a tantalising smile.

"Then we must choose carefully," the father-god said. "We must choose to only do things that are truly wondrous for our appetites, to make the venture worthwhile."

Chapter Twenty-Six

I was returned to our shared room beneath Aphrodite's temple atrium, to my own bed, but my consciousness was incomplete. I felt as I had whilst observing Medusa be saved by Poseidon in the twisted streets of the Labyr district: aware of my mortal functions, and yet detached from reality and unable to affect my surroundings.

I felt the envy that Aphrodite had planted renew within me, a cruel mistress who suddenly whipped me on. I had never believed I could control it, or defeat it; its presence had been so dormant of late that I naively believed it to have served its purpose. I thought it expired, but it was a near-dried flower watered just in time to bloom again and harvest vengeance against me. Poseidon was correct: the envy's resurgence was so potent, so bitter on my tongue I almost gagged. I was under twofold Olympian control: a semi-communion daze; and Aphrodite's bestowed manipulation. Whatever I was about to witness and react to, I should be controlled with the utmost Olympian will and attention.

I was able to rise from my bed and looked to Medusa's. It was empty. The solid, wooden door was slightly open, carelessly left ajar. I looked through the skylight: the moon shone brightly, not quite full, against a black and starless sky. It was late, the time at which all in temple would be getting their sleep before the morning rite.

My hobble had been temporarily alleviated; I could sense relief from the burden of my old injury, and nothing of the disappointment I normally expected when fully released from the Olympian communion and returned to my normal state. I opened the door wider and stepped into the corridor, silent as dust falling on fabric. The dark stone was barely lit, the wall-hung fire-lamps spread broadly apart. The route to the atrium took me along the full length of the corridor, a sickly tunnel of unromantic walling and bland, closed doors. Aphrodite's temple was a thing of refinement and symmetry on the surface, and routinely ordinary beneath the veneer.

In my trance I was pushed towards the steps leading upwards to the atrium. The particular quiet of the temple at night should have unnerved me; but I felt no dread, for either spies or for a more sinister presence.

As I emerged from underground and into the atrium, I found her. Medusa was alone and robed, on her knees and with hands clasped before the dominant statue of Aphrodite. No fire-lamps were lit on the columns that lined the room; she and the statue were bathed in moonlight alone. The altar at the foot of the god, upon which bloody sacrifices were sometimes made, stood clean of past offerings.

I made no sound as I stepped forward, fruitlessly hoping that she could see me in her peripheral vision. One pace, and no more, was permitted by the power that enshrouded me then. I was frozen to the floor, and yet my bare feet felt nothing of the stone. Calling out to her was futile, my mouth invisibly clamped shut.

I watched helplessly as she completed her prayer, the words of which were unheard by me. Her arms fell submissively to her sides. Her robe slipped off and revealed her naked form, perfect and astounding. Slowly, she turned her back to the statue. The branding of Poseidon's trident glowed beneath her breasts. The insignia burned molten orange, stronger than it had earlier that fateful night, but Medusa did not flinch or cry out in discomfort.

A third person appeared but a yard from her. He was derived from the very air about her, materialising from the tiny fragments of dust that naturally occupied the cracks and crevices of the temple's interior. They gathered and swirled together, until their chaos danced into mortal order. He faced her and I knew the man. Youthful, muscular, dark-haired and naked like Medusa: Hyperion, Poseidon's High Priest. His own chest glowed with the same trident, the two symbols partnered.

The light generated between them granted me observe a difference in the High Priest's eyes: they were Poseidon's own, which I knew well. Narrower than Hyperion's, the familiar streak of cunning and passion in Poseidon's were unmistakeable; they sparkled green with the depths of his oceans, matched by the wisdom of his Olympian sorcery. Disguised as his High Priest, Poseidon had evaded any barriers erected by Aphrodite. He had come for Medusa.

Their glowing tridents began to lose potency, dying like a fire past its prime. The sea-god incarnate cupped a hand to one of Medusa's ears and whispered words to her that I was not allowed to know. They both smiled, lovers-to-be in harmony. He stroked her face with care.

He pulled her gently towards him; she gave no resistance or rejection. Their mouths were near-touching, and yet they did not kiss. He put both hands on her bare buttocks and lifted her. Her legs, limber and slightly fleshy, spread willingly to wrap around his waist. Her weight was no effort for him and he held her with assured stability. With his coaxing, she positioned herself upon his hardening phallus.

She exhaled a shriek, which she quickly silenced. The undignified sound could have been mistaken for a bird of prey passing in the sky outside. She arched her back in pain and the beginnings of pleasure, and gripped his arms and brought herself forward. Her plumply perfect breasts squeezed against his pectorals. With her slowly writhing against his groin, he carried her towards the altar.

Then my own great indiscretion dawned upon me. For all my wisdom in matters divine, for all my faith, the greater power was my mortal credulity: I had thought her mine.

Chapter Twenty-Seven

While in full communion and only with my ears did I witness what remained of their long and crude lovemaking. I had been summoned by Athena herself. The ritual deflowering of hundreds of young women during the *Adonia* had not shocked me; but this seemingly consensual ravaging of Medusa made me squirm.

Her orgasmic gasps filled the room. I prudishly studied the high, curved walls of Athena's immaculate chamber. The god's clay figurines had grown in number. I searched for Medusa and I, but whether because the doomed fucking was impossible to ignore, or because the small statues had been removed, I could not find them.

Athena and Aphrodite stood over the god's viewing pool, watching Poseidon's seduction of Medusa reach its climax. Aphrodite's face was solemn. She might have looked away, so as not to subject herself to seeing her love for the sea-god be shattered and abused. Yet she insisted on the voyeurism: she stared into the silvery liquid, captivated. Athena watched her sister more than the goings-on upon the temple altar.

Poseidon and Medusa stopped. A post-coital silence echoed around the chamber. I wanted to see what the lovers did now: whether the sea-god disappeared immediately, leaving Medusa to flee the scene before being discovered; or if he stayed, drawing out the inevitable abandonment with some care.

Athena spoke softly to Aphrodite. "You have been boldly betrayed."

Aphrodite kept her voice even and restrained. "By he who I should not love, but do. And by she, briskly and sincerely nominated to be the next High Priestess of my Athens temple. Am I so dense to be played for such a fool?"

Athena stared at the pool. "This is my fault. Sacred vows have been spurned. Embarrassment has been brought to your door. The plan to trick Poseidon and protect Medusa, my bold proposal, has backfired. I ask your forgiveness."

Aphrodite's face crumpled with anger, ignoring Athena's request. "Look at them. They lie so flagrantly upon *my* altar, a bed for their gruesomeness. And look at her," Aphrodite said, throwing a hand towards me. "All of us totally bound, including her, imprisoned by Zeus' will. Able to do nothing to stop it."

I knew then that Zeus himself controlled my semi-communion daze. Such manipulation, I thought, and for what purpose?

"We will hold him to account for this," Athena said boldly. I detected defiance that was too great in her tone; as if she did not really believe the father-god's motives could be confronted.

"He will not let me punish her," Aphrodite said. "He will not let you, and you have as much reason as I."

"I certainly do. My former priestess, allowing herself to be seduced and putting up no defence. My shame is two-fold: upon my own house, and upon yours."

Divided by their birthrights and beliefs, they were now united by treachery and distrust.

Aphrodite's voice quivered with sadness. "She prayed before my statue, but not to me. To Poseidon. She made no effort to seek help from me, or from you. Only an appeal to him, to immediately satisfy her desperate curiosity. If she were truly a wonder of the earth, she would have remained virgin all her life, driving Poseidon and mortal men wild with speculation to the end."

Athena began to slowly circle her viewing pool, looking idly up at her figurine-lined walls.

"What is our father's plan?" She said rhetorically. "Why would he permit Poseidon to satisfy himself? And prevent Medusa from being protected at all? Perhaps Zeus influenced her giving way to Poseidon. And why would he allow you," the god suddenly pointed at me, "to witness the ordeal, and be unable to do nothing?"

She lowered her finger, which had not been gestured in accusation but in query. Something in the pool had piqued her interest, and the same finger was dipped gently into the shimmering mass.

"She has Zeus' favour," Aphrodite said bitingly of Medusa. "Like the accursed, cheating sea-god. They are made for each other. I should not care what happens to them, or whether our father's schemes have intended to cause us such great sadness. I should not care. But I do. This will not settle easily, Athena."

"Medusa carries his child," Athena said. "It will not be a normal gestation. Poseidon would guard her viciously from us."

Aphrodite looked at her urgently, the fire of revenge sure-owed ablaze in her dark eyes.

"We can do nothing to punish her," Athena continued. "But your High Priestess can. The rot must be stopped - her damage to your temple, and my own, can be limited. Justice may be ours."

"A cunning idea. How will it be done?" Aphrodite said, feverish with anticipation of what her clever, resourceful sister had evoked.

Athena smiled and came to face me. Her own mortal-form eyes danced, alive with discovery and learning. The god was enlightened, and she spilled her wishes to me.

"Do as I tell you, Miranda, and you shall be returned to my temple," she said, her voice filling the room. "Decline or wilt, and Medusa will go unpunished. Her actions will quickly set the precedent for the mockery of religion. You will spend the rest of your days in Aphrodite's temple, shunned and worshipping a god in whom you have no faith. Listen to my instructions: you will be released from Zeus' grip. Creep away from the tryst. Say nothing until morning. Then speak with Hydraphea, alone. Inform her of what you witnessed upon the altar. Betray Medusa, just as she has deceived us. Let her disloyalty not spread like a disease. You, Miranda, must be the cure for it. You are either a friend to her, or a friend to yourself."

Her eyes peered into mine, holding them with invisible force. I saw profound blackness in her pupils, pitched with a power that went beyond my understanding of her. Within that new territory beyond the apex that I believed to be fully defined, Athena shared a great secret with me. The god knew Zeus' mind: she knew of a great plan, nurtured and kept hidden from all but her by the father-god. She had known of it for some time; she had been entrusted by Zeus to know its mystery, to become an essential component of its workings. She supported it; she understood its far-reaching intent.

Athena did not dare speak of Zeus' scheme aloud, only for Aphrodite to seize it in her mania of rejection and scorn; only to ruin the great tapestry of heritage that was to be woven. The Olympian legacy Zeus had designed was all that mattered. Medusa's seduction, my obedience and her ensuing punishment were critical to its success.

Chapter Twenty-Eight

I awoke in the gloom of the temple atrium. I stood statue-still, but felt free from all Olympian grip. The moonlight still shone and the sky's blackness had no hint of daylight. While it felt as if much time had passed, little had.

The statue of Aphrodite had an ominous shadow cast across the lifelike face. Upon the altar the lovers Medusa and Poseidon were draped, they too unmoving. They were wrapped in each other, sleeping like sibling kittens curled into familiar comfort. They could have been young corpses who, having spent a short lifetime together in love, had chosen to die together for some cause: wayward to observers, profound to them. I crept away as Athena had asked, retracing my steps down into the bowels of the temple.

The god's ultimatum pounded in my ears: the price to protect Medusa was to forsake myself. In the past I had willingly shielded her from the constant attentions her beauty provoked; would I protect her now, now that she needed sanctuary from a power mightier than mortal desire? My greatest fear was the greatest of truths: had I been in her position, she would have suffered for me.

◆ ◆ ◆

I did not hear her return to our room. The heady after-effects of the semi-communion, followed by the full summons by Athena, had traumatised my body. I had near-fallen into bed, exhausted.

A strong sun, vengeful for the long night that had kept it at bay, woke me mid-morning. Medusa's bed was empty; whether she had slept in at all was unclear. I had not been woken for the rite: let the beast slumber, they probably whispered to each other; be thankful she cannot sully the ceremony.

I rose and the walls closed in. My long-injured leg felt stiff. I seized my walking stick and, with sick determination, I lurched from the room. I breathed in the air of the stone corridor and felt instantly more alert, as if our bedroom had harboured strange odours and memories of a life quickly torn away, never to be revisited.

I limped to Hydraphea's quarters, unknowing whether she would be inside. The door to her room was slightly open, as if expectant of an impending visitor. I stood on the threshold, hesitant to announce myself. But I did not need to: her voice came from within the room.

"Come in."

I pushed the heavy door and entered. The

room was vast, perhaps half the size of the temple's atrium. In the centre sat the High Priestess, alone. Her confidence upon that simple and backless seat was intimidating: she sat poised straight, ready to conduct business. Her room was sparsely decorated with tasteful ornaments. I was reminded of Menethus: Hydraphea's collection would not have been amiss on one of the trader's market stalls. The trinkets were well-kept and expensive, perhaps gifts from devoted admirers or lovers, from times long-since passed. In some I could identify provenance: colourful rugs and a large, golden bell, all from Persia; and glassware and porcelain, Greek in design. One piece resembled a phallus.

"Close the door," she said, and I did as told.

A silence lingered between us: she the conduit of Aphrodite's wrath, anger supported by Athena; and me, unwelcome guest enforced upon her.

"You can only have come here with something to tell me," she said pointedly.

"Last night I saw Medusa. On the altar. She was with Hyperion, he possessed by Poseidon. They were fucking."

Upon sealing my decision to side with the god, to speak what was the truth after all, I expected a great weight to be lifted from my shoulders. Yet I felt more burdened; Hydraphea's expectant stare wanted more.

"He came from the air," I continued, desperate

to explain all. "He appeared from the very dust off the temple floor. It was Hyperion, Poseidon's priest, possessed by the sea-god himself."

"You have already said so," Hydraphea said, here eyes locked with mine. Her reaction was impossible to read.

"If I do not tell you this, if I protect Medusa and say nothing, Athena will desert me. I will pray that mercy is shown to Medusa. My prayers used to count for much."

Hydraphea cocked her head slightly, measuring whether to grant me respect.

"Had I been in your position," the High Priestess said, "I would have done the same. Bring her out!" She commanded, not to me but to others unseen.

Two priestesses, clad in robes of plain white rather than the usual fuss of crimson, emerged from a room within the room. The entrance to this secret base was concealed by an illusory wall, camouflaged into the decor. I recognised the priestesses as Sephone and Lydia, long-standing devotees of the god and no friends to me. Between them stood Medusa, naked, wide-eyed and knife-edged with stressful anticipation. Her renowned body seemed dulled and spent, its usual sheen absent: Poseidon had consumed it. She looked at me with a longing I had never before seen: her natural fortitude that I had known her for, since our first meeting as children, had been displaced by dread. Love and fear, as the father-god had once commanded: now she knew both.

Hydraphea rose and went to Medusa.

"Please..." Medusa said, beginning her defence.

"Silence," said Hydraphea, softly hissing the command as she felt Medusa's bare belly. "You have spawn inside you. You have disgraced the god, and are cursed by allowing Poseidon to have you, to spill his seed inside your virgin womb. You have committed an abomination, and abomination is what you shall become."

Sephone and Lydia, now her captors, gripped Medusa's wrists more tightly.

Medusa stared at me but addressed Hydraphea. "Wha...what will become of me?"

"You will be exiled to the Isle of the Dead, on the edge of the Underworld. The lip of Hades' realm."

Medusa gasped. "Oblivion..."

"You will stay there. For as long as it is decreed."

She prayed openly as they took her away, in a tongue scant-learned from her days as a child of Tanis. I could make some understanding of it, the dialect being Libyan: requests for aid and forgiveness from almighty powers all bear a similar, ghoulish tone.

No time was wasted in ridding her from the temple. Soon a cluster of other priestesses and acolytes had gathered in the atrium to form a unit around her: to eject her for the hurt her beauty had caused Aphrodite; to make an example of treachery.

There was no speech, no words to coordinate this sinister ritual. The executers were well-drilled, prepared for the profoundly rare event as if it were a daily task. Hydraphea maintained a constant stare upon the god, her back to the ordered and intense proceedings.

Still naked and beneath the glare of Aphrodite's statue in the temple atrium, Medusa was wrapped in a shroud of white cloth, acolytes and preistesses taking turns to spin the fabric around her body from toe to head. They then forced her onto a wooden stretcher, and her arms and legs were tied to it. She writhed beneath the shroud uncomfortably, like a prepared Kemet corpse in the grip of a death-tremor. Her moans became muffled, her breathing urgent and stressed. The intent was not for her to die by suffocation, and her captors watched closely should they have the need to loosen the covering. Her breathing soon slowed as she became accustomed to the shroud's oppression.

Four priestesses hoisted the frame into the air, one to each corner.

"To the sea!" Hydraphea commanded, breaking away from her communion. Her piercing, roving eyes found me. "Miranda - join me at the front. You have done this temple a great service. The city shall know it."

She thrust me alongside her to lead the procession from the temple. Behind us only walked the four who carried Medusa to her doom, hoisted above their pretty heads like a new course being taken to banquet.

My crippled leg slowed our pace, and the High Priestess grew impatient. She spurred me on, her slender hand clawing into my back to push me. We proceeded through Athens' half-rebuilt streets, steering our short train of people west towards the port of Piraeus and the coast. Other residents cleared a path for us and looked on, unwilling to interrupt: Hydraphea's stern face silently told onlookers that this was not their business. When we approached groups or crowds, they quieted their own dealings and parted to let us pass.

"They're burying one of their dead," said a male voice from within one of these cliques.

"The dead don't whimper," replied another.

It was then that I heard Medusa's cries, miserable and childlike, emanating from the wooden stretcher held high. She could have been lamenting since we had left the temple, but I had not noticed until then. I was oblivious, heedless to all but Hydraphea's guiding hand and the thudding of my guilt, itself maturing fast as the sibling to trauma.

"Miranda…Miranda," she wailed softly. Her sorrowful voice was caught between a yearning for me and disbelief that I had destroyed our friendship. '*Help me, Miranda…why have you done this, Miranda…*' is what she was truly saying. I had taken a craven axe to our sisterhood and split it in two as a woodsman does a log. Aphrodite's dose of envy had left me ravaged; as spoiled as Medusa was by Poseidon. Now splinters of regret nestled deep beneath my skin; deep wounds that would be quick to lacerate, and take a lifetime to heal.

We navigated our way through the port of Piraeus, operational and in renewed state since the great flood. Soon we arrived at the same length of remote beach beyond the harbour, where the young women of the *Adonia* had washed themselves clean in the sea.

We slowed to a trudge along the moist sand, the tide too far out to lick our feet or flood our footsteps. Further up the beach stood a lone figure. Their features were vague but for the black robe that covered them from head to foot. I felt a terror grow in my belly, a nausea and tightening of my throat.

As we neared the figure, I saw it was a woman of familiar height and body. The black hood was carefully pulled back to reveal Ursula's face. She said nothing and bowed her head slightly to Hydraphea, one High Priestess to another. I wanted her to seize me then, to immediately take me away from this hideous procession, but she barely acknowledged my presence.

The four priestesses continued to hold Medusa aloft upon the wooden brace, facing the ocean. The water twinkled with sunlight dancing upon its crests, but the bright day could not have hosted a darker business.

Ursula was the first to speak. "I am told that Zeus himself summoned the ferryman. This is all arranged by his personal command."

Hydraphea said nothing. We waited for what seemed like an eternity. Hunger and thirst were quashed by an eerie determination to meet Medusa's fate.

The shape of a vessel appeared on the horizon. I could see it was no trading boat, no war galleon: it was shallow of hull, and manned by a single oarsman who stood at the stern. This lone sailor propelled and steered the craft using a lone pole, the length of which must have extended remarkably to plumb the depths and touch the ocean floor. The boat soon reached the shore, and even in my despair I marvelled at the skill and strength required to sail it without the fabric to capture the wind.

The vessel came to a stop and rested on the sand. The ferryman had come to collect his cargo. We all ventured forward. His stature was clearer to behold. A hooded cloak as old and grey as the boat he steered covered his body, which was entirely unseen. No face appeared from within the darkened cowl, no protruding nose or chin. No hands gripped the pole: I could see now that it was made of ancient wood and stood obediently in the water, unaided. The ferryman was entirely motionless: a still island in the shallows, mirroring the solitary Isle of the Dead he served.

"Miranda will accompany me," Hydraphea said. "This will be her final task for Aphrodite's temple. Then you may have her back, with my blessing."

Hydraphea and I approached the ferryman. Reaching the edge of the vessel, I tried to decipher his mysteries, whether he was man, beast or worse.

"Eyes down," Hydraphea said. From within her robe, she produced Medusa's *musalu* - the mirror inherited from her long-dead mother. "It is custom to include a token for the ferryman. Payment for transporting the exiled to the Isle. Something dear to them. I found this mirror in her belongings. It is perfectly appropriate - ideal that such a heinous device should compliment such a disgraceful crime. We want nothing to remember her by within those walls. No fragment of her treachery will be left behind."

She placed it gently on the bow, inside the boat. She stood back and looked at the ferryman, waiting for acknowledgement. The cloaked, sinister figure bowed slowly. Creaking noises were made, emanated from either the ferryman or from the boat's hull. Hydraphea and I returned to the small group. The High Priestess addressed the priestesses holding Medusa.

"Place her in the boat. Do it quickly, and deftly. Do not look at the ferryman. No harm will befall you."

The priestesses cautiously stepped forth. When they reached the vessel, the stretcher was lowered. They manoeuvred to be two either side of the boat and placed Medusa onto the deck, still bound to the wood, her feet facing the ferryman. They hurried away.

Medusa's presence on the boat was a trigger: immediately the ferryman resumed the same action that had brought him to the shore. Hands must have been released from the cavernous arms of the decrepit robe, for the pole was gripped. The pole was thrust into the sea, and the boat reversed away. The vessel turned and in moments the ferryman's cloaked back could be seen. The boat moved quickly, urged over the water with profound haste.

I collapsed onto the sand, overwhelmed by another summons for communion. I heard a howl of despair, carried on the growing wind and the rush of waves.

Chapter Twenty-Nine

P oseidon spat words to Zeus, who sat casually upon his great throne.

"This is outrageous," the infuriated sea-god said.

I stood close to the father-god, by his side and sharing his view of Olympus' main hall. He had summoned me himself, but not covertly; I was visible to all.

Poseidon took a step closer to the throne. He was flanked by Athena and Aphrodite, themselves raising no voices of dissatisfaction. Both their sets of eyes widened slightly as he advanced on the father-god.

"I will seize that old demon Charon and cast him back to Hades. I will split his boat in half, shatter it to pieces - just as she did to her alliance with my love Medusa." The sea-god raised a finger aimed at me, quivering with anger.

"This girl will not be alleviated of the trauma she feels by obeying us," Zeus said of me.

"Us!?" Poseidon fumed. "She has not obeyed *me*!"

Zeus continued more steadily. "She will not be released from it for as long as she lives. She understands it is the mortal's burden. They live, they carry joy and grief, pride and guilt. As do we, though we do not *live* - that is subservience. We *are* life."

I was to be part of the example set by Medusa's infidelity; her fate would be tied to my own, and in turn to the Olympians themselves. I was but a useful tool to them; an instrument to be played to form a terrific symphony of Zeus, which was to be fully revealed.

A familiar ripple of mortality spread through me, and for the briefest of moments I felt what it would be to have all my human senses intact on Olympus. The air was cool and replenishing; there was no smell to recall. The shudder I felt against my skin was uncomfortably welcome, like their puppeteering of me.

"I don't care about *her*," Poseidon said of me acidly. "This punishment is unreasonable and misguided. I cannot allow it. Medusa carries my child in her mortal womb. You would not slaughter it as an innocent."

"Your offspring with Medusa will thrive. And the punishment has only just begun," Athena said. The sea-god turned to her, his brow sunk low and dejected. "Despite your bewitchment and seduction of Medusa, my sister and I have been abused by her sacrilege. She must be a lesson to others, a warning. Her desecration of Aphrodite's temple and of my trust must be disciplined."

Poseidon looked at her with sadness that was as uncharacteristic as it was genuine.

"It was not bewitchment or seduction. It is infatuation. I beg you, wise Athena. I beg you, scorned Aphrodite. Punish me instead. I cannot ignore mortal beauty. Medusa is its very essence. Impossible for me to overlook it, to not crave and act on the opportunity to unleash my untamed desires. Please, understand this as the girl Miranda understands the mortal burden. Punish me instead."

Athena appeared moved by his entreating. But Aphrodite showed no such empathy, unwilling to resign what she considered to be her reckoning.

"Her punishment *is* your punishment," Aphrodite said softly.

"You will not intervene to save Medusa," Zeus added.

Poseidon turned his attention back to his brother, his face wild again.

"Oh yes," Poseidon said tauntingly, "I forget - all hail the *Great Plan*. Is it to honour the arrogance of both your daughters, or only your own? Is it a way of uniting their differing mother-lineage, of paying the debt of your own errant standards? What plan is it, Zeus, that you would deny my very right to exercise my power? What plan is it, that the hierarchy among us is ignored? Things will not continue like this, brother."

The father-god leaned forward emphatically, and announced his majestic intent to them all.

"Our legacy on mortal earth is my priority.

Our survival beyond the time when we are no more. We are not immune to Mother Death. And so I give you myth, our remedy and our legacy." Zeus paused, and sat back in his throne. "Myth," he repeated, louder and entranced by the concept, "to position us forever in mortal minds. Stories of our affairs, told and retold - perpetually commemorated by them. There is a price for it, and it is expensive to linger forever in mortal memory. Medusa's fate is currency with which to pay for our immortality."

Chapter Thirty

I awoke in Ursula's private chamber, upon her own bed of firmly-packed wool, within our first temple of Athena.

I felt pain, a dull ache about my waist and abdomen. I assessed the areas: mild bruising was present, from where I had been carried the entire distance from the beach to the city. Judging by the way the marks were spread across my body, I determined that I had been lifted over someone's shoulder to be transported like a sack of grain. I assumed it had been Ursula herself; no other person witnessing Medusa's terrible exile would have volunteered.

Golden daylight streamed through the open skylights. The radiance falsely indicated that all was well and that the earlier events of the day had been nothing more than a dream. I calculated that morning had long since passed. Night beckoned, and I shuddered at what reminiscent fears the darkness might spawn.

The memory of the communion lingered, but soon dissolved into the poisonous memory that was Medusa's fate. *'The punishment has only just begun'*. Athena's words rang around my head like the beginnings of a fever.

At the side of the low bed were a jug of fresh

water and, on a wooden platter, a small loaf of sweetly spiced bread. I ate and drank greedily, in a way that did not become the values of the temple I had finally returned to. My short time serving Aphrodite had turned me covetous.

"I will overlook your ravenous hunger, behaving like a starving animal," said Ursula firmly, echoing my own thoughts.

Her voice did not startle me. I found the High Priestess sitting in one corner of the chamber opposite the bed. She had changed from the black robe of mourning worn on the beach to one of familiar yellow, the colour of mature butter. Against the light stonework and in the dying daylight, she camouflaged herself well.

I slowed my eating. "Did you carry me back here?" I said.

Ursula rose from her seat and looked at me, not unkindly.

"I am not so old that I cannot carry one of this temple's sisters two leagues on my shoulder. We attracted curious glances. A small price for removing you from that serpent's nest."

'Myth...there must be a price for it...' Now the father-god's words echoed in my ears, prompted by Ursula.

"It has been decided that you will witness Medusa's punishment in full. It is the god's wish, not my own."

I felt taut with distress: the two-faced offspring of love and fear.

"Athena compelled me to tell Hydraphea of what took place between Medusa and the sea-god," I said. "I did as commanded. Now I must witness *more*?"

Ursula looked away from me, as if masking some long-held grudge from her own experience.

"What it is to serve Olympus. I have already pleaded with the god on your behalf, but she is unmoved."

"It is beyond her control," I said petulantly. "It is Zeus who wants this."

"Careful," Ursula said, warning. "I would not expect you to commune again. Your life hereafter will be quietly spent, doing all you can for the god and her hard-won city."

I said nothing, unable to find words to contend.

"Now that you have eaten and drank, we will waste no more time."

Hung on the wall opposite the bed were the ceremonial spear and shield, both golden and almost disguised by the dusk-light. The High Priestess removed the shield and positioned herself behind it, holding it upright so I might look into it.

"Sit before it. You cannot kneel, for your long-injured leg," she said.

I shifted my sore body from the bed and took to my knees on the cold, hard floor. Defiance to her words, small and at my own expense, was mine. I endured the discomfort: ancient and primal necessity for the loyalty to temple Athena.

The shield was plain and wholly reliant on its golden lustre to attract and retain the eye. I beheld my reflection, murky in the imperfect sheen of the metal. My sullen face filled me with sadness: disappointment in my lack of beauty; and distress in my condemnation of Medusa. The sound of the sea, which had crept into the silence of the chamber, sweated my brows with unease.

I became transfixed with the shield. My unclear reflection vanished, and the golden sheen filled my vision. It became brighter and soon was akin to looking into the sun. I closed my eyes, and the noise of the ocean grew louder.

I was no longer in Ursula's private chamber, but aboard the demon ferryman's creaking vessel. My presence was another variation of the communion, and yet I had received no summons. I was there, and yet not: I sat near Medusa's head at the bow and I reached out to touch her covered face; nothing but air greeted me. Medusa's mirror rested nearby undisturbed; discarded like its owner.

I looked at the tall figure of the ferryman: Charon, Poseidon had called him. He conducted his repetitive strokes within that ragged grey cloak:

I could see that skeletal hands dripping with decrepit flesh gripped the pole. Whatever creature the ferryman was, it had plenty of strength and Olympian blessing for its macabre business. Whether the ferryman knew of me, his new, ghostly passenger, I could not say; his task was undisturbed by my arrival.

The small boat had made astonishing progress. I looked out to sea from the bow. Edging closer was a small landmass, an island. The afternoon sky had streaks of cloud flowing towards the isle. They gathered above it, losing their whiteness and becoming grey as the dense wisps became mists. The weather over the ocean was fine, over the isle it seemed poor.

Medusa spoke, her voice parched for thirst. "Who are you, ferryman?"

Charon offered no reply.

"How many like me have you taken on this journey?"

Shallow waves clashed. Wind gusted briefly. Still no sound came from Charon, save for his near-silent, persistent propulsion.

"If you will not speak of yourself, tell me something of the isle. Is it earthly, or divine? What is its history?"

The ferryman remained speechless, and Medusa became cross.

"Perhaps you cannot speak. Perhaps you are a mouthless form. Regardless I cannot stand your silence." She paused and in a calmer, resigned voice: "My own history will soon begin. I will die as I am now upon the Isle, and I will be re-born there. I have been known as beauty. I will be known as terror. We are only truly born when we die."

The ferryman remained mute. The waves licked the ancient vessel's hull. Medusa continued ominously.

"This magic thought comes from Zeus himself. I have never been summoned for communion to Olympus, and yet I am a subject most revered. Bewitched and seduced by Poseidon, to be a portion of the gods' immortality. After my death I will be but myth."

"Quiet yourself," I whispered fearfully. I believed she spoke too blindly, no matter how truthfully. I wished I could stop her worsening her position.

"There is a voice upon the breeze," she said despondently, her nerve lost. "Miranda. But she cannot be here. I wish she were, but she cannot be."

I tried to touch her face again. There was no contact, but I let my insubstantial hand hover upon her, hoping for the sensation of touch. I wanted her to forgive me. Perhaps she thought to do so, but she never said it.

We reached the shore of the isle very suddenly.

Like the ambush of death upon the living, the grey sands and oily residue upon the sea-foam crests stopped Charon's boat with abrupt certainty. The ferryman finally rested, his ghoulish grip upon the pole eased. He stood statue-still, his task of fetching and ferrying Medusa across the water complete.

I stayed aboard and surveyed the landmass. Beyond the sands were jagged rocks: enormous and eroded into a sharp-edged landscape to keep the curious at bay, and the brought imprisoned. Shrubs and plants were few, and grew between the spiky boulders. Their colours were differing shades of dull green; some leaves displayed colourful spots, warning of poison.

The mists that lingered about the island, first seen from the ocean, were constant on land. The climate was warm and humid, the air dense with moisture; uncommon Greek weather. I felt the fine, thread-thin rain upon my face, and again marvelled: judging by my futile attempts to caress Medusa I could affect nothing, and yet I had felt the jolt of the ocean beneath Charon's boat. I could smell the damp and acrid odour of the island, like stale woodsmoke; and now I could wipe the moisture from the decaying atmosphere from my brow.

Looming beyond the rocks, perhaps at the centre of the island, was a mountainous region. The grey stone of the cliff-face blended well with the mists. The peaks were unseen. Squinting, I could make out a structure built on a plateau. Columns in the temple style were barely visible, and its high position was reminiscent of Athena's victory temple within the Acropolis overlooking Athens.

I failed to see a path from the shore, until two figures entirely clad in loose, white robes emerged from among the rocks. They walked assuredly, despite their heads and faces being fully covered. Their feet and hands were also hidden and it could only be assumed that they were mortal: women according to their protruding bosoms. They were as illusory as the path they followed.

They approached the vessel in a shroud of silence. Their feet made no imprints in the wet sand. I disembarked and stood beside the boat, expecting to be greeted. I held on to the bow to steady myself, waiting for my crippled leg to cause me pain; but the scar had vanished, and I could bend my leg with ease. A fragment of kindness amid this obscure sorcery.

"Who's there?" Medusa said. Nothing escaped her hearing.

The two figures ignored me. One raised a clothed arm, as if to command an invisible army. The cords that tied Medusa to the wooden brace were broken, for she immediately leapt up from her bondage. While ably standing atop the prow, she removed the cloth that had covered her body. She tore at it, desperate to be free of it, like a swimmer surfacing from a dive too deep.

Naked as she was when expelled from Aphrodite's temple, she breathed freely and escaped the boat. She stood so close to me I could smell her: instead of her usual pleasant aroma, she was now bittersweet - of burnt lavender and sweat. She looked wildly at her new surroundings. Her open-mouthed gaze paused upon the creature Charon, and she now understood the lack of conversation. Her roving eyes found her mother's mirror, the beloved and underused *musalu*. She gasped and made a stern attempt to seize it. But like my touch upon her had yielded no sensation for me, so did her effort to take the inheritance. She scrabbled for it, using both hands and clawing at the vessel with her nails. Her groans of frustration were startling, and she could not fathom the intangibility of something that was surely hers. The trinket now belonged to the ferryman.

With his cargo offloaded, Charon started his grim rhythm. The vessel edged away from the shore, returning to the water, its hull quickly beyond Medusa's reach. He steered east, in the direction of rocks that jutted out to form an arm of the isle. Soon the creak of his rowing was swallowed by the waves. He disappeared from view into descending mists.

Medusa faced the white-clad women. The one who had not broken Medusa's bonds had already begun walking back towards the path between the rocks.

The other spoke: a harsh voice and akin to Maestra's, but croaking with evil rather than playfulness. "Come, or I shall force you," she said.

I thought of our old teacher's alleged Stygian ancestry. Perhaps those ancient witches resided on the isle, as guardians of the forsaken.

Medusa did not defy the order. I followed, unseen by her and still ignored by the mysterious women. From the foreboding beach we followed a crude passage through the rocks. The way had once been hacked through the stone and ascended gradually, winding and snaking upwards towards the plateau. The spray of mist was ceaseless, and the harsh landscape changed from dustless granite to loose shale as we crept higher.

When we reached the bottom of the table-land, we were filthy with the spew of water and rock dust. It was clear that the building above our heads had once been a temple. The collapsed roof muddled any decoration that may have identified its origins or devotions; the columns that once supported it had been half-destroyed, their heights jagged and irregular. Broad stairs, ruined like the old temple, led up to the plateau.

At the top the extent of the temple was astonishing. It had to have been bigger than

Athena's within the Acropolis; its broken facade disguised its true size. Beyond the fractured pillars stretched a vast field of rubble. More of the same pernicious botanics seen on the shore were thriving, some having grown to great length and thickness. These serpentine vines had weaved and wrapped their way around fallen blocks of stone, gripping them with constricted claim.

The air was clear of vapour, as if the remnant columns formed a gateway between the constant island mists and the still, lifeless atmosphere within the body of the temple. While sunshine was forbidden through the clouds above the isle, over the temple it shone brightly. Detail of the stone used in the construction was now clear: what had once been white had been set upon by some organic disease, the filth of which caused a decay. The dark, greenish spores weakened the stone, gradually eating through it. The occasional crack, as a piece broke in two, crushed the otherwise suffocating silence.

The white-clad women veered towards an opening in the centre of the roofless atrium. They stood at its mouth, gaping wide for prey, and waited for Medusa. Her own pace became laboured when she saw the beginning of the descent into darkened chambers beneath. Knowing that any escape would surely be hopeless, she eventually stopped at the lip of the steps leading down. I stood behind her, still seemingly invisible to all. Shadows created by orange light quivered from the gloom below, striking the intact walls of perfectly squared stone; fires were lit down there. The speechless white-clad went first, and the other gestured Medusa to follow.

"What awaits me?" Medusa said fearfully.

The gesturing woman pointed again to the opening, and with greater force indicating displeasure.

We descended hundreds of shallow steps. Whatever had obliterated the temple above had left the infernal shrine below untouched. The source of the fire emanated from the very bottom of the pit, the orange glow strengthening with every step taken. Markings and carvings had been expertly scratched into the stonework of the passage walls. These were no pleasant decorations: crooked faces picturing what could have been victims of the inferno below; and languages that were unfamiliar, their spidery lexicon certainly written with sharp instruments or talons. The descent permitted these terrible features impose themselves; they encroached with an evil that would have leapt from the walls, had some conjured restraint not forbidden it.

Finally we four reached the bottom. An expanse as vast as the temple above greeted us, at the centre of which burned an enormous fire-pit. The heat was breathtaking and the noise roaring, the pool of fire outlined by its perfectly rectangular housing. The atrium's size could be further discerned by shadowed columns, themselves vaguely illuminated by the blaze. They stood guard over the blackness that lay beyond them, rigid soldiers defending either brickwork or oblivion.

The white-clad women stood apart from each other and faced Medusa, forming a gateway like oracles awaiting a truth-seeker.

Medusa shouted above the flaming noise, her voice a final dose of defiance in the face of inevitable fate. "I am not responsible for my beauty, but the gods must be for their endeavours."

The white-clad women removed their facial coverings. Athena and Aphrodite stood before us, flesh shimmering in the firelight. Neither looked at me. Medusa beheld them wide-eyed and aghast, surely recognising them from their statued forms in temple.

Athena had been the one to speak before and she did so now, her voice no longer harsh.

"You abandoned the sacred vows of my and my sister's temples. You adulterated with a god, discovered on an altar no less, bringing ultimate shame to both our houses. This, in return for the sanctity we bestowed upon you. The crime, intentional or not, is unforgivable."

"You, Medusa," Aphrodite said, a small smile creeping into the corners of her pert mouth, "shall be a byword for great beauty, and for great terror."

What words Medusa had spoken of her doom, claimed to have been enlightened by Zeus himself, became truth.

The flames within the great pit suddenly died down. There was sheer darkness, and then fires sprang from cavities in walls beyond the columns. Plain, darkly-coloured brickwork was exposed: unlike the oppressive walls surrounding the descending steps, these enourmous cuboids were unmarked, like parchment awaiting a scribe. The extensive perimeter of the atrium was revealed; the columns did not guard oblivion, they formed it.

In place of fire within the pit was a dark and viscous liquid, its mass slowly rising and falling in shallow waves. Wordlessly, the gods gestured for Medusa to enter the pool.

"I pray my fate pleases you," Medusa said softly.

Medusa stepped forth with a trepidation that was only exceeded by the Olympian will to propel her forward. Her lithe and enviable body came between Athena and Aphrodite. She went on and we followed, like acolytes behind a High Priestess during the rite, until she stood on the lip of the pool. The liquid receded, revealing steps.

Medusa descended. Her first contact with the substance produced no gasp of pain. She immersed herself up to her breasts, and then she disappeared beneath, dragged under and swallowed whole by the purulence. She did not resist its pull.

The wall-fires strengthened, setting the gargantuan dungeon ablaze with light. Flames reflected in the pool's black mass and the substance became shallower, as if draining.

The fiery light rescinded. New wonder had gathered in the centre of the empty stone pool: this nucleus had become the eye of the vortex into which the pitch muck had been sucked, leaving no trace of residue around it. This entity had the shape of a woman, curled up like an embryo near-gestated. But the body was imperfect: a swelling ballooned its lower half and the flesh, though obscured by the poor light, was not mortal.

Athena suddenly took my hand, grasping it as if she needed protection. As a familiar blackness began to cloud my vision, I heard the sound of snakes: hissing from an immeasurable number of angry serpents; and the *click-click* rattle of the kind found in the deserts far south of Greece.

The feeling of the god's hand in mine ceased. Contrary to Ursula's prediction, the summons for communion took me.

Chapter Thirty-One

The brightness of Zeus' great hall was too much for me to bear following the terrific murkiness of the subterranean shrine on the Isle of the Dead. I shielded my sensitive eyes, and caught glimpses of Poseidon, Aphrodite and Athena. Again I stood beside Zeus, for it was his summons I answered to again.

"I beg you kill her," Poseidon said softly to the father-god. There was defeat in his voice: no anger, no appetite for his usual fight. "I beg you end this ordeal. The point is made. The kingdom of the sea bows to those of justice and of beauty."

"Her punishment is my design, my command," Zeus said assuredly. "Like all proper penance, Medusa's retribution has been inspired by her life. Her birth and childhood in a place famous for snakes: now they embody her. The value she placed on the mirror: sentimentally as her mother's dying gift to her, and too full of dispassionate hubris to use it. Now, through a reflection is the only way to avoid her direct stare, which will turn mortal flesh to stone - a nod to your protection of her in the mazed streets of Athens, Poseidon."

Zeus looked intently at the sea-god.

"Those unfortunate to meet her stare will

look at her forever," the father-god said gravely. "In terror as Medusa the gorgon, just as so many did in wonder at Medusa the beauty. And her aptitude for combat and cunning: natural when a child, honed to be used precisely and honestly when in service to Athena. Now she is a most dangerous adversary - one that will attract brave men and women to the Isle of the Dead, to seek her out. To slay her. They will go for glory. They will go for power."

My eyes became wet, but not due to the bright brilliance of Olympus: I grieved for Medusa's fateful helplessness; and for my veneration, blind to the victimhood of others.

Zeus turned in his throne to face me, smiling. "I let your tears for her, and for yourself, flow in this communion. It is a favour seldom granted, so do not waste them."

The father-god returned his determined gaze to his brother and daughters, and he addressed them.

"One day Medusa's suffering will end. One brave man will seek her out - but not for glory or power. For two things - for love and for myth. Love, unadulterated by curiosity or lust. And myth, to fuel our timelessness. And this man shall be victorious, for he is my son. Perseus."

"In love he shall acquire glory and power," said Aphrodite with rare wonder in her voice. "More myth. More currency with which to buy our immortality."

Athena held out a single hand, and from it grew the figurine of Medusa. The statue depicted her naked; it was a final glance of her stunning beauty. Body parts faded away: her legs and arms became curtailed; and it became headless, her remarkable face vanishing. What remained turned a putrid colour: a rotting green and spent blue, with yellowish markings reminiscent of infection. Zeus nodded once, confirming his wishes and approving the statue's transformation.

Through the lens of my tears I noticed Aphrodite's eyes suddenly widen in horror: she looked at me aghast, and then at her father. Athena was not so shocked, her face calm and expectant.

"What have you done!?" Aphrodite said.

"Another thing for myth," Zeus said. "For us."

I felt a swell of tiredness within me, my heart taking a toll that I withstood but could not comprehend. I beheld my hands: they had become wrinkled with age. I put them to my face: it felt weathered with new lines and crevices. Olympus dissolved around me.

Chapter Thirty-Two

I was returned to Ursula's chamber, and the High Priestess gaped and trembled with astonishment, a lifetime's years having been added to me. I had been turned more old and wizened than Maestra. The High Priestess dropped the golden shield in shock, the clang of the metal on the floor heralding the Olympian spell.

She carried my newly frail body to a small room where I would reside until the cold season began.

Ursula and Maestra were unfailingly kind. Between them they fed and watered me as I lay crone-like in bed. Maestra kept my attention and distraction from my plight by reciting and editing recipes from her book of medicines. She spoke to me about her winter garden preparations, and how the rebuilding of Athens progressed. She did not question me; she seemed to accept my transformation as if she, like Athena, had expected it. She knew the gods too well, she could afford her detachment from them.

Ursula prayed at my side, though in the beginning I was too weak to join her. I slept deeply, and her interactions mingled with my dreams: herbs and potions featured in those set in broken temples; chants and smoke plumes in those which featured fire-stained walls.

I was no longer a young woman of less than ninety seasons, but an old woman of more than ninety years. Yet, I was not as frail or immobile as I first perceived. My strength gradually returned, and my body settled into the rhythm of what would surely be its final years.

One day, when Maestra had finished reading to me and we were enjoying a silence, I burned for an answer to a question that I thought her wisdom could give.

"Maestra, I must ask you something."

She raised a white, crow's-wing eyebrow at me.

"Questions always yield an answer unwanted, or an answer deserved," she said ruefully.

"When Zeus aged me, he said it was for myth and for them. I do not believe that is all he intended. What more could it be?"

Maestra considered the question. Through the skylights of my small room, I heard the laughter of children at play outside, passing our humble temple, and then the calls of a female adult herding them.

"Casting aside his intentions for his own ilk,

the father-god shortened your life as a mercy. Your rapid ageing is his way of sparing you from a lifetime of guilt for doing Olympian bidding and convicting Medusa, and a lifetime of mourning her victimhood. But Zeus' mind is changeable, he does not dwell on punishing us. This is not weakness. This is yet more instruction. More teaching that will eventually settle into mortal lore, and lead us into chaos and peace and back again."

I was eventually presented to the temple's priestesses and acolytes. With the aid of a walking stick, for although I escaped my youth I had not escaped my old leg injury, I shuffled to stand before the statue of the god. Ursula introduced me as a long-serving priestess from the Athenian temple at Pylos, a small city on the south-west corner of Greece. It was said that I had chosen to see out the rest of my days within the city won by the god; that I was to be afforded every courtesy; and that I was not to be chastised for missing rites. I did not care whether Ursula had lied willingly, or with permission from the god.

I recognised most of my peers, though kept up the act initiated by Ursula. Most could not see beyond my elderly frame and tree-bark face. Acantha was the only one to narrow her eyes in doubt, but even she most learned would have struggled to believe me a victim of such wild Olympian enchantment.

In the early days of my convalescence I kept to myself, only retaining Maestra and Ursula for company. I grew stronger, as if my extreme and sudden ageing was an illness that needed time to recover from. As I emerged more often from my private cell, I overheard whisperings among the temple's cliques. Word had spread that there was a new terror in the world; a new foe for the brave to face. They said she was half-reptile, with snakes for hair and a stare that turned you to stone. That she had disgraced Athena's and Aphrodite's temples. I could only assume that Aphrodite's priestesses, perhaps Hydraphea herself in unrestrained glory of her god's vengeance, had talked. Once I heard Medusa's name itself be mentioned among Athena's acolytes. I said nothing of it, but the indiscretion sprawled and led to calm and firm reprisal by Ursula to the entire temple: Medusa was a name no longer welcome within any temple's walls.

The seasons passed. I assisted Maestra in the care of the almond and olive trees, and the delicate task of planting amaranth seeds. When the weather turned hot again and the sun rose early and retired late, I had energy enough to harvest the amaranth myself.

In late summer, in the evening cool of the atrium, Ursula gathered us all before Athena's statue. A new celebration devised by the god had been confirmed: the *Panathenaia*. Before the last day of season's heat we would troop up the hill to the Acropolis, to the site of our grand, destroyed temple, its own re-building humbly slower than that of the city itself.

Sacrificial oxen would be taken, their blood used to make the ground fertile. Gifts of cloth and herbs would be displayed and burned respectively. The *Panathenaia* would be an offering to Zeus, and a petition for help from the people of his able but reproved daughter: the new, grand temple should be rebuilt without delay. And after it is positioned there again within the citadel, the *Panathenaia* would become an annual symbol, each celebration greater than the one before.

Hearing the announcement of the new rite aroused little joy in me. Once I would have been impatient for the procession; once I would have ensured the healthiest oxen were sourced, the finest cloth woven and coloured. Now the High Priestess' words provoked thoughts of Medusa: memories which had become dim in my distraction with my new, much-shortened life and much-changed body; a side-effect of Zeus' will. She came to mind with a vengeance, as if punishing me for forgetting her. Later that same night, beneath stars that shone brighter than I could ever recall, I took counsel with the High Priestess alone in her private chamber. I spoke quietly, and with finality. Age gives greater certainty.

"I want to gain passage to the Isle of the Dead," I said.

Ursula looked at me as if she had expected the question sooner. Her expression was neutral, neither prepared to fulfil nor deny my request.

"If you go, there is no way back," she said softly. "Before you went in communion, protected by Athena herself. Now you would go wholly mortal, and alone."

I allowed her words the chance to change the way I felt, but they did not.

"I once asked Maestra for further meaning behind Zeus' changing of me," I said. "She said it was a mercy for obeying the Olympian will to define their immortality, and for not having to endure a lifetime of grief for Medusa's fate. But I have found something more."

"And what is that?"

"I believe Medusa is an example of fear. I believe his sorcery of me is an example of love. Love and fear must be united."

The High Priestess studied me solemnly. "Why?"

"So we can embrace death, and not be tied to our flesh by regret. So we can surpass this mortality."

Ursula considered this. After a short time she said: "To prove this you must confront her?"

"Not confront. I only wish to be with her."

We fell silent. Should Ursula refuse me, I rehearsed asking Maestra or seeking out another person of profound wisdom for how to summon the ferryman and travel to the ill-omened isle.

Finally she answered. "The ferryman will want a token, a fee for his service. It must be something dear to you."

I sat on the bow of Charon's vessel, a year to the day after Medusa was strapped aboard it in exile. My naked body, withered and sagged, drank in the sun's rays, gorging on their nourishment. I rejoiced in the cool salt-spray the lively waves threw up. I made no effort to converse with the demon-creature; his voiceless company was perfect for the pilgrimage. My Athenian acolyte robe lay neatly folded upon the bow, my offering to the ferryman.

Ursula had summoned Charon with a method I did not witness. Now she stood on the shore of the same beach beyond the harbour of Piraeus, sight of her growing ever-smaller as the ferryman relentlessly pushed us across the water. She and I had shared few words on the journey from temple. She had stroked my face in a motherly way as the boat came into view and told me that, if I felt any fear, I should overcome it with her blessing. She said I had no reason to be afraid because I knew love.

On the Isle of the Dead nothing had changed, the landmass a slave to permanence. Charon left me as he had done Medusa, with unceremonious automation, itself a ritual of its own.

With only my skin to cover me, I retraced the mist-filled steps I had taken as a younger woman in the grip of a communion I did not expect to know again. From the shore I found the subtle path through the rocks, and followed it to the steps up to the plateau and the tumbledown temple. I moved nimbly, without a walking stick. My long-injured leg bit, but I endured the dull ache and compelled the affliction to keep pace, spurred on by my purpose.

The ascent to the temple exhausted me. At the top I caught breath, and then dragged myself onward, aiming for the dark mouth of descent in the centre of the long-abandoned atrium.

The same carvings pressed on me from the walls as I descended to the vast underground shrine. The bizarre faces grinned and frowned, and the peculiar letters danced in firelight. The field of flame had been re-lit. Ursula's words of reassurance began to dissipate.

I moved slowly and not without trepidation.

At the bottom of the chasm the pool of fire was ablaze and I began to sweat, heat and dread drying me out like a cow skin turning to leather. I walked towards the flaming pool, the sound of the fire licking the air from within its stone prison, roaring in my ears. I veered around the pit's edge and eventually passed it, finding the corners of the underground atrium black and cool, they were so far from the fire. I stopped and took breath, thirsty and seemingly alone in the immense chamber and with only the glow of the dense flames for company. I would die soon without water, an unwanted end.

The great hissing of snakes quieted my doubts. Behind me I felt a change in the air: a cool draft sent a shiver across my neck. I smelled something rank: a grossly rich odour of dead flesh.

Her voice whispered in my left ear. Its easy tone and natural sensuality had been marred by exhaustion and a constant, creeping whimper caught in her throat. I felt no breath, only a repeated, light flicker of a serpent's forked tongue as it tasted my wrinkled skin.

"I know you," she said. "My memories are unclear, but you taste of my past. Like a fruit short of ripening. Bittersweet."

I stood still, rooted to the floor. "I am what remains of your past," I said, whispering into the gloom.

The flickering, tasting tongue upon my ear

ceased, and the chill air behind me became warm. Her voice echoed through the gloomy shrine. She had moved some distance in a fraction of time, and in total silence.

"Why have you come here, Miranda?"

I slowly looked around, and felt my body relax. Wherever she had gone, she was not close.

"To be with you," I said aloud.

I again felt the air grow cold behind me. I froze and my aged spine stiffened in frightful anticipation of the terror unseen. She spoke again, her voice now to my right.

"Zeus wishes that my legend spreads. He has made me powerful. And vindictive. For good reason. He told me so himself."

Her snakes hissed in a messy rhythm, as if repeating the words of their mistress in their own fork-tongued language. When they silenced and only the roar of the fire-pit could be heard, I knew she still lingered nearby.

I knew it would be the demigod Perseus, son of Zeus and Danae, who would one day end her misery; who would one day strengthen the myth she had already become. But she did not know this, and it should be kept so until the moment came.

"I wish I'd had the strength to refuse Athena," I said shakily. "To have said nothing to Aphrodite's High Priestess. But my piety is too much for me to bear."

Across my wrinkled cheek I felt the caress of

her finger. Her flesh was cold as desert night, and it moved so slowly along my skin that tears welled in my dry, crone eyes.

"You had little choice," she said. Her voice cracked with what could have been emotion, but was more akin to intense thirst.

"Let me fetch you water," I said.

She laughed lightly. "I have no use for water. But I have use for company - who better than you to fully witness the myth that Zeus has created. Myth - the great device to secure the gods' immortality."

"I haven't long to live in this body," I said. "Down here in the dark."

Our faces met. Her eyes were closed. I recoiled and gasped, transfixed by her appearance: the snakes atop her head were woven among her old hair; they had been tamed by her, but her virescent, reptilian face bore the scars of a thousand bites. Her bare breasts, arms and shoulders were all else that was left of her glorious human body. Below her groin her legs began, but soon merged into a plump second abdomen. She supported her upper body on this bizarre tail, and I saw that it became slim and long, extending into the gloom so its end was unseen.

"Fear not," she said.

Her eyes opened. They were slim and yellow, inhuman, and they peered into mine. I felt my body instantly stiffen, her gaze persistent and not unkind. I tried to speak, but my tongue had turned to slate. We forget how death creeps upon us.

Sometimes the fire died, and light was let in from the sky high above the depths in which I stood, at one with the stone floor. It was in these moments that I saw her slithering and in full: swollen and still yet to birth Poseidon's child.

She had fashioned a bow and arrows from the thick vines and broken stones of the temple above. Lethal debris. Those who came to kill her for glory and for power, as Zeus had proclaimed, became the hunted themselves. They were mostly men, clad in armour they thought would protect them. Occasionally a woman came, equally assured but no less unfortunate.

Their death-screams became my atmosphere. Statues like me grew in number, her assailants frozen in stone by her stare. I had much company.

The passing of time became incalculable.

I heard voices belonging to well-equipped men. They were different to those who had come before. They spoke of needing her head. They were explicit and determined. One had a name splintered deep in my memory: Perseus. He was lordly, but not conceited. From good stock, but humble. Young, but dangerous.

Medusa's head was cunningly sliced and then it belonged to him. The sea-god's child she had carried for so long finally spilled from her womb, her open neck-wound the exit point. It was a winged horse and, as it shook the dark blood from its body, was revealed to be as white as Zeus' atrium. Beauty had become terror, and terror had given birth to beauty.

One of Perseus' compatriots took Medusa's arms as trophies, themselves not so affected by her metamorphosis. He lopped them off hurriedly and without much neatness. Athena's mutilated figurine of Medusa was now accurate.

Perseus took the winged horse, and they departed. The fire died. We remnants were enfolded in utter darkness and silence; death-quiet that did not know time.

Eventually I heard another voice speak to me. It belonged to the father-god. He wanted me to tell her story.

"Medusa's tale," he said. "Record the truth of it, set it in stone. Athena once told you: *your mortal life as one of my vessels shall be filled with love and fear in precise balance. You accommodate me and, you will one day realise, Olympus itself.* You are now *manteia* - oracle for all. You begin your own legacy as the gatekeeper of myth, guardian of our timelessness."

The father-god interrupted Mother Death. My tongue became flesh. My fingers became warm. I became mortal-form again: greatly aged, as I had been when Medusa let me join her.

I have no need for food or water; for as long as he needs me, a spring wells inside of me. The father-god is generous to those in his service.

Within the re-lit fire-chamber I did as commanded and recalled Medusa's life; our life. I scratched the words upon the walls.

Acknowledgement

Special thanks to my test readers, especially Les Smith, Julian Holder, Alex Meredith, Tom Grant and Alastair Bergner, and all at Cambridge for their input and suggestions. To the Easts for their kindness, and to Emma for her neverending forebearance and sharp eyes.

About The Author

Jon East

Jonathon (Jon/Jo) East was born in London, 1980. He began writing fiction in his mid-20s. 'Manteia' is his third novel. He lives in Cambridge.